MAGIC IN THE WORLD
and Other Stories

by Walter Lockwood

Chapbook Press

Schuler Books
2660 28th Street SE
Grand Rapids, MI 49512
(616) 942-7330
www.schulerbooks.com

Magic in the World and other stories

"The Great 83 Baseball Tour" was originally published in the December 1983 issue of *Grand Rapids Magazine*.

Layout and design by Magda Phillips

Cover photography by Susan Lockwood

Cover design by Sam Pierman

ISBN 13: 9781957169156

Library of Congress Control Number: 2022913827

Printed in the United States by Chapbook Press.

For my family—Pam, Ian, Alison,
Matt, Susan, and Katie.

Love and thanks to the patient readers and critics
of early drafts: GF Korreck for his discerning notes;
my wife Pam for her wise and dependable judgment;
my son Matt for his baseball savvy and story sense;
my daughters Katie, Susan, and Alison, my sister
Susie and my granddaughter Avery for careful
reading, listening, insights, and encouragement;
finally to David Wygmans and Dave Hendrickson
for their willingness to listen to stories read aloud.

CONTENTS

GOD AND JACK BUCK

The boy loved his gramp (to whom God, his gramp told him, didn't speak much) and loved visiting Florida during spring break because of baseball. His grandparents lived in a small house on the water in Madeira Beach with orange and grapefruit trees heavy with fruit that the boy would pick for breakfast each morning. His gram was sweet and plump as the apple muffins she baked for him. It was a relief to be away from school and especially their church for two straight Sundays.

In his eleven years the boy remembered God communicating only once with him, though not with words. That was just before his mother had died and his stepmother, the pretty Foursquare Gospel Lady, had come into the picture. His mother lay in a dark room suffering. Terrified of things he didn't understand, the boy had prayed with all his heart for a bright light to drive away the darkness of her pain. That night he'd had a dream of a giant sun filling the world with light, and in the morning he had wakened to a glorious wash of morning sunlight. His mother had opened her eyes and felt better. She had walked outside to the patio to sit in the sunshine.

The light, though, had faded away by noon and within a week his mother was gone, too. God had not communicated with the boy since then, but he noticed that others, especially his father (now that he was saved) and stepmother, long an active part of the Foursquare Gospel Church, were led here and there by God on a daily basis. God seemed to speak to them all the time, and they appeared to listen and give reports. "I had a word from the Lord about an investment," his father would say, or "The Lord let me know the sellers are good Christians. It's a used car we can trust." There seemed to be a language he'd learned from the church or maybe to impress her. The boy prayed each night, listened for God, but heard only the chimes in the mantle clock.

"God laid it on my heart that we should visit your parents," his stepmother had said before this trip. "There are so many things they need to hear."

The boy knew the sorts of things she meant to tell them because she often told him, too, and would sometimes make the back of his neck burn like prickly heat. Though she wasn't a pastor, she had a knack for bending any conversation into a sermon. She had the Bible memorized. She talked constantly about the joy of living according to God's will, yet she so often seemed solemn and joyless herself, causing the boy to forget how attractive she was. His gram, who got stuck with her more than anyone on these visits, would knead a ball of dough and listen politely to her evangelizing. His gram was a Presbyterian and his gramp a jazz musician who slept in on Sunday. They both seemed more joyful to him than either his father or his stepmother. And his gramp, like himself, was especially joyful about baseball.

Every day but Sunday, after the boy had fielded grounders in the driveway for an hour or two (tennis balls flung against the brick facing, Tigers vs. White Sox), the two of them would walk out to the Little League field down the block. His gramp had pitched in college and then for years in semi-pro. Though he was 60, he could throw a tennis ball with accuracy and blinding speed, especially from Little League distance. And in that way the boy, over several spring breaks and numerous summers at his grandparents' small vacation cabin in Michigan (staying weeks at a time without his parents), learned to hit a tennis ball and thus a baseball harder and truer than most boys ever do.

It was early morning of the fourth day of spring break when Jack Buck showed up. Jack Buck stayed at a beach hotel on Treasure Island where the boy's grandfather played the piano bar. Jack Buck was the radio voice of the St. Louis Cardinals, and the hotel was his home through the whole of spring training. He admired the grandfather's talent and spent many evenings listening at the bar.

They were hitting tennis balls that morning on the broad Treasure Island beach before the crowds appeared. The boy, who threw right but batted left, sent one drive after another toward the Gulf, some actually landing in the distant water.

At his gramp's bidding, he sent them to left field, then to right, and then up the middle.

A deeply tanned, silver-haired man in Bermuda shorts and an orange silk shirt came walking out to them from the hotel. "Stan," he said, approaching the boy's grandfather. "I've been watching from my balcony. Who the hell is this kid?"

"My grandson Tram."

"Tram?"

"Well, it's Tom, but he calls himself Tram after Alan Trammell."

"The new shortstop for the Tigers? Pretty big shoes to fill."

"Meet Jack Buck, boy. He announces all the Cardinal games."

The boy was stunned and speechless. He shook Jack's hand.

"How come you two play with tennis balls?"

"He keeps nailing me with line drives." His gramp laughed, lifting a yellow tennis ball from his ancient, floppy glove. "With these I get only bruises—no fractures."

Jack smiled. "Can he hit a baseball like that?"

"What the hell do you think we're doing this for?"

Jack motioned for them to go ahead with batting practice. Though nervous now, the boy kept pounding long line drives. After a bit, Jack walked out to the boy's grandfather and said a few things that made him smile and nod.

As he passed the boy on the way back to the hotel, Jack Buck said, "See you tomorrow, kid. You got a nice swing."

During dinner that night, the boy's gramp announced that Jack Buck had finagled passes for the whole family to Al Lang Field tomorrow, the Cardinals versus the Expos. The boy would likely meet some real big league players.

His stepmother's face turned stony. "Tomorrow is Sunday."

"Hey, honey," his father said cautiously, "how often does something like this happen? Can't we ease up a little? We're on vacation." He had once played baseball himself, though not in any exceptional way. He maintained that talent in a family often skipped a generation, so he was thankful for his father's mentoring of the boy. In spite of his new wife's attitude, he'd stayed a Tigers' fan, if a restrained one.

The boy knew to stay silent. A word from him could

provoke a barrage of Bible passages about obedient children being pleasing to God.

"Ease up? How do we ease up on faith? We've already made plans to visit the St. Petersburg church," she said with a calm voice and a drawn smile. "You know perfectly well what the plans are. And I'd like him there. It would bless him to go with us."

His gramp, who usually stayed out of things, said, "The game doesn't start till one. How about I pick all of you up at noon in front of the church. We'll be there in plenty of time."

"I certainly don't intend to go," his stepmother said.

"Nor do I," said his gram. "I have a dinner to fix."

"Well, we'd love to have you two ladies along." His gramp's tone was unnaturally warm and gracious.

"I have no desire whatsoever to see grown men playing a boy's game, especially on the Lord's Day."

"Well then," his father said, getting a little heated. "Just the boys will go. We'll meet you outside church, dad. You drive yourself home, Helen."

His stepmother's look was startled, disbelieving, prompting the boy to cheer silently. His father, before this surprising turn, had consistently let the strength of her righteousness subdue him. In three years of marriage, she had altered him in significant ways. The boy's real mother lacked her movie star looks, but she'd been an easy, sunny presence. Some days, especially Sundays, the boy woke up aching for her.

"I think we need to have a talk, Richard," she said quietly and rose from the table. But his father kept eating, refusing to follow her. His gramp grinned faintly but said nothing. Gram ignored them all. The boy sensed that something important was going on.

St. Petersburg had its own Foursquare Gospel Church (the boy had hoped to get a break from this), and it proved more wildly Spirit-filled than their own Foursquare up north, people erupting in tongues every few minutes and interrupting the ancient preacher who seemed happy to let the Spirit flow. He had a folksy Southern drawl and blurted out AMEN with a question mark for every point he made. The congregation echoed him noisily. Some stood, raised their arms, and swayed as if in a trance. As the boy's stepmother stood and did the same, the boy thought about her frequent trance-like moods (she maintained Christians were in the world but not of it, puzzling him). The music came and went at odd times, performed with abandon by an old black woman on a keyboard, a freckled girl about his age on an electric guitar, and a pale, blubbery woman on drums whose arms waggled as she played. People sang passionately, and some danced in the aisles. When noon came, the service was nowhere near being done. The boy's father glanced impatiently at his watch as prayers for healing and the laying on of hands began. A line of ailments stretched down the side aisle and around the back.

"Time to go," his father hissed, gripping the boy's arm. The stepmother, eyes sealed in prayer, lips moving soundlessly, didn't notice them until they were halfway to the door.

"Richard!" they heard her cry. But by then it was too late. The boy's grandfather, always faithful, was parked in front of the double front doors with the engine running. They piled into the Ford wagon and were off. The boy smiled when he saw his soft Mizuno baseball glove on the back seat. His father tore off his tie.

"Good service?" his grandfather asked.

"Quite nice," the boy said.

"We'll talk about it later," his father muttered.

"I told a lie," his gramp said. "The game really starts at two. Jack wanted us there early."

The boy had been to Al Lang Field before and considered it the next best thing to heaven. A partially covered grandstand wrapped the field from first base to third, with bleachers stretching into both outfields. A small crowd of early bird fanatics waited for batting practice to start. Just beyond the left field foul line, a marina gleamed in the sunlight, full of boats sheltering from Tampa Bay. The field was a miracle of perfect, cross-cut, shining grass with a hosed-down reddish infield of fine clay and sand. Covered green dugouts butted up to the stands with a few coaches and players wandering in and out. Jack Buck, dressed in a white shirt and blue tie, was waiting for them at the gate.

"Hey Stan, hey Tram," he said and squeezed the boy's

shoulder. His gramp introduced his father, who seemed as star-struck as the boy.

"Follow me," Jack said. "I got some friends I want you to meet." Instead of going in, he led them to the back of the stands where he unlocked a metal door marked PRIVATE. They walked a damp-smelling concrete hallway to a door that said HOME TEAM LOCKER ROOM. Jack entered, and they followed, in awe. The boy's heart was drumming in his ears.

The room was full of players getting into uniform. The boy couldn't identify them; he knew certain Cardinal players by name but rarely saw the team play. Jack Buck motioned to an older guy, fair-skinned like most redheads, with sunburned cheeks and pale white forehead.

"Red, I want you to meet some friends of mine. This is Stan Fields, the jazz piano man I keep telling you about, his son Rick, and his grandson Tram."

"Tram?"

"It's a nickname," Jack explained, "after Alan Trammell."

"Hey, son," he said, ruffling the boy's hair. "I'm Red Schoendienst. You must be a shortstop." The boy nodded. "I played some short but mainly second base. If you're any good, you'll need your own nickname."

"Keep an eye on this kid," Jack said. "I'm serious."

"Shit, Jack," Red laughed. "I'll be retired or dead by the time he's old enough."

"Okay, screw you, I'll do it myself."

"Get the kid a ball," Red said. "We'll sign it."

A stocky Cardinal with a boxer's square jaw tossed Red a ball. The boy recognized this one from baseball cards. It was Ken Boyer, the Cardinal manager. Red, who had once managed the Cardinals and would again, was now a coach. "This ball's pretty clean," Ken said. "You sign it, Red, then I will." Red had a ballpoint pen that they both used to scribble their names on the white of the ball. Jack signed it as well, and then walked it around the room to three more players.

In the dugout, where Jack led them next, Jack handed him the ball, and the boy read the names Lou Brock, Ted Simmons, Garry Templeton.

"We didn't want just any bum to sign this," Jack said. "Save room for a few Expos, too. I'll show you the ones."

The boy's father was dazzled. "Do you believe this?" he whispered.

Players were clearing the locker rooms now, stretching and running on the sidelines. The boy put his ball glove on. As the men of his family sat self-consciously side-by-side on the Cardinal's bench, players spitting and swearing and turning the air blue, a ball came skipping into the dugout. The boy made a dive and picked it off. He moved out onto the grass behind the foul line and fired it back to an Expo outfielder loosening up with a coach. The outfielder had DAWSON and the number 10 printed on the back of his jersey. The boy felt an electric charge run through him. He had just thrown a ball to Andre Dawson, the best center fielder on earth. Dawson smiled and whipped a grounder at the boy. Surprised and pleased, the boy back handed it and hit Dawson's glove with a bullet. Another came at him hard. He took it on a short hop and threw a strike to the big glove. The great outfielder laughed, raised a thumb to him, and went back to throwing to the coach.

Jack Buck took them to the Expos dugout to meet Dick Williams, the manager. He signed the ball. Catcher Gary Carter signed the ball. The boy looked at Jack and then out toward Andre Dawson. "Damn right, that's one you want," Jack said. "Go get him."

The boy jogged toward Andre Dawson who sat on the grass stretching his long legs. Dawson recognized him and smiled. The boy handed him the ball and pen, and he signed it "Andre 'Hawk' Dawson."

The boy read it. "Hawk?" the boy asked.

"I got a hawk eye at bat. My uncle gave me the nickname when I was a kid. What's your name, son?"

"Tom Fields, but I like Tram, after Alan Trammell."

"Gotta get a nickname of your own. Nice glove, nice arm. You look like you got some gifts. Yeah, you need a nickname that's just yours."

The boy went back to the dugout, sat down between his gramp and his father, and watched batting practice in a daze of wonderment.

As infield practice began and the game got close to starting, Jack Buck came by and said it was time he got to work. First, though, he showed them their reserved seats just behind the dugout. As they made their way through a guarded gate into the stands, the boy was shocked to see his stepmother sitting in one of those reserved seats. His father saw her, too, but looked away as if he hadn't. Before he departed, Jack Buck shook each of their hands. As he gripped the boy's hand, he turned to the grandfather. "Listen, Stan. This boy can play. I wouldn't tell you if it wasn't true."

"I agree, Jack. And thanks for all this."

Jack smiled and climbed toward the press box.

His father sat down next to his stepmother and said, "Hello, Helen. Didn't expect to see you here."

"I didn't expect to be. I'm not glad I am." Her voice was low and flat.

The boy and his gramp took seats next to his father, away from her.

"Why **are** you here?" his father went on.

"Just to see what it's like. I've been sitting right here in a dark cloud of profanity and ungodly talk of a sort I've never heard. It's no place for a boy. Let me take him home."

His father rolled his eyes toward a cloudless, pure blue sky. "We're not walking out on Jack Buck's hospitality. We're staying for the game," he said firmly. "If you can't take some cussing, then go on home. You'll never hear the boy talking like that, but we can't avoid the world, Helen."

The boy saw a tear pop out, but she quickly stood and left them there. He felt bad for her even though she was wrong. His father didn't say a word about her, but suggested they go down and get hotdogs, which they did, along with a couple of beers and a Coke for the boy.

The boy sat and watched the game, as fully happy as he'd ever been. The Expos won by two, but it didn't matter. On the way home, his father got talking about family things to his grandfather. "I'm not sorry I married her," he said. "She's made a difference in my life. I mean, I'm a believer and I've felt the Spirit working in my life often enough. But I must admit that, hard as she's prayed, I've never received the gift of tongues and likely never will. It's because, dammit, I'm not sure it's a gift I want. I fake a few things, too, like God telling me what to do about used cars. And I must admit that during those times she was praying and laying hands on me—well, she's just so drop-dead gorgeous, ask any guy in the church—I'd find myself scheming about how to get in her pants. You can see my spiritual life has a ways to go."

The boy's grandfather laughed heartily.

His father turned to the boy sitting in back, his baseball glove still on his hand and the autographed ball buried in it. "Sorry, son. Never mind that." He looked back to the grandfather. "The Foursquare Church is not really my cup of tea, either. I'm sorry I've made the boy go there and to that funky Christian school. Maybe I need to change some things."

"It's not so bad," the boy said truthfully. There were, like most places, some good people and some bad ones. Like his father, though, he knew he'd never have the gift of tongues or hear God speaking to him on a regular basis. He was certain, however, that God had communicated with him clearly a short while ago—this time through Jack Buck, the radio voice of the Cardinals, speaking words the boy would treasure in his heart.

His stepmother, soon after the trip, became pregnant and gave birth to a girl, and then another one just thirteen months later. The boy adored his little sisters, both wild rapscallions, tomboys who gave their mother fits. By the time they went off to school, they both could swing a good bat, and their mother's movie star looks showed signs of erosion. Maybe as recompense, though, she discovered (credit life itself) kinder and more effective ways of sharing her faith with people.

40 years passed by in no time, and Tom Fields (who on the baseball diamond, once his church background leaked out, became known ever after as Foursquare Fields) realized in a calm, philosophical way that his dreams had not all materialized. Yet he had held firmly to remnants of them, in particular the autographed baseball from that remarkable day at Al Lang Field. He hadn't sealed the ball hermetically for preservation but had allowed his children and friends to touch it, hear the story, and read the famous names. Most of those players were dead now and the signatures fading. Six Hall of Famers had signed the ball as well as two who'd come close. The ball was no doubt worth a fortune, but it wasn't for sale—not at any price.

MAGIC IN THE WORLD

The magical marks were called letters, and they made words. That much Olivia knew. Some were straight and stick-like, some curved like snakes, some round with tails. Some seemed to be others upside down. How many of them were there? At three she learned to sing their names and learned there were only 26. That surprised her—she thought there were at least a hundred or more, (whatever a hundred was). Each had a sound—no, several sounds.

Her parents read to her every night, but she would never be able to learn this impossible thing. She memorized *Barney Beagle Plays Baseball* listening to her father and mother read and reread the book and then pretending to read it herself—all 79 pages. But she knew (as did her parents) that it wasn't reading. At four she began to recognize cat, hat, bat, and rat. They were all the same except for the starting sound. The recognition of it was like a light bursting in her head. Her parents bought a book of alphabet sounds—phonics, they called it. It was the wisest book she'd ever known. Within two weeks the miracle of reading came to her, the great mystery unlocked, and she quickly forgot she had not always known it.

Of course, she kept doing it, loving it. She read *The Eye Book* to her sister Anna who was a little over a year younger and envious of Olivia's abilities. By the time Olivia was five, she was reading chapter books about boxcar children, about a family in a little house on the prairie, and especially about horses. Words and pictures and magical worlds came to life in her head, and she played and read with Anna (who quickly learned the secret, too) and was happy.

And then one early September day, she was sent off to an old brick building called Jefferson School, and she met Mrs. Mulligan, her new teacher. Her non-magical education had now begun. Mrs. Mulligan was nice but quite old and set in her ways. Through each fall, year after year, she taught a long segment on the Indians of Michigan. She hung faded posters of a Potawatomi village. The students built little brown butcher paper teepees and napped beside them on their roll-up rugs. And no one but Mrs. Mulligan read stories because kindergarteners couldn't read. Olivia tried to tell her that she read whole chapter books, but Mrs. Mulligan knew that such things were impossible.

"In first grade you'll begin to learn reading," Mrs. Mulligan wisely said. "You're quite smart, Olivia, but you need to be patient. How would you like to wear the feathered headdress today?"

In first grade, Olivia began to notice a feel to school like ponies walking in a ring. Miss Rose was young and quite pretty except for her sharp nose that reminded Olivia of a nuthatch beak. Each morning Olivia would dutifully get up at 7:00, brush her teeth, wash her face and dress in her school clothes. She ate Special K and a muffin with peanut butter, gathered her schoolwork and pink lunchbox into a Barbie backpack, took Anna's hand (Anna now had Mrs. Mulligan and was building teepees out of brown butcher paper) and caught the school bus, both of them enduring the clamor to and from school, though Anna went only three days in a week.

She took *Little Women* to school one day for silent reading time, and Miss Rose phoned her mother and asked that Olivia not read so far ahead of her class. Instead Miss Rose would double up on photocopied work sheets to keep Olivia busy. This child's work made Olivia so angry she wanted to pinch Miss Rose's pointed nose. Her parents were beside themselves about what to do. At home, Olivia was reading *Swiss Family Robinson*, and Anna was racing through one chapter book after another. The two made up plays using characters from the books they read and their Playmobil people and plastic horses. Olivia sometimes suggested Anna's lines because she remembered so many, and Anna dutifully delivered them. Their playtime was the most important part of their day, though they had to wait through long hours of school to get to it. Their parents still read to them, which was a joyful thing, and took them to the library on weekends to replenish book supplies. Olivia loved learning but not going to school.

Life continued plodding on, day after day, in this divided way. Her father sometimes read poetry to them and often wrote his own. His job was building guitars, which he did in a metal building behind the house. Her mother was a pianist who taught piano to various students in their home. Both Olivia and Anna were her students, too. Anna took to music a bit faster than Olivia. Olivia loved it but preferred words. Mother sang beautifully, taught them duets for church, and, of course, accompanied them.

One evening after he'd read some poems, their father asked them an odd question: "Do you remember in the very beginning of the Bible where God asks Adam to name the animals? Well, imagine that one day God brings out an elephant and a mouse and tells Adam to name one Ping and the other Pong. Which should he name which?"

Olivia thought a moment, smiled, and said, "I'd name the mouse Ping and the elephant Pong."

"Yes, I'd do the same," said Anna, nodding.

"But why?" father asked.

"Ping sounds little," said Olivia.

Anna nodded once more. "Pong sounds much bigger."

"That's curious," father said. "They're almost the same word."

"Yes, they are." Anna frowned as she thought about this.

"O is bigger than i," Olivia said. "But I'm not sure why."

"Bring me the answer tomorrow."

By chance, Miss Rose, without intending it, provided the answer the next morning. She was having her first grade students fill out a worksheet called *Having Fun with Noisy Words*. To demonstrate she read them a poem (something she rarely did) that went like this:

> "Pop, pop, popcorn,
> Popping in the pot!
> Pop, pop, popcorn,
> Eat it while it's hot!
>
> Pop, pop, popcorn,
> Butter on the top!
> When I eat popcorn,
> I can't stop!"

Miss Rose looked pleased with the grins and titters from

her class. "Words sometimes sound very noisy, don't they? If you really listen, do you hear all that noise?"

Olivia got excited for the first time ever in Miss Rose's class. She raised her hand. "Yes, I hear popcorn," she exclaimed. "Every P is a little explosion from my lips. The O is big and round in my mouth." She demonstrated with an exaggerated "POP," and her classmates laughed out loud "My lips and tongue and teeth and mouth are like musical instruments, Miss Rose. I never knew it before!"

This appeared to be more of an answer than Miss Rose wanted. Her smile tightened as Olivia went on.

"Now I can understand a story my father told. He told us God asked Adam to name an elephant and a mouse—and to choose the names Ping or Pong. Naturally, the mouse would be Ping—do you get it?— and the elephant Pong because one vowel is made with a tiny closed up mouth and the other with a great big open mouth. I see it now!"

Miss Rose seemed not to understand. "I don't recall God ever asking Adam to name an elephant and a mouse, especially not silly names like Ping and Pong. What in the world are you talking about, Olivia? We're discussing poetry, not the Holy Bible. Honestly, your mind works in the strangest ways."

And for the rest of the morning, Olivia said no more. At lunchtime recess, she found Anna crying underneath a large maple tree. She sat down beside her and put an arm around her shoulders.

"What happened, Anna? Are you okay?"

"I hurt my knee. Jacob Brown said you were weird, so I kicked him. He pushed me down and took my pudding cup."

"Jacob Brown's way bigger than you. He's in my class, and he's a rotten skunk. I'm going to go find him and take away your pudding cup."

Anna cried a little more. "Don't, Olivia. He's mean. I just want to go home."

"We can't. The bus doesn't come until later."

"We could walk. I think I know the way."

Olivia sat considering it. Miss Rose's class was the last place on earth she wanted to be today. But they wouldn't get far before they'd be caught and brought back. That is, unless they traveled a secret way. Her imagination happened to be full of the Swiss Robinson family, shipwrecked on a deserted island—with a thirty-foot boa constrictor coming after them and bloodthirsty pirates, too. She smiled at the thought of Mr. and Mrs. Robinson and their four boys living alone in a tree house they'd built themselves, and later, when the rains began, a dry and cozy cave they'd discovered in a mountainside. The father and mother taught the boys everything they needed to know.

The same creek that passed behind her father's guitar workshop also meandered, he had told them, through the ravines and beneath streets of the town. The creek ran under a street a block behind school and out into a deep ravine on the other side. If they followed the creek, she guessed they'd be home before school was out.

Olivia saw a classmate of Anna's nearby and motioned to her. "Carolyn," she said to the small, pigtailed girl. "Anna and I are feeling sick. When you get back to class, tell Mrs. Mulligan that we had to go home, would you please?"

Carolyn looked blank. "I guess so. What's the matter?"

"We both feel like throwing up."

Carolyn backed up a step, nodded, and ran off. In a few minutes the bell rang ending noon recess, but Olivia and Anna stayed put, crouched behind the thick maple tree. When the playground was empty, Olivia took Anna's hand, hurried toward the street and crossed into the ravine without anyone seeing them.

"Our backpacks are still at school," Anna said fretfully.

"No one will take them, Anna," she reassured her. So they scrambled down a dirt path to the spot where the little creek streamed out of a metal culvert. "We'll just follow the creek to our house. It's easy, and no one will see us." They set out, pleased that a small path continued for a while beside the creek. The woods around them filled with the music of birdsong. Though the day was sunny, the ravine was bright sometimes, dark and shadowed others. She decided not to tell Anna about the thirty-foot boa constrictor or the pirates. Beneath the birdsong she heard something more constant, a creaking sort of hum.

"What is that?" Anna asked, tightening her grip on Olivia's hand.

Tall grass grew beside the path. Olivia bent down and spotted small winged insects clinging to the stalks of grass. "Look, Anna. I thought I knew the sound. We have these in our yard."

"Oh, they're crickets! They sound funny—like our noisy gate."

"They sound like their name."

"They do!" Anna's face lit up. "Do you think when Adam named them, he heard that? Cricket! Cricket! It's just right. Maybe that's what Dad meant with Ping and Pong."

"Of course he did, except that was about littleness and bigness. I figured it out today. You're very smart, Anna."

"You're much smarter, Olivia," she said.

As they walked through the increasingly dark and snarled ravine overgrown with wild grape vines, they passed time by listening carefully for sounds. Frogs startled them, vaulting into water just as they approached. Olivia saw a bullfrog crouched inside a hollow log, eyes just above the surface of the water. A low croak rumbled out of his bulging throat.

"Bullfrog croaking in a hollow log," Olivia said, and for the first time ever, she was sure she'd made a line of poetry.

She was sure, too, that this adventure had become scarier than she'd expected. A snake streaked by them in some short grass. Anna screamed. Olivia pulled her close and thought for an instant of the thirty-foot boa constrictor.

"I didn't know this ravine was so deep," she said, trying to sound calm but feeling quite uneasy. "That was just a baby snake sneaking away through the grass. We scared it." She smiled a little, hearing the hiss of all her s's. Some words were such physical things, almost like little bodies. There was so much rightness in the world!

"Are we okay, Olivia?" Anna asked in a small voice. "Are we lost?"

"I don't think so, but I wish Mom and Dad were here. I thought this would be easier."

The path ran out, and they found themselves on the edge of a large, swampy pool with green lily pads thick at the edges. A crow squawked loudly in a tree just above, startling them.

"What is that?" Anna said fearfully.

"It's just a noisy crow. Look up in that tree."

Anna looked, and there he was. "I guess he has the right name, too."

"Adam was smart," Olivia concluded.

They pushed through high grass and thick tangles, making their way slowly around the green pool. The ground began to grow soft and muddy and squished under their tennis shoes. They froze when they heard something large crashing toward them through the brush just ahead. Olivia pushed aside a grapevine and whispered, "Look, Anna." There stood three of the softest, most velvety creatures she's ever seen, one with mossy antlers and two without, feeding on small shoots, unaware of the girls. Olivia's heart stopped pounding; she squeezed Anna's hand and began to breathe again.

But the calm didn't last. Out of nowhere, a huge black dog came bounding and howling down into the ravine. The deer bolted and vanished in a flash. Anna took a step back and her right foot disappeared in the mud and her leg followed—right up to the knee. She shrieked, and Olivia pulled on her arm as hard as she could. The mud at last let go, and both girls tumbled sideways into the grass.

"Oh, I lost my shoe," Anna said, tears filling her eyes. "It's my best one."

"Maybe I can get it out." But as Olivia reached toward the rapidly disappearing mud hole, she saw the black, terrifying monster of a dog not ten feet away, staring them down. Anna gripped her arm and began crying in earnest.

"Go away! Shoo!" Olivia shouted.

The dog studied her as if amused, barked twice resoundingly, and then turned and climbed back toward the top of the ravine. Olivia watched him until he was out of sight and then hugged Anna.

"He's gone, Anna, but I think your shoe is lost."

"I still have my sock," Anna whimpered. "I think I can make it."

"I don't know. Let's get around this pond and see."

Beyond the pond, the water narrowed to a creek again, but there was no path. Olivia looked ahead and began to see how foolish she'd been to lead her sister into this place. She looked toward the steep incline the black dog had climbed and saw it actually was a path, slanting and zigzagging, with bared roots looking almost like steps. And then she heard music. Listening closely, she recognized an old, old song her father sometimes played. Whoever was playing now, though, was making the song much sadder and full of misery than her father ever did.

"Let's go up and see who it is," she said.

Olivia pulled Anna to her feet (one leg caked with mud), and they began climbing the path out of the deep ravine. The incline was steep, and they both had to use their hands to help pull their way up. As they neared the top, Olivia saw a fieldstone chimney and then a sagging roof. The music was much closer now. She hoisted Anna up and over the last bit of worn path and saw the back of a small log cabin, weathered and dark with age, bordered by a long row of stacked firewood. Nearby stood a wooden shed the size of a garage with a roof slanting toward the ravine and a black stovepipe rising from it.

Olivia held Anna's hand and cautiously made her way around the woodpile and into the front yard—a little patch of sparse grass surrounded by a ragged assortment of spindly wildflowers. The front porch of the cabin ran its full length, and on it, in a cane-backed chair, sat a man playing a guitar as old and worn as he was. The man looked like no one she'd ever seen. His skin was black, his face covered with a wild white beard that was really more green than white. He wore a painter's cap that had been white but now was turning green, too. His lips were thick and smiling, partly obscured by a bushy, greenish moustache. He may have heard them approach, but he didn't open his eyes or stop playing until the sad song was done. She watched his hands on the guitar and saw they were turning green, too. His fingers flashed on the strings, and she felt her heart ache at what he played.

The music stopped, he opened his eyes, and when he saw the two of them, he smiled broadly. Olivia knew at once they were safe.

"Well, now," he said. "Who is this come visiting old Uncle Dummy?"

Olivia hesitated, surprised at his strange name. "I'm Olivia. This is my sister Anna. Why are you green?"

He laughed heartily. "Never seen a green man before?"

"Not ever."

"Well, I'll tell you about that. But first tell me why you're here."

"We were hiking in the ravine, but a giant black dog came down and scared us."

"A giant black dog, was it? Was he chasing some deer?"

"Yes, he was. And I think he meant to eat us."

"Mercy! Did he look anything like that old black dog?" He pointed to the end of the porch where a black, normal-looking dog with floppy ears lay calmly gazing at them, his head on his paws.

"Maybe a little."

He grinned and pointed to the cane-backed chairs on either side of him. "You girls been having some adventures, I can see. Sit and rest a spell. That old ravine is hard on a person. No school today?"

Olivia looked at her feet. "We have a half day off." It wasn't exactly a lie but almost.

He chuckled merrily. "Did that myself—one too many times. Well, little lady," he said to Anna. "I bet you stepped in the wrong part of the swamp. Lose your shoe?"

"The mud took it," Anna said.

He pointed toward the shed. "There's a hand pump. Big sister Olivia, you work the handle for her so she can wash off. Then come rest on the porch, and I'll get you ladies a glass of milk. You like milk?"

"Oh, yes, thank you," Olivia said.

When Anna's leg was clean again and her sock rinsed out, they went to the porch and sat on either side of the chair that held the guitar. Uncle Dummy soon came out with two glasses of milk and a paper plate of cookies. He set the milk on the porch rail in front of their chairs so they could sit and drink. He sat between them and passed the cookies—gingersnaps a little stale, not her favorite. Anna loved gingersnaps and ate two before Olivia had nibbled the edges of one. She felt she should make conversation.

"Why did your parents give you such a funny name, Uncle Dummy, sir?"

He laughed and said, "I named me that, honey, not my parents. They named me Mose. Mose Harris."

"I like that much better."

"Why are you green?" Anna asked.

He laughed again. "It's from corn straw, honey. The corn straw dye turns me green! I even smell green."

And it was true. He smelled green, like the inside of a barn full of hay.

"See that little shed over there?" He reached behind him and grabbed a straight broom with a long, honey-colored wood handle leaning beside his door. "I make my corn brooms there, just like this one. I make a few brooms and then sit and play my old guitar, which is turning green, too. I used to be a black man, but now I'm a green man." He chuckled merrily at that, his eyes dancing.

Olivia discovered she was eating her second cookie. The milk was cold and fresh.

"While you're having your snack, why don't I play something I bet you never heard before." He stood and went to the edge of the yard and picked something. When he sat again, she saw it was a long, thin blade of grass. He pressed it lengthwise between his thumbs and put it to his mouth and blew. A high, shrill sound emerged that in a moment became the strangest, funniest church song they'd ever heard.

"I know it—it's *Jesus Loves Me*," Anna said.

"This grass flute's part of my nature band," he said. He reached out from the porch and pulled a leaf from a birch tree, held the edge to his mouth and played *Happy Birthday*. Olivia laughed, delighted, and he followed with a moaning church hymn on a saw and fiddle bow he kept hung on a nearby nail. But that didn't end it. He played rhythms on soupspoons and got both girls up to dance. The green man could make music out of anything. Olivia was bewitched. Finally he lifted his guitar and set it on his green knees. "I'll sing you a church song that's plain old fun. You go to church?"

"We sing at church. Our mom plays piano for us," Anna said.

"Our dad plays guitar," Olivia told him. "He makes guitars, too."

Uncle Dummy smiled broadly. "Does he now? Imagine that. What is his name?"

"Martin. I saw his name on your guitar. Did he make it?

May I see what it says?" Uncle Dummy held out the guitar to her, and she read "Christian Frederick Martin and Company, established 1833, New York, New York."

"A little girl like you can read all that?"

"Of course," Olivia said. "We can read books."

"My, oh my, that's a miracle. I'm guessing your daddy's name is Martin French. Martin French makes a fine guitar. My guitar is way, way older than your daddy, honey. It's a different kind of Martin. I know your daddy, though—played with him a few times in the city park downtown. Your mama's name is Jenny French."

"You know us!" Anna exclaimed.

"Well, I know you now. And after I play this song, I think we should phone your daddy and mama and let them know you're here. Do you remember the phone number?"

"Of course!" both girls answered at once.

Uncle Dummy smiled, settled the guitar on his lap, and began to play a rhythm that sounded like a train. This time he sang along in an old sandpaper voice that made them laugh to hear. And though it was rough, it was right and wonderful to hear. With the guitar chugging away at a good speed, he sang:

> "This train is bound for glory, this train.
> This train is bound for glory, this train.
> This train is bound for glory,
> Jesus made a place in heaven for me.
> This train is bound for glory, this train."

And he sang the verse two more times with variations in some places, but in the next verse the guitar train picked up speed and instead of words they knew, Uncle Dummy sang in a strange language he made up as he went (or so it seemed), and instead of singing the melody, he traveled all around it, using words like "Dooya, dooya, babba doo bop. Yoodat, shobop, dabba doo bop. Dot dot dot, reeba doo bop!" And his voice turned into a trumpet, and then a bass fiddle, and then a saxophone with a brash and wicked sound.

And as Olivia watched and listened in wonder, there came a moment—one that would happen only a few times in her life—when in a blast of light she could sense a simplicity beyond all understanding, a glorious oneness, a magic holding the world in place, safe in the boundless sky.

And once Uncle Dummy was done, they clapped happily, and then he made the phone call. Their parents came in minutes, along with four police officers that Olivia told Anna were pirates. There were tears and some scolding, but they were safe and relieved. Their parents hugged Uncle Dummy, and their mother kissed his green cheek.

When the semester ended in December, Olivia and her sister left Jefferson School, and their parents took over their schooling. Learning became magical again. Their father explained that Mose Harris called himself Uncle Dummy because, though he had a thousand gifts, he'd never learned to read.

Sometimes their mother drove them over to visit Mose, listen to him play, and sing with him. Sometimes he rode his bicycle to them. He was greener than ever and always kind. And just in case the subject should come up, they had the book of phonics handy at all times

"Help me do it by myself," became the motto of their little school. And Olivia and her sister lived by that and grew in a thousand ways.

THE JESUS BOYS

Jesse Bodine, having tried and failed to enroll himself in a new school (it was already May), approached the block-long midway of Silver Beach Amusement Park overlooking the public beach and Lake Michigan, a hundred steps below the bluffs where the St. Joseph business district and rich-looking Whitcomb Hotel loomed over the waterfront. They'd arrived two days before, settled in a shack with two cots and a hotplate, a luxury after the ten days he'd spent sleeping in their aging Studebaker, thawing out and eating in school while his pa sat in a South Bend jail. Two long concrete piers, one with a lighthouse, stretched out into the lake from the mouth of the St. Joe River. Near the south pier stood a weathered dance pavilion with the stylish name, Shadowland.

Jesse passed the spindly underpinnings of a wooden rollercoaster and then a tall ferris wheel visible from miles away. The carnivals they'd moved with on and off were always the traveling kind, forever tearing down and setting up, but this one stayed put. It had a solid feel he hadn't known before. He moved onto the midway—a boardwalk with a flat roof sheltering a shooting gallery, a Guess Your Weight concession, the usual variety of game booths like others he'd worked, a carousel of hand-carved horses, and the revolving barrel entrance to the Fun House with a mirror maze and an evil, laughing mechanical clown.

The crowd was a good size for late afternoon in the middle of May. From down the midway, Jesse heard the rough bark of his father's voice from the midst of a gathering.

"Hey, take a chance, boys, take a chance!" Thurman Bodine crowed. "Knock the bottles down and win a real live chameleon on a leash! Hey, you, son," he called to a young man built like a wrestler. "You got an arm on you like a damn gorilla. Win that little lady a chameleon on a leash. Come on, son, come on, you're big as a bull!"

Jesse approached his father through the crowd. The gorilla, a stocky kid who looked two or three years older than

Jesse, with a cute redhead at his side, took the bait. He paid a dime, wound up, and threw the ball with all his might. Two of the five bottles fell. He shook his head. His second throw missed everything. The third hit near the mark but tipped only one bottle. The other two stood as if nailed down.

The kid said, "Those bottles are lead weighted."

Thurman, hard and stringy and bent like a catalpa bean, smirked at this. "Let some real man try. You throw like a fairy princess." At that moment he spotted Jesse. "Hey, you!"

Jesse looked up, acting surprised.

"You with them matchstick arms," Thurman went on. "Come over here and show this big boy how to throw a baseball."

Jesse moved closer, acting nervous. "Me? What do I have to do?"

Thurman shoved three balls at him. "Knock them bottles down in two balls or three, you win a chameleon. Knock them down with one and you win that giant panda worth ten dollars. All for a single dime, son."

"All right, I guess." Jesse put the balls down on the counter and reluctantly dug in his pocket. He handed over the money, picked up one baseball, gripped it lightly, two fingers across the seams. He backed up several steps, wound up with a big, high baseball kick, reached back and threw the ball with an easy, fluid motion. It took off from his fingers like a rocket. All five bottles exploded into the canvas behind them.

"That was dumb luck," the gorilla said. He glanced at the redheaded girl and reached into his pocket for more money.

That evening, Thurman had a crowd around him. Jesse, with two giant pandas sitting at his side, rolled a baseball in his hand while his father went on working the crowd.

"Who'll bet a dollar against this skinny arm? Who's got a dollar says this boy can't knock down all them bottles with one ball from way across the midway?" He turned his yellow eyes to Jesse. "You throw free. Give me a chance, boy—you're already cleaning me out."

"I can't do it from way back there," Jesse said, shaking his head.

"It's my money. You got nothin' to lose, and you get a buck if I win."

Jesse lifted a ball uncertainly.

"Damn! I found me Dizzy Dean and Bob Feller wrapped in one!"

Several men stood at the counter setting out dollar bills, each of which Thurman covered. At the edge of the crowd a dapper man in a blue striped suit and graying beard hiding his bowtie watched with curiosity. He studied Jesse as he backed up across the midway, doubling the distance of the throw. He found a spot he liked, took that easy windup and let the ball fly. The bottles exploded but two were left standing. The crowd erupted with cheers and applause, and the men at the counter collected from Thurman, who looked crestfallen.

Someone in the crowd cried out, "Hey, Dizzy Dean, how about doing it just like that again only for two dollars?"

Thurman shook his head and raised his hands in defeat, yet the bettors egged him on. He kept shaking his head, but it was clear his resolve was crumbling. "Oh, what the hell—this here's why I'm a poor man. You better get my money while it lasts, boys."

Quickly, the bets were down, and Thurman looked to the boy again. Jesse shrugged and lifted another ball and sent it screaming at the bottles. All five went down in a perfect strike. The crowd muttered in disbelief as Thurman raked up the winnings.

The dapper man took another long look at Jesse and then wandered down the midway.

At closing time, Thurman went into the tent behind his booth, lifted a small bottle of whiskey hidden in cigar box, and took a long pull. He sat down on a stool and counted out his dollar bills as Jesse watched.

"Hope nobody seen you come in here. They'll learn quick enough you're my trained monkey."

"I'm hungry, pa."

'Where were you? Going for supplies don't take half a day."

"Just looking around town. I got everything on the list." Thurman took him hard by the arm and twisted. The boy cried out in pain. "I tried to sign up for school—I'm almost finished with the year, pa!"

"You had enough school, you hear me?"

"But the law says I gotta go to school."

"The law don't say nothin' if it don't know where you are. Now you've gone and told them, you damn jackass."

"Don't worry, they didn't take me. It was the wrong school. That shack's in Benton Harbor, not St. Joe."

"Good thing." He snorted his contempt. "The wrong school…you're dumb as a stump."

Thurman paused, releasing Jesse's arm, and slowly lifted his dirty eyes to the tent flap. In the opening stood Bobo Pride, the manager of Silver Beach. He wore a tight suit, straw hat, and a gold stickpin in his tie. He had a bulldog's face and a cigar in his fist. Beside him stood Busby Snipe, a soft, fat man who managed the park's money.

Bobo lumbered up to Thurman and stared down at him. Thurman leered back.

"Two days on the job, Bodine, and you already broke my cardinal rule. You work for me, not for yourself. This is a clean operation. I heard about you…you work people for anything you can get. If you don't knock it off, I'm throwing your sorry ass out." Bobo stared hard, but Thurman didn't blink.

Busby spoke up for the first time. "I was watching him, Bobo. They were betting on that boy's arm. Ask the boy."

Thurman glared savagely at the fat man. He spat near the fat man's shoes and turned to Jesse. "Get outta here," he snarled.

Jesse slid quickly around Busby and out the tent flap. He wandered onto the lighted midway and back of the food stands where a truck was parked for unloading. A bald man in a blood-stained apron rolled a dolly full of boxed hotdogs down the ramp of his truck. He passed in front of Jesse and into the back of a food tent. Jesse looked up into the open truck, glanced around, slipped up the ramp and snatched a box of hotdogs. As he jumped down, he ran head-on into the dapper man with the graying beard. Jesse cried out, tried to get around him, but the man blocked his way.

"Put it back," the man said quietly.

"I'm just helping unload."

"No, you're not. Put it back before there's trouble."

In shock, Jesse turned, climbed the ramp, and slipped the box into the truck. The dapper man waited for him to return.

"What's your name, son?"

"Jesse Bodine."

"You stealing because you're hungry or are you just stealing?"

Jesse shrugged, not looking him in the eye.

Ten minutes later, Jesse sat across from him at a picnic table under a light, wolfing down hotdogs and Nehi orange.

"In case you wanted to know, I'm Major Gates."

Jesse kept his eyes lowered. "I'll pay you back for this."

"I was watching you work that crowd today. A boy like you needs a healthier livelihood."

Jesse kept eating, didn't respond.

"I know a lost sheep when I see one."

"I ain't lost, and I ain't a sheep."

"No? Well, maybe not. But how'd you like a better job?"

"I got a job."

"That's a con game, not a job."

"It's none of your—" Jesse stopped talking for a moment and looked at the man. "It ain't a con. Those bottles are lead weighted, but I knocked them down fair. Pa don't cheat."

"I saw you throw. I believe you knocked them down fair. What do they pay a boy like you here?"

"I guess that's my business." The man stared at him. "Pa pays me fifty cents a day…most days."

"I'll pay you four dollars—every day. If you're good, you could make a hundred a month."

Jesse was stunned. "Doing what?"

The man handed him a business card. Jesse stared at it:

THE ISRAELITE HOUSE OF DAVID
         PRESENTS
EDEN SPRINGS AMUSEMENT AND
BASEBALL PARK
EAST BRITAIN AVENUE
BENTON HARBOR, MICHIGAN
MAJOR GATES, MANAGER

"Doing whatever I ask you to. Eden Springs is across the river in Benton Harbor, four miles away."

"Pa'd never allow it."

"Well, you go and ask him and find out. Is this pa of yours a halfway decent man?"

The question made him uncomfortable. "He fixed army trucks in the war. He was good at it, but then he got shell shock." It was the one favorable thing he knew to say about his father.

"Well, then…" the Major offered his hand, and Jesse took it. "Give it some thought. That's one fine arm you have there…for just a boy. You about 15?"

Jesse snorted. "17 in a few more months."

The Major smiled at him, turned and ambled away toward the parking lot.

Jesse walked beside his pa through the dimly lit riverfront part of town toward the bridge to the river flats of Benton Harbor where the shack stood. His pa had sold the Studebaker to pay for coming here and starting over. Businesses were closed and dark except for Henry's Bar and Grill, the last place before the bridge.

"You go on home," Thurman told him. "I'm stopping here."

"I'll never find that shack by myself in the dark, pa. Let me come in and wait for you."

"God almighty, will I never be done looking after you?"

Jesse followed him in, and they sat down at the empty bar. Besides the bartender, who wore the nametag HENRY, there were only four old men at a table playing euchre. Thurman ordered a shot and a beer, and a root beer for Jesse.

As Henry poured the shot, Thurman asked, "So where's the money come from in this town?"

"Whirlpool, Auto Specialties, fishing boats. Why, you looking for work?" He opened a root beer.

"Maybe."

"Of course, there's the House of David, too. They got their finger in a lot of pies in St. Joe and Benton Harbor."

Thurman tossed down the shot and took a deep breath. "I heard of the House of David. They're holy rollers…those nuts sitting around growing beards, waiting for the world to end."

"I guess that's them, but they don't do much sittin' around. They got the biggest Olds dealership and the biggest open air farm market and cold storage plant in the whole country. And a motor court motel and Eden Springs Amusement Park, of course, and that baseball team of theirs. Those boys can play…"

"And I bet they pay Henry's Bar and Grill for spreading the word," he said with a sharp laugh. "I just can't stomach their kind of Bible thumpers. And I hear they got a wicked king."

"King Ben? Hell, he's been dead for years. He liked sex, I heard, but made his followers go without."

Thurman guffawed. "Go without? The good Lord hisself can't make that happen!"

"Well, all I know is those folks make money. Even through the Depression—the one that's supposed to be over now." He gave a snort. "I guess they got a fortune hid somewhere because they've never been much on banks." Henry shook his head wistfully. "That Major Gates—he's one of their top boys, I hear—talk about a smart cookie. King Ben never had his business sense."

"Major Gates?" Jesse asked.

"That's what they call him."

Thurman tossed down his beer in a long swallow and pushed the glasses toward Henry to refill. "Damn...I better start growin' me a beard."

In the shack (rented to them by Bobo Pride), Thurman made Jesse fry him up eggs and potatoes, even though it was way past midnight. He was drunk, now sucking the last inch of whiskey from a bottle, and turning meaner with every swallow. The place had no amenities besides a hot plate, a hand pump at the tin sink, and a tumbledown outhouse.

"What kind of son are you, anyway?" he slurred. "You never had a job in your life but knocking over bottles with a baseball. Worthless as tits on a nun." He tossed the empty bottle; it hit the wall near Jesse and somehow didn't break. Jesse gritted his teeth, scraped the eggs from a skillet and dumped them on the plate in front of Thurman, who set to shoveling them in.

"Damn you, pa! I ain't worthless. I work hard, and I got a new job if I want it."

Thurman laughed and kept eating. "You? Hell, what kind of job would anybody give you?"

"Working at Eden Springs Amusement Park! For four dollars a day—maybe a hundred a month. The man—that Major Gates—gave me his card and said to ask you."

His voice came out low, threatening. "What's this? Who done this?"

More cautious now, Jesse held out the business card. Thurman snatched it away. "Him…"

"Israelite House of David. God almighty! A man don't take all the trouble to raise up a son, just to send him off to dance with the devil! Clean up the mess and get yourself to bed, boy. Your pa tells you what you can do and can't do, and the answer is hell no." He tore the card to pieces.

Rage exploded in Jesse's head, and though he knew he was big enough now to do damage to his father, something always held him back.

The next morning his pa came to at 10:30, looking like he'd just returned from the dead. He scratched his head and moaned. They had to be at work by noon. Jesse was frying bread for the two of them and coffee was heating on the hot plate.

"You still alive?"

Thurman just growled and scratched. He sat up on the edge of the bed with his head hanging down. "In the night I got to workin' some things out. I was thinking you should go see about that job. Since I can't bet on your arm no more, we're gonna need money. I figure the devil's got more money than Bobo Pride, so go talk to that Major Gates. Don't waste no time about it, neither."

Jesse took a moment to absorb this, then felt a glimmer of something he hadn't felt for a long time—not since his ma had been alive. "Sure, I'll do it, pa. I'll do it right away."

Thurman stared at him with narrow, burning eyes. "You're doin' it for one reason—because I told you to. And don't think about keeping back money from me. You'll get what I think you need and nothin' more."

Jesse nodded and flipped the fried bread onto a plate.

It took him an hour of walking to find Eden Springs. He'd passed a school on the way and figured next time he'd borrow a bike. He stood in front of the park, staring at the arched gates as a Greyhound sightseeing bus pulled up close to him. Tourists came spilling out.

Inside the park, Jesse wandered about, wide-eyed. This was no ordinary amusement park: he passed in front of a large stage and amphitheater where a band in uniform was playing ragtime, led by a flamboyant conductor with a beard down to his chest. A miniature steam train passed by, pulling a load of children over a long, meandering track. He passed by a bowling alley, a beer garden, a penny arcade, a midget auto raceway, a zoo and aviary—all set into acres of landscaped grounds. He half-whispered "Ma should've seen this."

In awe, he wandered across a track and jumped at the shrill whistle of another steam train. He got out of the way, looking sheepishly at the engineer, who tipped his cap.

"You there, boy—do you want something?" Jesse spun around and saw the face of a girl about his age. She sat in a booth, selling tickets for the steam train. She wore a pink dress and straw hat, a small, elvish creature with strawberry hair gathered under her hat and green eyes that crackled with challenge. He stared at her.

"Are you deaf?"

"Don't call me boy. You're no older than me."

"If you like that train so much, why don't you buy a ticket?"

"I'm here for a job."

She laughed. "There're no jobs for Gentiles at Eden Springs."

Jesse stuffed his hands in his pockets. "I don't know what you mean."

"Gentiles—anyone who's not of the Israelite House of David. What's your name?"

"Jesse Bodine. I'm looking for some guy called the Major. He said I could have a job."

She pondered that a moment. "That'd be Major Gates. You'll most likely find him over by the baseball park. I can't imagine him offering work to any raggedy Gentile boy named Jesse Bodine." But she smiled a little. "My name's Miranda Honicutt."

His voice came out flat and defensive. "You think I'm lying, don't you."

A brown-bearded man in his mid 20s approached with a cash bag handcuffed to his wrist. "Any trouble here?"

"This boy said Major Gates offered him a job."

The man looked Jesse over. "Well, it's a mistake. We don't have any job openings at Eden Springs."

"He gave me his card."

"Let's see it."

"I...I lost it."

"Better be on your way, son. There's no job for you here."

Jesse reddened, glanced at Miranda who was grinning at him. He turned abruptly and hunched toward the front gate. As he passed under the arch, he felt a tug at his shirt. It was the girl.

"Do you always give up so easy?"

"I know when somebody's trying to make a fool of me," he snapped.

"Don't listen to that Nathan Short. It's not his say who gets a job. Anyway, he's just acting important in front of me." She grabbed his arm and yanked him in the direction of the baseball park. "It's my break time. I'll show you where the Major is."

She led him down a path and into a nearby ballpark with a fair-sized grandstand and maybe 20 players working out in various parts of the field. Most of them had the long hair and beards of Israelites.

"Do you like baseball?" she asked. He gave her an annoyed look, but she went on talking. "I do, but I like movies better."

"I don't go much."

"I'm not supposed to, but I sneak off. Have you seen 'Star Dust' with Linda Darnell? I've been four times."

Jesse shook his head, uncertain of himself with this self-assured, talkative girl.

He spotted Major Gates standing with his foot on the bench of a dugout, watching the infield warm up and talking to a man in a House of David baseball uniform. The man was big, with a thin, pointed beard and a long rope of hair hanging down his back. The Major looked up as Jesse and the girl approached.

"Well, well. John, here's someone I want you to talk to." He moved out of the dugout, held a hand out to Jesse. "I didn't think I'd see you again."

Jesse shook his hand. "My pa said it was all right."

"This boy said you offered him a job," Miranda chirped.

"I did."

He took Jesse by the arm and led him to the big man he'd been speaking to. "John Banner, this is Jesse Bodine. He's a young man with a future, I think. John manages our team, son."

"You been recruiting again?"

"I want you to see him throw."

John looked wary. "This is no young man. He's a boy."

"As a favor to me," the Major said.

John glanced at Jesse and then away. He rummaged in a bag for a catcher's mitt and moved wearily out of the dugout. "You ever played organized ball before, son?"

Jesse shook his head.

"You own a glove?"

"It's at home," he lied.

"That's a good place for it."

The Major stepped in. "I never told him what sort of job he was applying for, John. You certainly have some old glove or other lying around."

John shot the Major an irritated look and motioned for Jesse to follow him out on the field. "Hold up, boys," he shouted to the infielders. "The Major's recruited a young arm. Move over a minute and see what he can do."

The third baseman, a stocky stump of a man with a wiry red beard and hair tied back with a rawhide string, fired a cannon over to first and turned to Jesse with a grin.

"Deets," John said to him, " lend this young fella your glove. He left his at home."

Deets tossed his glove to Jesse. "You just up from the Little Leagues, son?"

A laugh went round the infield as the players knelt or sat on the bases. John went to the plate, took a mask from the catcher, a tall, skinny black man with a sleepy smile, short hair graying at the temples, and tossed a ball out to Jesse, who caught it awkwardly.

"You ever **been** in the Little Leagues?" John asked. Jesse shook his head. "I guess the Major must've spotted something the ordinary eye can't see." He squatted down. "Just hit the glove if you can."

Jesse walked onto the pitcher's mound, bewildered by the height of it and by the rubber. He felt around for some comfortable spot, finally settling his right heel in the toe hole in front of the rubber. He looked at the glove, took his long, leisurely windup, and let fire. The ball sailed three feet over John's head, hit the concrete at the base of the backstop and rebounded halfway back to the pitcher's mound.

"I can't throw way up on this hill with my foot in a hole. I need some level ground."

John glanced over at the Major and stood up. "In baseball, you throw downhill, son. Try it again."

Jesse went back to the rubber, tried to find a comfortable spot and couldn't. He moved to the grass behind the mound.

"You can't throw from way back there."

"Why not?"

"It's not legal, for one. And the batter has another ten feet to figure you out." Jesse began his windup anyway, so John quickly crouched and held up a target. The boy fired the ball from the flat grass. John never moved his glove—never had to. A puff of dust or smoke rose out of the pocket as the ball buried itself. John got to his feet, pulled off the glove, shaking out his hand.

The Major smiled. "I saw him knocking down bottles at Silver Beach."

"You throw a curve?" John said to Jesse.

Jesse shrugged, uncertain. "Sometimes I make it move to get all the bottles to fall. That one was straight."

"Was that your hardest?"

Jesse grinned and shook his head.

"Well, praise the Lord. Hop, come over here and catch this young fella." He tossed the mitt to the catcher, who pulled it on and squatted behind the plate like a big grasshopper.

"Deets, let's see what he does with a batter in the box."

"Only if he'll throw from where he is. He'll kill somebody otherwise." The third baseman picked up a bat and went to the plate, looking like he meant to eat the kid alive. He waggled the bat, raised it high behind him, and took a huge cut at the first pitch, twisting himself into a knot. He looked down in disbelief at the ball stuck in the catcher's glove.

Hop, the catcher, chuckled merrily. "Extra ten feet musta throwed you off, huh, Eddie?"

Jesse set his jaw and threw another. In the next dozen pitches, Eddie Deets managed to foul off just one. Finally, he tossed the bat down in disgust, amid general hilarity.

Jesse caught the eye of the girl, standing near the dugout. Smiling at him, she pulled off her straw hat and pushed back loose strands of her tied-up, pretty hair.

That afternoon, Hop Hopson, against his will, stood at the mound working with Jesse, showing him how to toe the rubber and push off to get more body into the pitch. Jesse tried it, but his foot kept slipping off.

"Boy, you got a smart arm and ignorant feet. You ever pitch from the stretch?"

"What's the stretch?"

Incredulous, Hop said, "When you got men on bases. You pitch from the stretch so you can hold 'em on."

"I think I saw it before."

"How many ball games you ever played in?"

"Some. Not many." He felt Hop's stare. "None."

Hop tossed up his long arms in exasperation. "How'd you blow a dozen pitches by Eddie Deets when you never played in a game before?"

Jesse grumbled, "I never said I played baseball. That was the damn Major's idea."

"Just you watch who you're damnin'. The Major is the only one keepin' you here, young fella. You'll practice baseball and get paid for a day's work. If you can find something better, than go do it. Otherwise shut up and do what I tell you to."

In a low, sullen voice Jesse said, "How come he hired me?"

"The Lord blessed you with a gift. Throwin' a baseball is the only reason you're here, not your personality. And it so happens I know everything there is about throwin' a baseball, so if you listen it might be worth all the bother and irritation you're causin' me. I'm only doing this for the extra pay."

"But I don't know that much about baseball, Hop."

"If you like it around here, you better learn quick." He slammed a ball into Jesse's glove. "And you call me Mr. Hopson." He let out a big sigh "I bet a dollar you don't even own a glove. Just keep that one. I don't use it much."

Jesse looked down at it with puzzlement.

Several hours later, Jesse sat on the grass near the dugout, wrung out and weary from throwing. Hop was fishing in a canvas bag, checking catching gear.

"How come you don't have a beard like the others, Mr. Hopson?" Jesse asked.

"Because I ain't one of the Jesus boys. I'm a ringer, along

with about a third of the team. The Major, he likes to win, so he pays for outside help. I got no problem with House of David folk. They got some strange ways, but they're good folks, mostly. They don't fuck or eat meat or drink liquor, which ain't natural, but they don't mind if I do, so we get along all right."

"How come you call 'em the Jesus boys?"

Hop grinned a little. "That's what Satchel calls 'em when he comes through here with the Monarchs. It's their beards and long hair. Satchel Paige. You heard of him?"

Jesse hadn't, and Hop sighed with disbelief. "Well, he's someone you better learn about, because once you see him pitch, you ain't never gonna be the same."

Jesse was back in the shack by six. He had four dollars in his pocket, but wasn't about to tell his pa he got paid by the day. His pa returned at midnight, drunk. All he said was "That goddam Bobo Pride is watching every move I make. There's suckers everywhere, and I can't skin a nickel. Coming here was a bad mistake." Then he collapsed on his cot and passed out.

Jesse left for Eden Springs at eight in the morning, borrowing an unlocked bike from the school and hanging his baseball glove on the handlebar. Hop was waiting for him outside the ballpark. He walked him over to a nearby tennis court with a concrete block practice wall at one end. Hop set a hard rubber ball in his hand. "This here's your morning work. You throw this against that wall and catch it on the way back. You just keep doing it till I come to get you. Don't stop. We got a game at one."

Jesse pulled on his glove and whipped the rubber ball against the wall. It came back faster than any baseball, bounced under his glove and ended up in the tennis net. "Over and over," Hop said. "Grounders, line drives—field 'em all and keep throwin'."

By 12:30, the House of David stands were full of a loud and good-natured crowd. John Banner, Eddie Deets, and second baseman Bert Burns, the House of David pepper team, were out in front of the first base stands doing their pre-game routine to the delight of the fans. The three got the ball moving so fast the eye couldn't follow it. After a minute, Jesse realized the ball had vanished—they were playing shadow ball. Right then the pepper team froze like statues; John reached into Eddie Deets' beard, plucked out the baseball, and put it in play again.

Grinning and stirred up, Jesse looked over the opposing team, a local semi-pro bunch called the St. Joe Auscos. He wore his House of David uniform for the first time. It was baggy on him, but he wore it full of pride. Hop came up, getting into his catching gear.

"You warmed up?" Hop asked.

"I can't play. I ain't good enough."

"You shore ain't. But long as the Major likes you, you'll do your part. You're throwin' the invitation pitches today, God help us."

Jesse was stunned. "Huh?"

"You'll find out. Just follow me."

The home team lined up with hats off along the first base line as a small brass band—all Israelites—played "The Star Spangled Banner." Once it finished, the crowd whooped it up. The team—Israelites and Gentiles both—gathered in a circle and bowed their heads. Jesse watched and did the same.

John Banner spoke in a solemn voice, " Lord God, we just ask you to be with these boys today. We're about at .500, Lord, but the season is young. Help us keep in mind that we play for your glory and not our own. In the name of Jesus Christ we pray. Amen."

A shout went up from the team, they broke out of the circle, and Hop Hopson walked to the batter's box and began joking with the umpire. John Banner handed Jesse the game ball, slapped him on the back, gave him a shove toward the mound, and Jesse found himself moving all alone onto the field as the rest of the team settled in around the dugout to watch.

"Ladies and gentlemen!" the announcer's voice boomed. "Welcome to the first game between the Benton Harbor House of David and the St. Joe Auscos! Today the home team is offering not just one pitch but a full at-bat of invitation pitches to the visitor's lead-off hitter!" A cheer went up. "Doing the honors will be the House of David's newest and youngest player, Jesse Bodine!" A smattering of applause rose up, but it felt like electric current in Jesse's veins. "Young Jesse'll be the only House of David defender on the field except for his catcher, Hop Hopson. He'll be facing the Ausco's leadoff hitter, shortstop Art Moon!"

Jesse turned the ball in his glove, toed the rubber, feeling sick. He looked hard at Hop now crouched behind Art Moon, who was a small strike zone making himself smaller. As Jesse struggled to get a comfortable footing, Hop stood upright, turned to the umpire and said something. The umpire smiled uncertainly, and then shrugged his approval. Hop waved for Jesse to back up. Confused, Jesse shuffled to the back of the mound, looked around at Hop who was still waving him back. Jesse moved to the spot he'd thrown from the day before, nearly a third of the way to second base. Hop nodded, got in the crouch again, smacked a fist into his mitt, flashed one of their two signs, and the ball game began.

The announcer's voice returned to the PA system. "Ladies and gentlemen, Jesse Bodine will toss the invitation pitches from a full 70 feet away! Good luck to you, young fella!"

The crowd clapped hard, energized by this new wrinkle. Jesse stared into Hop's glove, shook out his long right arm, raised it above his head then back, kicked, and fired. Moon, fooled by the distance and Jesse's speed, watched the first one streak by.

"Stee-rike!" the ump called.

Hop guffawed, stood, and made the long throw back. The crowd was even more alive now. Jesse caught the ball with two hands. Feeling dizzy and sick to his stomach, he looked toward Hop, wound up again: his arm bent like a buggy whip, and he sent the ball screaming toward the batter. Moon was ready this time and took a wicked cut as the ball hammered Hop's mitt.

The crowd was up and shouting. Hop was laughing out loud. He tossed the ball back to Jesse and raised a fist. Jesse smiled nervously and dug in for the next pitch. Hop set up on the outside corner. Jesse stared in, then wound, kicked, and fired straight at the mitt. As the ball crossed the corner, Moon reached for it with a weak, off-balance swing. He topped the ball and sent it spinning on the ground toward the mound. It took one high bounce, then a second just in front of Jesse, who shut his eyes and ducked away. The topspin sent the ball careening past his ear toward left field where there was not a soul to pick it up. Jesse saw it reach the outfield grass and keep on rolling.

John Banner screamed from the dugout. "GET IT, BOY! NOBODY OUT THERE BUT YOU!"

Jesse glanced at him, scared, as Moon rounded first and streaked toward second. Feeling like a stone statue, Jesse somehow got his legs moving and took off in the direction of the ball, now resting partway to the fence. The crowd rang with laughter. Jesse reached it, picked it up, dropped it, picked it up again, turned and threw with everything he had toward Hop, who was blocking home plate with Moon barreling down the third base path like a small pickup truck. Hop kept his mitt at his side, decoying him into staying up. To Moon's shock, the ball arrived an instant before he did. He plowed over the top of Hop, driving them both into the umpire, who went down in a heap along with them.

As they slowly untangled, Hop—the wind knocked out of him and half bent over—held up his mitt with the ball buried in it, and the umpire, up on a knee, raised his fist. The crowd went crazy.

John Banner came out to check on Hop and motioned for Jesse. John looked around at his gathering players. "Boys," he said, "you just witnessed the ugliest out you'll ever see on a baseball field."

The shortstop, a smooth glove man with braided blonde hair, laughed and said, "That boy's got a smokin' gun, John."

John looked hard at Jesse. "And nothing to go with it. Don't you boys go puffing his head up." John pushed Jesse toward the dugout. The Major came down out of his box seat, reached over the fence and shook the boy's hand. "Best way to open a game I ever saw. You have some showman in you, son. They'll be buzzing all afternoon over that one!" The Major laughed and turned back to his box, where Miranda sat smiling.

A starter named Horse Anderson took over for Jesse. John Banner motioned for Jesse to sit down on the bench beside him. As Anderson threw warm up pitches, John watched him closely but spoke to Jesse. "I don't care how much of a novelty the Major thinks you are. I'm not letting you embarrass this team. You ever turn your back on a ground ball again, you can hand in your uniform and go back where you came from. Don't expect to pitch anything but home warm up shows till you learn to play ball the way it's supposed to be played. You aren't here because I want you to be, understand?" Jesse lowered his head. "Old Hop about got his head taken off because of you. You just aren't worth it."

Jesse stayed in the ballpark after the players and crowd had gone. He threw the hard rubber ball against the concrete wall below the net behind home plate. He fielded the ball and threw again and then again. He saw Miranda out of the corner of his eye but kept practicing. She carried a basket hung on her arm, came near him and stood watching. He stopped.

"I'm practicing. What do you want?"

"I brought a picnic. You must be starving."

He threw the ball against the wall again and caught it. "No, I'm fine."

"Pride goeth before destruction, and a haughty spirit before a fall. I happen to know you haven't eaten since you got here today." She moved into the dugout and set out the food—bread, radishes, potato salad, some sort of meat, and a bottle of spring water.

He looked hungrily at the spread, then stubbornly away.

"We're vegetarians…all the Israelites are. I know you aren't one, but you'll like the food anyway. I can tell a meat eater by his smell."

"There's meat right there."

"That's mock turkey, made from soy beans. The body is a temple to be kept pure. Did you know God saves the soul and the body, too?" She unclasped her hair and it fell to her waist; "You like my hair? It's never had scissors touch it, except now and then when something grows funny. We leave our hair as God intended."

Jesse looked at her hair, her main glory. "I guess I'd eat a little if you quit preaching long enough."

Miranda laughed. "Oh, you haven't heard any preaching yet. You just wait. Your destiny is tied to us, Jesse Bodine."

Jesse looked at her, snorted a small, amused sound, and began eating.

"I know that because I'm psychic. I have gifts the others don't have. You won't ever meet anyone like me."

"I guess you finally said something I agree with."

She sat down on the bench near him, watching him eat. "How do you like Eden Springs?"

"I like it fine, but I like baseball more. I want to be good."

"The Major thinks you might make a good Israelite, too."

"What? He said that? I got my doubts about that."

"So do I. You must be a good pitcher if he's saying it. He wants me to be friends with you. I'm his daughter—adopted, not blood. I told him you're a strange boy. I'm not sure you like me."

"I like you well enough. I gotta get to know you."

"Truth is, I'm glad you're here. I've got nobody to talk to except House of David people. But I can't tell them half of what goes on inside me." She stopped talking for a moment, picked up an apple slice from the basket and took a small bite. "Sometimes I wish I was an outsider like you. I wish I was free."

"You don't know what you're talking about. Who says I'm free?"

"Do you know Israelites believe the world is going to end soon?"

"The world has a way of not ending when people say it will."

"Well, I think it's too wonderful to end."

Jesse stared at the grass. "I guess I wouldn't go that far."

"I don't know anybody who really wants it to end, even the Major." She ate the rest of the apple slice. "I want to be friends with you, Jesse. Okay?"

He shrugged and lifted a buttered slice of bread. "I guess so."

Two weeks passed, and Jesse threw only one ball in a game, a single invitation pitch, a strike. He didn't travel to away games on the bus. It appeared John Banner had no intention of playing him until he was forced to. Jesse worked with Hop every day but travel days, and those days he worked on his own. Hop would stand at home plate hitting hard ground balls toward the pitching mound. Jesse misplayed every third or fourth one, but he knew his glove was getting better. Each ball he caught he fired into a net standing at first base.

"Don't you never close your eyes, you hear?" Hop shouted. "Don't you never even blink! Ain't nobody plays baseball with their eyes closed!"

"When can I learn how to bat?"

Hop laughed. "Hittin' a ball's too complicated for you. I ain't no miracle worker. You're gonna learn to bunt for now and nothin' else. I'm teaching you survival. So just shut up and field that damn ball."

"But I gotta learn everything there is!"

Hop nodded patiently and hit the ball again.

Jesse was going for his bike (stowed in a cedar hedge) to ride home to the shack when he saw Miranda coming his way. He couldn't read her look.

She grabbed the sleeve of his sweatshirt. "The Major told me to bring you over to talk to him."

"What's going on?" Something heavy began pressing down in his gut.

"How should I know? Have you done anything wrong?"

"I'm just learning to play baseball. What's wrong with that? Maybe he thinks I'm not good enough for the job." Fears bounced about in his head like bumper cars. He thought of the bike and his anxiety grew.

"Come on with me," she said.

From his first day here, Jesse had noticed the mansion at a distance, down the road from Eden Springs, but as they came close he saw it was a castle made of wood, massive, with domes, spires, balconies—all surrounded by elaborate gardens, like needlepoint tapestries, right now being planted and weeded by a crew of workers.

"What is this place?"

"The Shiloh Mansion. It's meant to be like a heavenly mansion. I'll take you to the door and show you where to go. I hope nothing bad happens."

They ascended the semi-circular staircase onto the long front porch with carved pillars, rails, and lintels. She took him inside and pointed him to a glass door just to the left of the entrance. Jesse hesitated at the door and knocked lightly. A plain-faced young woman in a yellow dress opened it.

"Jesse Bodine?" she asked. He nodded, and she led him

to an inside door. She rapped twice and opened for him. Jesse stepped into the Major's office. He saw the Major behind a huge dark desk with carved legs. He also felt the presence of another. In an armchair near a window sat his father, shaved and hair slicked down, his hands clasped together.

"Pa. What're you doing here? What's happened?"

The Major answered. "You father has come to talk business with me. I thought you ought to be present."

His pa sat calmly. He lifted a newspaper folded beside him. "Yesterday I read in this newspaper about my boy playing baseball, the youngest on the team."

"But the story ain't right, pa. I ain't really playing— just learning to play. I only throw invitation pitches now and again."

"Hell, that's still something. Can't a man take an interest in his son's career?"

"Certainly a man can," the Major answered. "What are you thinking about, Mr. Bodine?"

"Any father worth his salt would take an interest. I taught that boy everything he knows about throwin' a ball. He has talent, sure, but he ain't got a lick of sense for business, so someone needs to look out for his interests."

"I see. And does Jesse turn over his earnings to you?"

"I give him back his fair share."

"Yes, I'm sure you do."

"I'm out of work at the moment, see…"

"Pa, what happened?"

The Major went on. "Just what's on your mind, Mr. Bodine?"

"He's a young Dizzy Dean, is what he is. That kinda talent is worth considerable more than four dollars a day."

The Major smiled, understanding. "Four dollars a day is all he earns for good reason. I have to pay a man to teach him all the things you didn't—things like the rules of the game."

"Four dollars is plenty good, pa."

Thurman leaned forward in the chair. "I was thinkin' ten dollars a day would be more in line."

"Absolutely not."

"Pa, please. I want to keep this job."

Thurman looked at Jesse, his eyes changing in a puzzling

way, his eyes not their usual hard steeliness but instead worried or humbled or something unlike him. He leaned way back in the chair, staring up at the ceiling, and then did a strange thing. He gave out with a short, muffled sob, something Jesse had never heard from him before. "Major Gates, I'm ashamed for my scheming. It's just that we're losin' our house in a few days, and I can't figure nowhere to turn. It's my desperateness making me this way. It's fair what you're paying Jesse. The world is full of trouble—I know it for a fact because it's coming down on me."

The Major folded his hands, staring hard at Thurman, taking stock for what must have been a full minute. "Well, I'm sorry, too, Mr. Bodine." He stood and went to a window, looking out at the gardeners at work. "Your son is a special interest of mine. I care about his wellbeing, and I suppose because of it, I should care about yours, too. Let me give it some thought. Maybe I can help."

To Jesse, the Major's help bordered on the too-good-to-be-true. He hired Thurman as a mechanic to repair steam trains. And Thurman seemed to remember how that sort of work was done. He was paid six dollars a day, and the Major provided them a small tourist log cabin on the edge of Eden Springs with an inside bathroom and kitchen with stove and ice box. Bobo Pride and his shack were no longer of consequence.

Miranda came by to see the place and seemed relieved for Jesse. She told him his pa was skilled at his job (this from the Major) and things were working out so far. Within a day, Jesse made off before daybreak to return the bike to the school, wiping his conscience as clean as possible.

His pa still drank at night, but he was quieter about it. Sometimes he would talk, saying he was learning things about Israelites that weren't all bad, like the fact that they shared their wealth. "It's a real good deal for folks who don't have nothing to start with," he said with a chuckle. Jesse still felt some wariness born of long experience, and tiptoed carefully around his pa as he might around a sleeping Doberman. But things were different, and maybe this time lasting.

The ball team was playing a little above .500 when word came that the St. Louis Cardinals were offering an exhibition game with the winner of the Midwest League. The Monarchs were well out in front, but Jesse heard the desire in John Banner's voice. He wanted his team to play the Cardinals. In their history, John told them, the House of David had played just two exhibition games with Major League teams and lost both by close scores. It was time to change that. Hop let Jesse know privately their pitching was too thin right now to get them there. Jesse wasn't sure what to do except keep on working.

In a weekend home game against the Chicago American Giants, another all-Negro barnstorming team like the Monarchs, something happened to turn the tide. It was a bright June day, and the stands were packed with as many black folks as white. Jesse was catching balls coming in from the outfield and flipping them to John Banner who was hitting practice flies. In the home bullpen Hop was warming up a black man with puffs of gray wool sticking out of the sides and back of his House of David hat. His name was Lester Birdwell, a knuckleballer the Major had just picked up out of desperation to help them out. They'd played four games in three days. Lester was at least fifty, with slow, skinny legs and a potbelly. Hop claimed he still had a dipsy doodle pitch and a decent knuckler in spite of being officially retired.

Jesse watched the game, as always, on the opposite end of the bench from John Banner. By the sixth inning the Israelites were hitting the ball hard but were only up 8 to 6 because Lester's dipsy doodle was wearing out. He couldn't get the ball over, and proceeded to walk the bases full. John trudged out to pull him, looking troubled.

Hop joined him at the mound and said something that made him mad. Jesse couldn't hear from where he was. He noticed John was wearing a glove.

"Banner for Birdwell," John shouted to the umpire.

Jesse's mouth dropped open. John Banner was an aging first baseman, no pitcher at all. But he took the mound as if he knew what he was doing, threw warm up pitches, not one a strike. He settled on pitching from a windup with the bases full, kicking in an awkward, low-slung way, and delivering side arm fastballs.

A batter watched four straight balls go by him, all outside

by a foot and a half. The lead was cut to one. John called time out and slunk to the bench. "Bodine, we're down to you, I guess."

Jesse stared wide-eyed at him, taking a moment to understand, but then jumping to his feet.

John mumbled a small prayer out loud. "Lord, if we ever needed you, now's the time." He slapped the ball into Jesse's glove. "You got six pitches to get warm. Can you do it?" Jesse said he could. "Show me I'm not making a terrible mistake. You do what Hop says and don't try anything cute."

The three Chicago runners sat on the bases while Jesse warmed up. He toed the rubber, trying to get comfortable. He knew he should throw from the stretch with runners on, so he tried it. The first pitch sailed over Hop's head, and the Chicago crowd started whooping it up. The ump threw out another ball. This time Jesse hit the backstop. It raised the roof. Two more sailed to the screen before he found Hop's glove. A mocking cheer went up at last.

Hop jogged out to him and said, "You throw to where I spot you and keep your eyes open. You'll be okay."

Jesse inhaled as if coming up from underwater. He felt queasy but pushed it down. Hop slapped his shoulder and trotted to the plate. The runners were up and ready. The batter, the cleanup hitter, watched him with a smirk. Hop set up on the outside. Jesse kicked and fired a fastball. The batter committed too soon and cued the ball off the end of the bat, right at Jesse. It took a crazy whirling dervish bounce, but Jesse stayed in front of it. It came up, caromed off his wrist, and smacked him hard in the eye.

All four runners made tracks. Dazed, Jesse spun in a circle, looking for the ball. He finally saw it, dove, and winged it submarine style to Hop. The sliding runner knocked Hop over, but an instant too late. When the runner saw the umpire's fist go up, he exploded to his feet and began a fury of protest. Shouts of disapproval rose from the Chicago crowd.

Jesse didn't remember much beyond lying on his back with John Banner's big face going in and out of focus. He blinked a few dozen times and tried to sit up. John pushed him back down, motioning for someone. Jesse saw a circle of bearded, wild-haired Jesus boys framed against the cloud-streaked sky. Eddie Deets bent down and pressed a towel full of ice to Jesse's injured eye. Jesse pushed the ice away and got to his feet.

"That's only one out," he said. "I gotta get two more."

Somebody laughed. Jesse's knees buckled, and Hop steadied him. He walked him around in a slow circle until Jesse got his bearings.

"I never closed my eyes, Hop. I never did."

Hop chuckled. "That's a fact…"

John Banner stood watching with hands on his hips. "You better sit down now and ice that eye."

"I been hit harder. It don't bother me."

John grinned a little, slapped Jesse on the butt, and headed back to the dugout.

Hop went to the plate, crouched behind the batter, set up low and outside, high and inside, high and out of the zone, and every place he put the glove, Jesse hit it. Six pitches—two call strikes and four futile swings—and the American Giants went down with the bases full.

Jesse pitched the rest of the game, laid down a bunt for an out (a moral victory), gave up just one dying quail hit, and saved the game. After the final out, John Banner strode to the mound and gripped Jesse's hand as if it were a trophy for league championship.

That evening a full moon shone down on a secluded spot of woods with a pond near the amphitheater. Jesse lay in the grass, his head on Miranda's lap. She held a cold compress to his eye.

"This is the best summer of my life," he said.

"I had a dream about you last night."

"Was it good?"

She hesitated. "At first it was. You were bathed in light like a saint of God. But then a shadow came over the land and covered you, and I couldn't see you any more."

"I'm right here."

"I know. I'm glad."

She lifted the compress to check his eye and winced as she touched the swelling. Their faces were close. Jesse stared into her green eyes as if he'd never seen them before.

"What?" she asked.

"Nothin'." He rose up a little and lightly touched his lips to hers. He lowered his head to her lap again, still staring at her.

"What was that for?" He could see she was pleased.

"For no special reason."

"If we're going to kiss, it has to be in secret or we'll both get in trouble."

"It wasn't a thing I planned."

She sighed. "If you had, I wouldn't mind. But Israelites aren't supposed to even think about it. Trouble is, they're always thinking about it, especially the men. Nathan Short watches me through the window when I'm going to bed."

Jesse got up on an elbow. "He does that?"

"I never let him see much."

"Damnation!"

"What?"

Jesse sat up now, perplexed. "Well…I guess I don't think much of Nathan Short any more."

She smiled and squeezed his hand. "Me either. Don't you ever worry about Nathan Short." She touched his cheek. "It's near curfew." She stood up and stretched, looking up at the moon. "You pitched like a warrior today. You were Joshua at the walls of Jericho. Your star is rising, Jesse Bodine. Can you feel it?"

He stayed sitting, looking at her. "I don't know. I'll have to see."

She shook her head, amused, then waved and took off running toward the entrance to the park. Jesse watched her disappear and lay back down, looking up at a few scattered stars.

John Banner said Jesse had an arm made of piano wire—he had the arm to pitch relief every day if he was needed. The team won the next eight straight, and Jesse saved four of them. He went along on the bus now, and some nights they stayed in motels and ate in restaurants, and the House of David paid for everything. They had moved into second place in the league, six games behind the Monarchs. Jesse could feel something different in the air, something new. And he was part of it. The Major still paid him $4 a day, but added $20 for every game he played.

His pa was quiet a lot now. On a night that Jesse played late under the lights, he came home to find his pa standing beside the bed just closing his battered cowhide suitcase. Jesse handed over his earnings, and Thurman grunted and nodded. "Ain't you somethin'. Quite a celebrity."

"I just play baseball, pa."

He lifted up Jesse's chin. "Damn, is that a beard you're tryin' to grow?"

"No, I don't shave yet."

"God almighty, they got their hooks in you. Well, suit yourself. You're big enough now. You'll fit in all right, I guess. But this ain't no place for me. I can't stomach the holiness. I gotta go somewhere. I gotta move on to other things."

In shock, Jesse said, "Why, pa? Where?" He had hoped a thousand despairing times for a parting like this, but now it sounded strange and wrong.

Thurman laughed. "Who knows? I got some cash in my pocket. I'll maybe get on a bus and see where it takes me."

Jesse glanced over at the old suitcase again. The look of it made him sad and uneasy. "We got it good here. You're a good mechanic. We got us a decent cabin. Why would you leave when things are good?"

"Listen, boy. You like to stay put like your ma. I get crazy if I can't keep moving. That's the way it is. You let the Major know tomorrow what I decided." He lifted the old suitcase, stood a moment checking the lock under the handle, reached for his jacket, said "So long," and was gone, gone without emotion, gone for once without destruction in his wake.

But that would descend on Jesse later, well after two in the morning, when hands began battering the cabin door as if they meant to break it down. Jesse cried out, leaped from bed and lifted a frying pan for protection. "Who the hell is it?" he yelled out.

"The Major! Open up!"

Jesse went to the door in his underwear and opened to a half dozen crazy-looking Israelites, some in pajamas, though the Major was dressed. So was Nathan Short, but he looked as though he'd been dragged by a horse. A chain hung from his wrist, and his eyes had a dazed, bloodshot look. Two of the Israelites took Jesse by the arms and held him tight.

"What is it? What's going on?"

"As if you didn't know," Nathan Short growled.

"I don't know." He couldn't keep the fear from his voice. "Major?"

"Where is your father, Jesse?"

"He left with a suitcase."

"When?"

"When I came home after the game. He told me he couldn't stay put like me. He said he knew I wouldn't leave. So he was taking a bus but didn't say where."

"That's more than four hours ago," Nathan said. "Somebody jumped me in the train office, tied me up to a drain pipe, then cut the handcuff with a bolt cutter. He had a cloth over his face, but I saw it was Thurman Bodine. He made off with my cash bag and two day's take from Eden Springs, more than $2500."

Jesse's knees sagged, but the men held him up.

The Major had them put Jesse down in a chair. The boy held his head with both hands, shaking it slowly, moaning. Through half-closed eyes, he saw the Major watching him carefully.

"We wouldn't have found Nathan till morning, but a sister heard him banging a heel on the drainpipe."

"I kicked that pipe a thousand times before someone came. I had a rag stuffed in my mouth and could hardly breathe. Can I call the police now, Major?"

"No. No police. This is Israelite business, and we'll take care of it."

"But Bodine is getting away!"

"He won't get away, Nathan. He'll have to reckon with us and with the good Lord."

"And spend all our money before he does. I bet this boy had something to do with it."

"Why would he still be here if he had?"

"Maybe he has a plan to steal more and meet up with his father."

"What about it, Jesse?" the Major asked.

"No, sir." His voice was faint. "My pa's done some things before, but never like this. This place here was good for us. I don't understand him." He grew more emotional. "I'll work to pay it back, Major. I promise I will."

Nathan laughed bitterly. "That shouldn't take more than 20 years." He looked to the Major. "I never saw anybody rise above bad blood. You trust that boy more than I ever would, Major."

"Have some charity, Nathan. It's a miracle of grace he's here at all."

"He's been hanging around Miranda, too. I don't approve. He's a Gentile and a bad influence."

"I asked her to make friends with him. That's my doing—though I suspect it may not suit your plans." He moved toward the door. "I want all of you to go home to bed. I need some time to think. Jesse, you come see me in the morning. I'll send for you when it's time."

His night was long, sleepless, and full of dark, rat-like thoughts. An owl screeched three times from a tree nearby and then went silent. His pa had left him to face this. He cursed his own blood and wiped angry tears from his eyes.

It wasn't Miranda but Nathan Short who came for him a little after ten in the morning. Nathan just said, "Follow me," and nothing else. He let him in through the front door of the Shiloh Mansion and left.

In the Major's office several serious-looking bearded men sat in chairs near the big desk. One was John Banner.

The Major looked businesslike but drained of color as if he hadn't slept. "As much hope as I've had in you, Jesse, this group of elders has decided that you are not of a character suitable to our House of David colony, even as a Gentile employee of the baseball team."

"I can't play?" He was dumbstruck. His knees went weak. He saw John Banner look down at his hands.

"I'm sorry things turned out this way." The Major held out a blue business envelope. "This is two week's severance pay. You'll need to vacate the cabin within a few days. We wish you well, Jesse. We know you didn't choose your father."

A thought he'd almost begun to believe in was draining away like blood from a gutted animal. He backed up from the blue envelope. "No. Put it toward what my pa stole."

The Major said nothing for a moment, then nodded and slid the envelope into an inside pocket. The meeting ended with that.

He wasn't surprised that Bobo Pride refused to hire him, but he managed to find work two nights a week at Shadowland cleaning up after weddings. The Salvation Army ran a mission on a main street of Benton Harbor. Because he was polite and didn't drink, he was trusted to help out serving food twice a day, and he slept there in a large room jammed with metal bunk beds which filled up each night with drunken men, crazy men, down and out men, black and white men, all blending in a nightmare chorus of snoring, farting, moaning, and cursing, scented with methane, sour bodies, cigarettes, and alcohol. Sleeping in the old Studebaker had been better than he knew.

Mid-July turned cruelly hot, and some nights he slept on the beach just to breathe fresh winds off the lake. Wherever he slept, he used his small duffle bag of belongings as a pillow. Hop's glove was in it, safe under his head. He still had the hard rubber ball, and practiced in an alley behind the mission for hours at a time. Now and then one of the men would watch with puzzled admiration.

On a sweltering Thursday, he lifted a scoop of goulash to a plate and saw that the plate was held by Hop Hopson, dressed in a bright flowered shirt and yellow pants. "Hey there, son," Hop said. "You want to see some good baseball?" He handed him a ticket that read ISRAELITE HOUSE OF DAVID vs. THE KANSAS CITY MONARCHS. July 19, 1 p.m. Hop continued, "Meet me at the Monarchs' dugout after the game." He smiled and passed the plate to the man behind him. "I miss you, boy. Do me a big favor and be there. Satchel's gonna pitch."

"Okay, Hop." His voice seemed more breath than sound.

"Glad you're still around." He gave Jesse's shoulder a bump, then turned and went out.

He hadn't expected the walk through Eden Springs to be so strange when just a few weeks before it had been a haven and a home. But he felt like an outcast, an enemy. He passed by familiar nameless faces that paid him no mind. He saw a man he knew as Earl driving a steam train. But Earl didn't look his way. He couldn't remember if Earl ever looked his way, but it hadn't mattered before. He was worried about seeing his former teammates, and thought he'd sit toward the

Monarchs' side of the stands. He worried about the Major—and worried more about Miranda, from whom he'd heard nothing since he was told to go. He felt more alone than he ever had, even though he'd almost always been alone.

The path to the ballpark was like walking in a troubled dream. The three gates, he saw, were lined up twelve or more deep. The crowd would be big, as it always was with the Monarchs. He gave his ticket to a girl at the gate and passed inside, glancing at the field and seeing the pepper team already at work. He saw Hop and a back-up catcher warming up Horse Anderson and Lester Birdwell in the bullpen. Hop saw him and gave him a smile and a nod. His heart lifted a bit. He moved around toward the Monarch side and took a seat amid a crowd of dressed-up Negroes having more fun than anyone on the Israelite side.

He'd seen local papers and knew both teams had gone into minor slumps because of the heat and pitching shortages in a grueling game-or-more-a-day schedule. He knew that Satchel, in his mid 30s now, sometimes pitched two games in a row. Only five games separated the two teams at this point, so there was even more reason for a crowd.

Jesse settled in to watch Satchel work. It was fascinating. His kick was high, higher than Jesse's, and he held his pitching arm straight down, then swung it forward and released the ball late, more from the side than over the top. There was something about that long arm moving slow and firing so hard that baffled hitters. The ball was by them in a blink. Then he might throw something off speed with the same motion, and the batter would be around before the ball arrived. He struck out the side in the first. In the second, John Banner reached first because a high inside pitch brushed his beard. Satchel protested; Jesse could hear him yelling at the ump.

"Man's got a two foot beard flappin' in the breeze. That ain't really him I hit. Beards that big oughta be totally e-legal!"

The ump ignored him, signaled John to first, and he trotted the base line laughing and pleased with himself. The Israelite crowd grew animated along with him.

Still grumbling, Satchel scuffed at the mound, rearranging dirt, then went into a stretch as John continued grinning at his Israelite fans. Everyone in the stands knew the aging first baseman was too slow to steal a base, so it was no surprise that Satchel paid no attention to him. John came off the bag three casual steps, still looking smug. In the next split second Satchel picked him off clean as a cobra strike. John stood in shock. He kicked the bag, looking like a jackass now, and the Monarch laughter rose like a wave. Jesse joined in, clapping his hands.

A big black man with a heavy moustache sat beside Jesse. The man said to no one in particular, "If that boy had white skin, he'd be makin' more money than Babe Ruth."

No one could touch Satchel that afternoon. He had more pitches than Jesse knew about, and he rarely missed his mark. The Monarchs went up 8 to 0 in the 6th, so the Monarch's manager pulled him to save some for another day. The game ended 8 to 2.

Jesse waited for the crowd to thin out. When he saw Hop coming toward the Monarch's dugout, he slipped over the wall onto the field. It was then he spotted Nathan Short beside the Major, moving toward the home dugout. Miranda, in her straw hat, followed behind Nathan. She saw Jesse, and their eyes met for a second or two. Then she looked away, disturbed or embarrassed, he couldn't tell which. It caused him pain, but he pushed it aside.

Hop wrapped a long, thin arm around Jesse's shoulder and led him toward Satchel, who was standing for a photo. Satchel gave them a grin. Hop shook his hand.

"Nasty, Satchel—mean as a snake." They both laughed. "Anyways, I want you to meet my friend Jesse Bodine."

He took Jesse's hand. "You're more a boy than I thought, but ole Hop wouldn't lead us astray."

The team manager came up to Hop, who introduced him as Newt Allen, a dark-skinned, cordial man, a former infielder Jesse had read about.

"I hear you can throw," he said.

"I can."

Newt smiled. "Well, Hop's joining the Monarchs today— but only so long as you're part of the deal. It's good with us if it's good with you. Our catcher's about wore out, and our backup's got a bad hamstring. Hop says you been savin' games for the Jesus boys."

Jesse looked to Hop. "You're leaving them?"

"I am. Those are good boys, but I don't like what the Major done to you, especially after all the work we put in. Anyway, the Monarchs pay better. If you say yes, I say yes."

"But ain't this an all-Negro team, Hop?"

Hop laughed and so did Satchel. Newt didn't. "It's a fair question. Truth is, we had one other white ringer before, so you ain't the first."

"Hell," Hop said. "I was the only colored man on a white team until Lester come along. I survived all right."

Jesse took a deep breath. "Okay, then."

Newt clapped a hand on his shoulder. "Praise God! Hop says you're staying at the mission. Go get your stuff together, and we'll pick you up out front. You just been made an honorary Negro."

The scene in front of the Salvation Army was memorable. Jesse boarded the big Monarchs touring bus, toting his duffle bag, amid a cheering crowd of ragged men proud of one of their own. Players leaned out bus windows, waving. And once Jesse was snug in a seat beside Hop, the bus began to roll down a road few boys like him would ever travel.

It was a dizzy, whirlwind life, always taking to the road. The Monarchs paid him $25 a game, play or not, provided food and hotels, often in the seamier parts of town where black ballplayers were heroes, played night games under portable lights they carried on the bus. He slowly learned to ignore the ignorant slurs of white people, even toward him. On occasion, when Hop felt the spirit moving, they went together to Pentecostal churches along the way. By season's end, Jesse could play without embarrassing himself, and he showed some signs of swinging the bat.

His pitching, thanks to good teachers, got much better. He saved 8 games for the Monarchs, who won the league by 12, played the St. Louis Cardinals and beat them 3 to 1. Satchel pitched the entire game for that win. Jesse never got in, but he sat there, contented to watch a master at work.

Over that summer, he paid $300 more to the Major against his father's debt. In the fall, the Major tried to rehire both Hop and him, with the added incentive of winter work in a House of David business. Both of them said no, and as it turned out, once the war started up in December, the Israelites wouldn't field another team until it ended four years later. The Monarchs, depleted by players going to war, found Jesse's youth and Hop's age strong attractions. Jesse played for the Monarchs as a reliever and starter from 1941 through the '44 season when he was drafted into the army. His best friend Hop caught him the whole way.

Over time, even though Jesse knew all too well his life had been a long struggle (he somehow paid off his father's entire debt), he found he was blessed with a past of such rainbow color that his stories stood apart. His grandchildren never heard a word from him about the war; instead, he told about traveling with carnivals, tossing balls to win bets, living in a mission while still a boy, learning real baseball from the great Hop Hopson and the Jesus boys at Eden Springs where steam trains ran and castles stood like heavenly mansions. Most of all, he relished telling about the barnstorming days with Satchel Paige and the Monarchs as an honorary Negro, and about the outstanding day they beat the St. Louis Cardinals 3 to 1.

When they asked their grandmother if such amazing tales could be true, she'd smile, push back a loose strand of her tied-up hair, and say "Oh my, yes. I was there as a witness."

YARD GIRL

Even in 1956 I knew that manual typesetting was a thing of the past, something I'd never be able to use. Yet I didn't regret taking ninth grade printing. I did my first piece of serious writing on that composing stick, laboriously inserting one letter at a time into a block of type in order to communicate with a girl. Our teacher was Mr. Gage, who was in his early 50s but looked ten years older. He dressed as if he knew he was obsolete. He wore old gray suits with lumpy shoulders, ink-stained around the pockets and sleeve ends. A tear in the back seam of one of his suit coats widened as the semester progressed. He taught mechanical drawing, too, as part of the Roosevelt Junior High Shop Program. Mechanical drawing would soon be as obsolete as manual typesetting. Mr. Gage spoke to us in a dreary monotone without jokes or smiles. Teaching ninth graders seemed to be his cross to bear, though he was spared most lecturing by the hands-on nature of his classes. He would set us in motion and then go read a newspaper.

We spent our first two weeks of class organizing our California Job Cases. I figured Gage intentionally messed up the cases so we'd need more time to straighten them out. I did learn a few things early on: upper case letters were called that because in the Standard Job Case (an older style), the capital letters were in the upper half of the case, the small letters (lower case) in the lower half. The California Job Case put small letters on the left, capital letters to the right, numbers along the top, and punctuation spread around, 89 compartments in all. There were probably two thousand little pieces of lead type and spacing slugs to sort and organize.

My best buddy Frankie Romano, a skinny, wiseass Italian who attracted girls for reasons I didn't understand, sat to the left of me. A creepy kid named Mervyn Bateman sat on my right. His eyes were slightly crossed and never seemed to be looking at you. Directly in front of me sat the only girl in the class, Rhonda Moon, a tall girl with very grownup breasts whom I found attractive in a rough-edged way. She wore the same clothes (long, faded plaid skirt, threadbare white blouse) two or three days in a row, and was not one of the popular girls or even middle of the road. I knew she lived west of school on one of those dreary streets near the river and the railroad yard where her father had a job. He was a maintenance worker whom I'd noticed because he was nearly seven feet tall, angular, bent, and steely looking. I saw their ramshackle house whenever I fished the river with my Uncle Ed, my father's youngest brother. The place was swarming with kids who looked poor and scruffy. The neighborhood was known by the VIPs of our school as the Yard (I lived five blocks east of the Yard, five blocks west of the VIPs).

Rhonda stared intently at her California Job Case, her fingers flying, and in three class periods her case was perfectly organized. She turned to me. I had another week, at least, to go.

"Need help?" she asked. "I love to sort things."

I looked up and saw that Gage had left the room. "Yeah, if you don't mind."

We switched cases, and she went to work. I glanced at Frankie, who gave me a knowing nod. I could tell he was thinking about her breasts. Mervyn Bateman nudged me and slipped a creased, hazy photograph onto my desktop. It was a naked woman with her legs spread wide. He pointed to Rhonda, grinned, and folded it up again.

"What the hell was that?" I whispered.

"Poontang," was all he said. His grin increased, revealing snaggy yellow teeth. I soon found that he carried eight-pagers with him, tucked in his books (Frankie and I were deep into *Mad* comics). I learned some strange things sitting beside Mervyn. Education came in many forms at Roosevelt Junior High.

Bass fishing in September was best when the river was low and fairly clear. Uncle Ed, my fishing partner, was built like a bulldog and held the record for home runs on our local semi-pro team. Four years in the Navy had killed his chances for the Major Leagues, but he kept on playing semi-pro until he was well past 50. He was a hero of mine back then, especially when he gave me a pair of his own spikes and taught me how to judge a long fly ball. He also could catch fish in a mud puddle. He claimed he could think like a fish, especially a bass. We never came home empty-handed.

We shared the same last name, Sunday, and I was proud of it because of him. My father, on the other hand, was older and less colorful, but maybe more solid. He owned a typewriter sales and repair store in the shopping area three blocks away. He was another one—like Mr. Gage—blindly plodding toward obsolescence. My mother, who stayed home to raise my two younger sisters and me, considered him a great catch. That, more than anything, kept him working hard to make a go of life. He had a strong tendency to get down on himself, but she was forever lighting up his darkness.

Uncle Ed picked me up in his truck early one September Saturday and drove down to the rapids just below the Yard. We wore old tennis shoes and shorts, first turning over shallow rocks to catch hellgrammites (the world's best bass bait) in a wire screen, and then wading below the rapids with fly rods. The smallmouth bass lurked there in the fast water, watching for live food rolling out of the rapids. Within a half hour, we each had two decent fish. Then Ed changed baits, hooking up a nightcrawler in hopes of a walleye. I watched his line drift through the deep holes, taking a turn at a bend. Something hit his crawler like a freight train.

"Jesus," he said, "It's Moby Dick." His pole bent close to breaking; he fed out line and couldn't gain any back. He began edging toward shallow water, following the fish downstream to keep the line from snapping. I reeled in and followed him. Twenty minutes went by, and we still hadn't seen anything of the fish. Ed didn't tire easily, but I could tell his arms were wearing down. Ten more minutes passed and suddenly the thing quit moving; Ed began slowly hauling it toward shore. When we saw the orange fins, he cursed in disgust.

"It's a goddam carp," he muttered. "Big as a horse." He heaved the monster up into the mud and rocks of the shoreline; it flopped a couple of times, exhausted, then resigned itself and went limp. It had to be four feet long and God knows how many pounds. Its mouth was huge, grotesque, a giant suction cup.

I heard excited voices and then saw two ragged-looking boys, maybe 8 and 10, standing on the bank, gaping at the giant fish.

"You boys eat carp?" Ed asked, meaning it as a joke.

"My ma knows how to fix it," the older one said.

"Hell, take it then, if you can lift it," Ed said.

The boys scrambled down the bank, grabbed the fish by the gills and tail, and struggled away, dropping it every few feet but determined to get it home.

Ed shook his head and turned back toward the rapids. "Those are poor folks," he said. "I wouldn't eat a carp if I was starving."

We fished another hour and ended up with seven bass. As we were getting ready to leave, I was surprised to see Rhonda Moon coming down the shoreline toward us. She was barefoot and wore shorts and a flannel shirt. When she recognized me, she seemed surprised.

"Oh, it's you," she said. "Hi, Ray."

"Hi, Rhonda."

"My mother sent me down to thank you for the fish. I didn't know it was you."

So those boys were her brothers. "Glad you could use it. My Uncle Ed here caught it. I never saw one that big."

"Thanks a lot," she said to Ed. He nodded, and she turned to go. "See you in school, Ray. Your job case is finished, by the way."

"Hey that's great, Rhonda. Yeah, see you in school."

Uncle Ed looked at me and rolled his eyes. "They got about eight or nine kids in that family. I guess that's a lot of mouths to feed."

I nodded, embarrassed for her.

Rhonda told me she was taking mostly Shop classes and some art, too. In printing class, no guy could come near her speed at setting type. She was smart in mechanical ways and quietly friendly when I talked to her. I labored away at my first project, Lou Gehrig's farewell speech in Yankee Stadium. It brought tears to my eyes at first, but by the time it was set, locked up in the galley, and printed on Gage's old manual letterpress, I could say it in my sleep and never wanted to see it again.

On our walks home from school, Frankie was pushing me to take Rhonda out and try feeling her up. He'd had some success in that area of romance, but I'd never even made an attempt. He suggested trying it at the movies, since I only had a learner's permit and no access to a car. He also told me a dark front porch worked sometimes, too, if you were quick about it. I told him I wasn't attracted to her, even though it wasn't really the truth. I wasn't sure what the truth was.

At about the point I'd finished printing Lou Gehrig's speech, Mervyn Bateman disappeared from class. Gage kept taking roll and asking about him, but nobody knew a thing. About two weeks later, he reappeared, looking down in the mouth. Before class started, Rhonda turned to him.

"We missed you, Mervyn. Where you been?"

She might have missed him—I hadn't.

He dropped his eyes and shook his head. "My ma is dying of cancer. I stayed home to help."

Rhonda's face went very pale. "Oh my God, that's awful. What kind of cancer does she have?"

Mervyn glanced at her chest, prominent now with her body turned toward him. "Breast," he said.

"That's terrible. I'm so sorry. Tell her I'll pray for her."

"Yeah, I will."

"Hey, Mervyn—man, sorry," I mumbled. It was inadequate but at least a reaction.

The news spread all over school before the day was out. There was talk of taking up a collection for the family, and Rhonda volunteered to do it in the Shop classes. In the next few days, she worked harder than anyone, pulling in more than $80, mostly in one-dollar bills. After a week, the teachers, administrators, and students had kicked in close to $300. Mr. Gage agreed to present the envelope of money to Mervyn during print class. He had him come up to the front of class.

"Mervyn," he said, with some faint emotion in his voice, "this is something we've all done to help out your family. Please take it to your mother with our prayers and good wishes." He handed over the thick envelope, as Mervyn stared holes in the floor.

"Thanks, Mr. Gage. I just can't believe it," he said, his voice quavery.

For some reason, we all applauded.

A day or two later Mervyn disappeared again. Mr. Bacon, the Roosevelt principal, waited a week and went over to the Bateman house to check on the mother's condition and Mervyn's absence. He found the place deserted. A neighbor let him know they'd moved to Detroit but didn't know where. He also found out Mervyn's mother was a bartender and not the least bit sick.

The outrage that followed was understandable, but Rhonda seemed more devastated than angry. I caught her after school and ended up walking her home.

"How could he lie about something like cancer?" Her voice was low and desolate.

"He's a crummy con man. "

"Ray, I talked all those people into giving money—money that was hard for some of them to come by."

I barked out a semi-laugh. "I only lost 50 cents."

"Well, I put in $10 from my own bank account." I could tell she wasn't feeling sorry for herself, just dismayed at human nature.

"Jesus, Rhonda. That's terrible. I'm sorry."

"You don't need to be. I did it. I trusted him."

I felt so bad for her right then that I did something rash: I asked if she wanted to go to a movie some time. I think it shocked her. No one that I knew of had ever asked her out. Her mood seemed to soften as we went on walking.

"Really? A movie? How would we get there?"

"My mom could probably drive us. I don't have my license yet. When the movie's done, we could walk to my house, and she'd drive us back to your place."

She smiled just a little, and it was then I started having second thoughts. But I'd already committed, so I figured, what the hell, going out with girls was definitely something you needed to practice—like basketball. "I'll ask my mom and dad," she said, and then waved to me, turning up the gravel path to her rundown house. I could smell fish cooking.

I made the mistake of telling Frankie my plans. We were practicing cross country that week on a local golf course with too many hills. We both hated the sport, but it got us in shape for basketball. Frankie was a sprinter, faster than I was, but

I was better over the long haul. He stopped to catch his breath way too often, and I waited for him. This day his head was sticky with black, sweat-drenched curls.

"When you gonna give Rhonda Moon a try?" he asked, bent over and breathing hard. "If you don't, I might horn in on you. I don't mind Yard girls."

"I'm taking her to the Liberty on Friday. 'Forbidden Planet' is on."

He straightened up and flashed me a huge grin. "Finally old Ray Sunday is getting some action. I was beginning to wonder about you." He punched me in the arm. "Here's how you do it, buddy. See, when you get about twenty minutes into 'Forbidden Planet,' you—"

"I don't need to be told how to do it, dumbbell."

"Sure you do. Listen, I know what works. Twenty minutes in, you sneak your arm around the back of her seat and rest your hand on her shoulder." He pantomimed the motions. "If she likes you, she will lean closer to you right away. Then give it about ten more minutes, and put your other hand on her forearm laying there on the armrest. Start rubbing her arm gently and work your way up. When you get to her upper arm—the soft inside part of it of course—the back of your hand will accidentally start brushing the side of her boob. With Rhonda, you can't miss. Try that for a while. If she doesn't stop you, move the hand onto her lap and inch your way up."

"What happens if she shoves it away?"

"You sit and watch space monsters, whatta you think? It might take a few dates. I sometimes don't hit it on the first try."

"Thanks for that priceless advice, pal." I punched him in the chest and took off running.

"Any time, you homo!" he yelled after me. "Wait up!"

Our 1956 version of social media was called slam books—6 x 9 spiral notebooks with the name of the originator on the front and questions about people and relationships on the inside. The slam books got passed around, mostly among VIPs and VIP wannabes, for their anonymous opinions. Frankie caught me in front of school with a slam book in his hand. He opened it and shoved it at me.

"Read this shit, Ray."

I glanced at the cover: *Slam Book of Tina DeYoung.* Tina DeYoung was a cheerleader—cute but gossipy. There were rumors she had a thing for me. I read what Frankie was pointing to. Tina posed the question, "Ray and Rhonda? Could it be a match?" The answers were scrawled on the next few pages: "Not a good fit." "She's stacked. Bet he's noticed." "A literary brain and a machine shop girl? Strange mix." "He's too sharp for her." "She has hair on her legs. Yuck!" "Ray must see something we don't." "He's slumming." "Come on, Ray. Look again." "Her old man is a janitor at the Yard. Get serious, Ray." The crap went on for another couple of pages. Meanness never gets obsolete. I gripped the whole section, intending to tear it out.

Frankie was horrified. "Jesus, don't wreck Tina's book!"

So I didn't—just heaved the slam book into his gut. "Some great friend you are," I snarled at him.

"Hey, Ray, come on. I only told a couple of people."

I walked away, furious with the world, including myself for the monumental social blunder I'd allowed myself to make.

My mom had to haul along my sisters to pick Rhonda up because Friday was my dad's bowling night. My sisters, Jenny and Marie, were 8-year-old twins who'd put my nose out of joint when they were babies but over time had become two of my favorite people. Jenny was sweet and sunny like my mom. Marie could be moody, but she hugged me hard every night before she went to bed. I read to them almost nightly—more than my parents did. I was crazy about both of them, and so was Frankie, who hung around our house more than he did his own. He was an only child, which seemed strange for an Italian family. His dad was a heavy drinker, someone I usually tried to avoid—and so did Frankie, who now and then said he wouldn't mind living with us.

Our '49 Ford was a two-door coupe and would be tight with five of us. I figured I'd squeeze in back with the twins, and Rhonda could have the front. I pointed my mom toward Rhonda's, and when she parked in front of the tumbledown house, she didn't bat an eye. She'd lived through the Depression on a farm, so she knew what struggle was. The girls waited anxiously in the back seat, excited to see my date. I'd been to two dances (the whole of my dating experience), but the girls hadn't gotten to meet either date except in photographs. This was a big deal for them.

I went to the front door, which looked as if a dog had been scratching at it for the last five years. I couldn't find a doorbell, so I knocked. Mr. Moon answered; he was taller than the door opening and dressed in a white shirt and dress slacks. This was apparently a dress-up occasion for them. Seven young boys were lying around a console radio, listening to "The Lone Ranger." They only glanced at me. I saw the two who'd lugged home Uncle Ed's carp.

"You must be Ray," the huge man said. He held out his mitt-like hand, and I shook it.

"Nice to meet you, Mr. Moon." As I entered I saw Rhonda getting up from a long dining room table where two women sat, one no doubt her mother. The house smelled of cooked cabbage. The women looked a lot alike. You could tell they'd once been pretty but most of it had worn away. My own mom was about the same age, yet much fresher looking.

Rhonda came up to me smiling. She looked very nice—she was in what I guessed were her Sunday clothes, a soft blue sweater with some miles on it, and a long black skirt along with bobby sox and saddle shoes.

"Ray, this is my mom and my Aunt Carla."

I nodded and smiled at both of them. "Nice to meet you." The two glanced at each other and smiled as if they approved.

"Now what are the transportation plans again?" Mr. Moon asked in a no-nonsense voice.

I turned quickly to him. "My mom's waiting out in the car—with my little sisters, sorry to say. They had to come along because it's my dad's bowling night."

"She bringing Rhonda back home?"

"Yes, sir. We'll walk from the Liberty to my house—only three blocks—and mom'll drive us back here. She wondered, though, if Rhonda could stop a minute for some cake."

"Sounds okay," he said. "Take good care of her. I want to know I can trust you."

"Yessir," I said sheepishly. "Rhonda and I are just friends."

"Good. Keep it that way."

Mrs. Moon came over and straightened out a small cross hanging on a chain around Rhonda's neck. "Have fun,

Rhonda," she said. "You two enjoy the movie."

It was clear this ordeal was a first for everyone. But Rhonda and I got out the door somehow. When she saw my sisters, she brightened and insisted on sitting in back with them. The girls were thrilled and giddy. It seemed to be love at first sight, Rhonda chirping that she'd always wanted little sisters. My mom was her usual sweet self and asked Rhonda all about her family. I found out a lot in those few blocks. She had three brothers and no sisters. Her aunt and her four boys lived with them because her husband had died in a work accident. Rhonda's mom stayed home with the kids, and her aunt cleaned houses. "Sometimes I feel lost in all those boys," Rhonda said, "but we're all doing our best. We have to look out for family."

My mom made her approval of Rhonda abundantly clear to me. I wasn't nearly as hopeful about my classmates, though, and wondered how many of them would be at the movie, since space aliens were a big deal in 1956. The Liberty was a neighborhood theater with a small lobby and refreshment counter with a glass and stainless steel machine spewing out fresh popcorn. To my relief, Rhonda didn't want anything, so I led her in and took middle seats close to the back. At first glance, I didn't see a soul I knew, but I wasn't trying to make eye contact. Within a couple of minutes, the lights went down, a Tom and Jerry cartoon played, followed by some previews. One was for a movie called "And God Created Woman," starring Brigitte Bardot, a French actress who, even in a preview, showed more of her body than I'd ever dreamed of seeing in the Liberty. It shocked the whole audience and turned me into a jello dessert. My heart was banging like a snare drum. I glanced at Rhonda who was stunned, expressionless. Just as suddenly, Brigitte Bardot was gone, and previews for "Giant" came on, with Rock Hudson and James Dean in cowboy hats. What a relief. But the violent surge of hormones had shaken me. I spotted Frankie way down in the front row, whispering in the ear of some girl I didn't recognize. He already had an arm around her. Frankie and I would doubtless be seeing "And God Created Woman" together, but without dates. It was something I could never take a girl to, ever.

"Forbidden Planet" came on, and it was cheesy but interesting. Leslie Nielson and his crew were flying Starship C-57D to the planet Altair IV to discover the fate of a previous expedition led by Walter Pidgeon, known as Dr. Morbius. He naturally had a sexy daughter named Altaira, who caught Leslie Nielson's eye. I wondered where, on a planet of strange, alien creatures, she had come up with her sexy harem outfits. The background music was very weird electronic stuff, appropriate for space, I guess. Rhonda seemed to like Robbie the Robot best of all. While she was grinning at something Robbie said in his mechanical voice, I slipped my arm around the back of the seat and rested my hand on her shoulder. It took every ounce of courage I had. She glanced at me, still smiling about Robbie, and didn't seem bothered. I felt her lean into me a little.

I let ten minutes go by, and then I put my other hand on her forearm. Her blue sweater seemed soft as rabbit fur. I followed Frankie's advice and stroked her forearm up and down. I could feel the armpits of my shirt getting damp. Slowly I worked upward on her arm; soon the back of my hand was brushing her incredible right breast. A surge of electric current coursed down my spine into my lower body. Images of Brigitte Bardot undulated in my head. Rhonda was engrossed in the film, seeming not to notice my intentions. In my haste, I decided to skip a step and slipped my hand over her breast and squeezed gently. I moved my palm around, pushing aside the cross, faintly feeling her nipple through the sweater and bra. She stiffened but didn't push my hand away. I glanced at her; her eyes were wide—like some small creature in the lights of a speeding semi. But she still didn't push me away. The thought playing in my mind was, "It's okay, she's a Yard girl." I looked at her again, jarred when I noticed tears pooling in the corners of her eyes. I jerked my intruding hand away and grasped several of her fingers.

"Jeez, Rhonda," I whispered. "I didn't mean it."

She nodded, took a deep breath, and together we watched the rest of the movie without unlocking hands, even when they began to sweat. For a while I felt as much of a creep as Mervyn Bateman. But as we walked home, she was surprisingly calm and understanding—in every way more mature than I was.

"I didn't mean to get teary," she said. "You just surprised me. I don't think we know each other well enough for that."

"Honest, Rhonda, I don't know what I was thinking of. I've never done it before. I think it was that stupid Brigitte Bardot preview."

"I'm surprised they'd show a movie like that at the Liberty."

"Yeah, it's shocking." Actually, I couldn't wait to see it.

"I know my body is mature for ninth grade," she said, "I'm slowly getting used to boys acting odd about it. My cousin Ricky is only 12. He broke the lock on our bathroom door so he could pretend to walk in by accident when I take a bath."

"What a little creep!"

She laughed. "He's just curious. Boys are very curious— more than girls. I keep the shower curtain closed now. My dad has promised to fix the door."

This was the closest thing to a sexual conversation I'd ever had with a girl. The trouble was, she seemed more like a woman, and I felt a lot like a kid.

We ate cake at my house, all gathered around the kitchen table. My sisters were in nightgowns, ready for bed, but my dad wasn't home yet, so they went with us to drop off Rhonda. Before she got out of the back seat, both girls hugged her. It made me shudder to think of some guy in the future doing to them what I'd just tried to do to Rhonda. We were sex fiends, for the most part.

I walked her to the scratched-up door, and she gave me a quick kiss on the cheek.

"It was a nice night," she said. "Thanks for asking me. I love your family."

"Yours is really nice, too. Sorry I messed things up."

"You didn't really."

"You're very nice, you know it?"

She turned and opened the door. "See you in school, Ray."

It was the one and only date I ever had with her. The slam books the next week were full of the two of us, and I didn't have the strength of character to ignore them. After all the years, I'm still disgusted with myself.

The school sponsored a Sadie Hawkins dance called the Sparkle Spin a week before the semester ended. Tina DeYoung asked me, and, relieved to be asked, I said yes. We'd both been elected to the royal court of the dance, so it seemed logical to go together. The affair was formal with corsages and boutonnieres, (suits instead of tuxes, thank God), the full financial disaster, especially for girls. I was pretty certain I wouldn't see Rhonda there.

The last thing I did in printing class was to set in print something I'd written myself. I'd stayed friendly enough with Rhonda, but there was a difference—a distance I was maintaining, and she'd picked up on it. She knew all too well about social status, so I guess my attitude didn't surprise her. Still, she stayed cordial to me through the rest of the semester, and it caused me some grief.

Here is what I wrote and printed: "Mystery person: She is a better person than I am, kinder and more generous and caring. When I hurt or disappoint her, she lets it go. She is smarter than I am, especially about people. She isn't stuck up or in love with herself. She is pretty on the outside and beautiful on the inside. If we had an election, I would vote her queen of Roosevelt Junior High. Who is she?" The piece seemed to puzzle Mr. Gage, but it was the first paragraph of writing I'd ever wrenched out of my heart. I asked Rhonda if she'd proof it for me, as she usually did. When she'd read it two or three times, she smiled and told me, "Whoever she is, she's lucky to have a friend like you. I hope she finds out how you feel." I never told her who it was, but her innocent humility touched my heart.

As Tina and I sat next to each other that same day in the library, she noticed printed copies of the piece in my notebook and grabbed one. I let her go ahead and read it. She finished and stared at it for a while. "That's the nicest thing I ever read, Ray," her eyes still on the paper. The back of her neck was flushed, and I realized what she'd assumed. It certainly didn't hurt our relationship, which heated up a good deal leading up to the dance.

My mother, puzzled at my choices, asked about Rhonda Moon. I told her we were just friends. My sisters were hoping to see her again and expressed their disappointment with me.

Tina's father, a local urologist, came with Tina (in her massive pink formal) in a Cadillac, stopped for a few minutes at our house for the corsage ceremony and photographs, and then dropped the two of us at school, where our matchbox gym was brightly hung with crepe paper and balloons by the hundreds. A dance band of five older guys (The Mellowtones) played slow, romantic numbers. We danced almost every song together, and got as close as her dress would allow. Her breasts and brain were both normal ninth grade size, but in the magic of the evening it didn't matter.

Rhonda Moon: it was not a name to inspire poetry. Yet she stayed stubbornly in my head as school plodded along. At the end of the school year, our paths diverged. It was inevitable. Rhonda went to a technical high school downtown. I went to a nearby public high school for college prep. Now and then I would see her when Uncle Ed and I fished the rapids. She would stop and talk, always glad to see me. The boys were often hanging nearby—growing up fast.

When I graduated and was headed to college on a scholarship, my parents gave me a Smith Corona portable typewriter that I pounded on for twenty years until the typeface wore off. About the time I got my first computer, the early 1980s, my father's store had closed up forever, the typewriter now a dinosaur. By then I was a television writer, living in Los Angeles. For years I'd written my rough drafts on yellow legal pads, revising over and over until I was ready to type. The pads were a tangle of cross outs and arrows and insertions, and I loved looking at the mess I'd made. Every change was visible. When I managed the transition to composing on the computer, everything became miles faster and more fluid, but the stages of development disappeared. My Smith Corona still sits in the attic. I recycle my computers.

I'm old, though most days I don't feel it. I walk now instead of run. My pal Frankie has been dead ten years. Once, in the previous century, I married a pretty actress who worked in a sitcom I wrote for, but the marriage ended after eight years and two kids. The kids try to stay in touch, though they live in France and Canada. Some time ago I heard from a former classmate that Rhonda Moon owned a successful medical appliance design company near Lansing with two of her brothers. Her family's house, I knew, had been gone for eons—part of an expanded railroad system. Over time, I'd lost all track of her, though she'd never left my mind.

And it's sad to me. She was by far the best human being at Roosevelt Junior High, one I willfully let drift across my path and then away without her ever knowing the depth of my admiration, and (I confess it now) my unworthy but enduring love.

THE LOOKING GLASS

As Leo waded knee-deep in the clear, swift-moving river with trees and sky shimmering on the surface, into his head sailed a poem he'd written years before for his daughter Tess at twelve—her looking glass telling what it saw. He spoke the few lines he could remember:

> "I am her friend and enemy.
> I lift her hopes, I break her heart.
> I watch the child face fade away
> and beauty mutate into art."

Here in this old holy place, he felt the familiar ache of loss as he stared into the glimmer of a river he'd fished all his life. He saw distorted reflections of himself and the foliage above him as he cast his line. He'd written the poem when Tess and her mother still lived with him. Tess was in college now on the West Coast, lost to him for the most part, though she had recently taken up writing and was interested in his thoughts about it.

He was no Norman Maclean purist when it came to fishing. He loved this small river, not home to trout but smallmouth bass and northern pike. The water was crystalline with a bottom of rocks and sand and many deep, silt-filled holes beneath fallen trees and at the outer reaches of bends. He wore work shorts, a grey Tigers' tee shirt, and old tennis shoes, fished with Mepps spinners, and pulled along a stringer of bass secured to a belt loop. He was one fish from his limit and farther upriver than he'd ever waded.

Though the Looking Glass flowed into the much larger, murkier Grand in the nearby village of Portland, the spot Leo now occupied, four miles upstream, showed almost no evidence of human habitation. Moments before, he'd come upon a small doe wading across the stream; she'd ignored him, climbed up into the trees, and disappeared. Muskrats and herons were about, and he'd felt no desire to turn and make his way back to the car. It was near dinnertime, and his meal tonight would be fresh bass fillets, a pleasure he could forego until he'd explored the river to his satisfaction.

His father, born in Portland, had introduced him to the Looking Glass as soon as he was old enough to navigate the water and handle a spinning rod. They'd fished it together for years until his parents had moved south. Then he'd learned to fish the river alone and for a few years with his daughter. He preferred company, but only if that company was quiet and appreciative—like his father, like Tess. Through his life this ageless river had run its winding way. Fishing alone here was poignant and bittersweet.

Ahead, he saw a sharp bend and a deep hole with a rotted tree trunk at the downstream side. As he raised his rod to cast, he caught sight of a long, narrow mowed yard that swept from the riverbank up to a wooden stairway ascending the easy rise of a hill into a stand of trees. Through the trees he could see the windows of a house. Someone had built on this pristine frontage. He saw flower gardens hugging the perimeter of the property and lawn furniture in a cluster. Disgruntled, he turned his attention back to the hole and the tree trunk and cast his line, dragging his spinner through the dark water of the bend.

A fish struck almost instantly, and his rod bent in half. The line sliced sideways, then rose from the depths as the smallmouth leaped, blasting skyward in a shower of gleaming beads.

Leo fought patiently, guiding the fish away from the fallen tree, slowly drawing it toward shore and at last sliding a hand beneath it, a three pounder or more——large for this river. He ran two fingers through the scarlet gills, held the bass aloft to remove the hook, and then, his heart still pounding, heard a woman's voice.

"You're fishing on my property," she said.

His head snapped up. She was kneeling on the edge of a flower garden, in leather gardening gloves, and holding up a trowel.

"No one owns the river," he muttered, sliding the fish onto the full stringer.

"True enough from a legal standpoint."

"Is there another standpoint?"

She laughed and stood up to face him. She looked to be in her early 40s, about his age, slightly overweight in a bountiful way, dressed in a bathing suit with a flannel shirt buttoned over it. "You've caught one of my fish. I charge a fee for that."

He grinned uncertainly. "And what would that be?"

"We'll need to negotiate."

She seemed serious, making him faintly uneasy. "Well, can we sit down to do it? I've been wading against the current all afternoon."

"I'll agree to that." She pointed to the circle of chairs. "There's a cooler with a bottle of Chardonnay or a beer if you'd like. Not a soul has been by here all day, not even a kayaker. I built this place to get away from people, but sometimes I feel marooned." She dropped the trowel and removed her gloves. "My fee is your company."

Leo laughed, felt his shoulders relax. He tied his stringer to a thick tree root partly under water so the fish stayed in the river. Wet to the waist, his shoes gushing sand and water, he climbed up into her yard, propping his spinning rod against a tree. "I'm not dressed for socializing."

"Look at me."

"I smell like fish."

"Well, I've been grubbing in the garden. I'm sweaty and my knees are black."

He took a chair, and she sat down opposite him, brushing off her knees. "I've hooked that fish twice and lost him. You make one cast and nail him. There ought to be a law."

"You and the law."

She smiled. Her face was tan and attractive, pleasantly soft under the chin, framed by thick auburn hair. Her eyes were intense and faintly intimidating. "I'm a lawyer." She leaned sideways and opened a small cooler.

"Of course."

She pulled a wine bottle out of the ice. He nodded his approval, and she twisted off the top, pouring generously into two stemless plastic glasses. He took one and held it out for her to touch in a toast.

"To the kindness of strangers," he said.

She took a sip. "My, you fish and you're literate, too. I'm

pleasantly surprised." She bent forward and offered her hand. He took it. Her flannel shirt opened a bit, revealing the soft swell of a breast in a yellow halter top. "I'm Sarah Benjamin."

He stared at her intently. "We've met before."

"Oh? I hope that doesn't sour our relationship."

"Should it?"

"Well…there are men who resent me. I've made a career of representing women in divorces—to their benefit."

"This is very bizarre," he said, lifting his glass and looking into the pale liquid. "My ex-wife was one of those women. You're known as Sarah the barracuda."

She went silent for several moments and sipped her wine. "Yes, I've heard that. I find it offensive, but it doesn't hurt business. May I ask your name?"

"Leo Adams."

"I remember. You're the writer. May Adams was your wife. You have a daughter. May was one of my first clients— must be nearly ten years ago."

"And I admit you did well for her. May deserved what she got. So did I, for that matter."

"Ah, the plaintive sound of a repentant male."

Not liking her sarcasm much, he said, "My daughter used to fish this river with me. Just one of the many things I managed to piss away."

She drank more wine and leaned back in the chair. "Sorry to sound cynical, but I don't give much credence to the hand-wringing of men. There are a few honest exceptions, but not many."

"Your own devoted husband, no doubt."

"A nice thought, but no. He's my ex-husband, and he's no exception, believe me. He's a first class bastard—the reason I went into divorce law."

"I take it you haven't remarried."

She laughed sharply. "I have no faith in marriage. My job is setting women free. Men are not naturally monogamous or trustworthy. As I remember, you were a case in point."

Leo took a swallow of wine. She poured him more without asking. Chastened, he said, "Wow. Sarah the barracuda."

She smiled pleasantly. "Not very hospitable of me."

He shrugged. "My wife deserved better."

"She did, indeed."

He felt her eyes scrutinizing him; when he looked up, he was surprised to find the laser stare replaced by something softer—puzzlement, perhaps. He took another sip of wine and set the half empty glass on a small table. "Well, I have a long haul back to my car."

"Oh, stay a few minutes. This isn't a note to end on. My bluntness is professional habit. I apologize. I honestly wish you'd stay a little longer. I'll show you the house—I helped design it—then I'll drive you to your car."

He wanted to get his fish and leave, but something forceful in her was holding him there. "It's a tempting offer."

"Good." Her smile showed relief. "Grab the wine bottle and follow me."

The house was not the lavish, leisure class mini mansion he'd expected from a lawyer at the top of her game—it was modest sized, built of honey-colored logs with glass overlooking much of the winding river and a porch wrapping three sides.

"I'm impressed," he said. "It fits here."

"Coming from a serious fisherman, that's a compliment. I outbid a developer for this property, by the way. There's a lot of acreage, and it's staying wild except for that strip of lawn we just walked up."

"God bless you for that."

"Oh, He has—mostly through the generosity of men like you."

Leo laughed hard and kicked off his shoes before they entered. "You're deadly. Am I safe here?"

She smiled. "As safe as you care to be."

"Hmmm."

The interior of the house was rustic, simply furnished around a large stone fireplace and expansive windows overlooking the wild scene. The kitchen was more lavishly outfitted, designed for a chef, with commercial appliances and gleaming pots and pans hanging above a granite-topped center island.

"You have taste. Any rooms for rent?"

Pleased, she said, "We'll see how things go."

He looked around for a place to sit. "Sorry—I'm still pretty wet."

"Sit here at the island. Or I can throw those shorts in the dryer, and you can wrap up in a towel."

"This is fine."

She smiled as Leo took a stool and set the wine bottle on the stone countertop. They both drank, and she poured more. Sun streamed through the windows in wide bars. She turned her stool so the light wasn't in her eyes.

"I know May has remarried. Have you?"

"Haven't dared."

"Good. Because I have something to ask that may benefit both of us—or not. I don't have time or patience to do this discreetly. The fact is I haven't been to bed with a man in quite some time. Would you consider it?"

He stared at her for several moments. "Is there some kind of irony I'm missing?"

"No, I'm perfectly serious."

"Do you just pick random fishermen?"

"No," she said patiently, "You're the first. I'm very selective, and that creates problems. I feel a strong attraction to you. It doesn't happen often, and I don't have time or energy for mating games. I'm guessing you don't either. I'll tell you what I want, and you can say yes or no."

"A lawyer to the core."

"True."

"No hidden clauses or strings attached," he said.

"None, unless they're your strings."

"Meaning if I happen to fall for you, I'm out of luck."

"I can't imagine it happening," she said.

He looked into her unflinching stare. Her eyes seemed to pull the words out of him. "I must admit it's flattering. I'm in a dry spell of my own right now."

She nodded, satisfied. "I'll open another bottle of wine."

Still hesitant, he said, "I've never known seduction to unwind like this."

"It's not seduction, Leo, it's mutual consent. But enough talk—you need a shower, and so do I. It's just off the master bedroom and big enough for two, if you don't mind me joining you." Stretching like a cat, she smiled and twisted off the top of another bottle of Chardonnay. She unbuttoned the flannel shirt and shrugged it off. The yellow bikini bottom was tied high on her hips. Her breasts were large, her body pleasantly overripe, too ample for such a bathing suit, but the abundance dazzled him.

"I used to be leaner. I've mellowed."

He got off the stool and stood facing her. "I'm still trying to catch my breath."

"So diplomatic." Smiling, she moved close to him, touching her breasts to his chest. He leaned toward her lips.

"I'd rather we didn't kiss."

"What?" She might as well have slapped him.

"It's pointless, isn't it, when there's nothing between us?"

"I'd like to think we might inspire something."

"Such a romantic."

"Such strange ground rules."

"Well, I'm always open to renegotiation."

He took a heavy breath. "Point me to the shower."

He followed her, watching her drop the parts of her bathing suit as they went. She adjusted the water temperature as he undressed. She squeezed a body wash into her hands and, looking him up and down, began to soap his chest. "Everything okay?"

"Hell if I know."

With a sigh, renegotiating silently, she pressed her mouth to his and found his tongue. A missing piece fell instantly into place. "Men are such delicate mechanisms," she whispered.

"Is it any wonder?"

And they made love standing in the shower, lingeringly toweled each other off, and then went to her bed with the cool-looking gray sheets, where she spread herself out like a Venetian courtesan.

She powered the narrow road toward his car with unnerving speed. They'd had to backtrack because he'd forgotten the fish and his spinning rod. They'd lingered far longer in bed than she'd planned. She was expecting a business associate at nine. They both were famished, for which she was apologetic.

"I rarely lose track of time like that," she said, her attention drifting from the road.

With one foot on a non-existent brake, he replied, "I'll consider it a compliment."

She seemed charmed, but her mind was obviously on other things. She talked because he was there. "I'm so pleased you released your stringer of fish. My bass is back where he belongs."

It was true, he'd released the fish, but he hadn't told her why. Her bass was back in the river, but no doubt traumatized, if such things happened to fish. Trapped on the stringer, the fish had waited as a snapper devoured the other four tied beside it. Leo had found the struggling creature alive amid the bones and ragged shreds of meat—a grim parable of some sort, though its meaning eluded him.

"I know you're quite famous," she went on, uncomfortable with his silence. "I'm afraid I haven't read your books."

"I'll send you one."

She reached into the console of her Jeep and handed him a business card. "Here's how to reach me. If you should ever want to drop by, weekends are best. Call first, though."

He slipped the card into the shallow pocket of his tee shirt. "Weekends. Right."

"Maybe you'd write a poem for me."

"Odd you should say it. I have one started."

She brightened. "Honestly?"

"In my head."

"In case I don't see you again, let me hear it."

"It's only a few lines of doggerel."

"Please," she said impatiently.

"Well—if you want, but be merciful:

'Your body, the ripest of peaches—
Kept for your chosen alone.
And, as with peaches, fair lady,
Beneath the sweetness is stone.'"

Though he didn't expect it, she laughed delightedly. "Oh, clever! Well done! It's charming…a bit brutal, but true. It's me. I hope you'll send me the finished work."

She veered sharply into the small municipal park. His Land Rover was the only car left in the lot, so she pulled up close beside it. Leo got out, removed his gear from the back, and leaned into her window. She obliged him with a kiss.

"This is very good for the soul," he told her, and found

her lips again, "it inspires illusions of caring."

"I'm not into illusions, Leo, but thanks for the time. It's been…a lark." And with that she waved and sped off, pea gravel ricocheting off his car.

He changed clothes in the open, climbed behind the wheel and looked out at the Looking Glass, its surface ablaze with the red and orange of the setting sun. As his thin fog of smugness dissipated, he found himself regretting he'd ever fished today, especially so far upstream. He grieved the carnage he'd been party to.

She'd enjoyed his silly poem, wasn't offended in the least. He'd pleased the queen, and she'd found their time a lark. He thought about his compulsive refashioning of life into words, about how much of himself he gave to the work of it. It was part of his being, but he wondered if his passion for words and an audience could ever replace the living people he'd lost along the way. This swift-running river had long filled him with clarity and reverence, yet now, with the smell of her still on his skin, he wondered if words had the strength to redeem holy places.

THE DREAMS OF OLD MEN

for Jack Kimmell

Barton Locke felt angry, humiliated. He was only 70, yet here he was in a wheelchair in the Care Unit of Golden Sunset Nursing home, victim of an idiot on a mountain bike clipping him and fracturing his fibula as he rode his daily route on a designated bike path. The hospital had kept him a week because of swelling and then shipped him off to recuperate in this holding tank for almost-dead people. The halls were full of them sleeping in wheelchairs. His room was little more than a broom closet—two hospital beds with privacy curtains to draw around them, two television sets hung from ceiling mounts over the foot of each bed, one visitor's chair. Barton was tall and loosely built, too large for the wheelchair. He wore a yellow bathrobe over a Hawaiian shirt and shorts, a deerskin slipper on his right foot, and a cast sock on his left. *Crime and Punishment* lay open on his lap.

As a smiling, heavyset woman in a sweat suit entered the room with a walleyed pug on a leash, Barton swept the fingers of both hands through his flowing white hair.

"I'm Alice from Pet Pals Volunteers," the woman said in a chirpy, kindergarten teacher voice. "You must be Mr. Locke. "

"I must be."

"This is Buster. He's come to visit you."

Barton lifted his book to reading level. "I don't like dogs. "

Her smile broadened, and she laughed. "Oh, Mr. Locke. Everybody likes dogs."

"He stinks. Please get him out of here."

Disturbed, the woman turned and pulled Buster out of the room. A moment later, a silver-haired nurse with protruding teeth and a nametag identifying her as MARTHA came in, set down a paper cup of pills and glass of water on Barton's bedside table.

"I understand we're cranky today," she said.

"If you mean me, I'm happy as a clam."

"You should try to be a little more appreciative. After all, she and Buster are just trying to add some happiness to your day."

Barton smiled. "They did. I was happy to get rid of them."

"Oh, I know you don't mean that." She shook her head, turned, and went out.

Barton returned to his book, but a moment later Nurse Martha wheeled in a slumped, scowling old man, parked him beside the unoccupied bed, and pointed him toward the television set. With a remote she turned the set on. The man glanced up and in a phlegmy voice said, "Did I ask you to do that?"

"Most of our patients like it for company."

"Judge Judy is your idea of company?" He attempted to move the wheelchair toward the window, but his right side was useless. He tried with an immense effort, but finally gave up, angry and disgusted. "Jesus. Somebody put me out of my misery."

Barton looked more closely at the man, curious now. He was older than Barton, slouched in the chair with chin propped on his chest. His thick, drill sergeant look—hair cut in a precise flat top—seemed familiar. "You realize, Nurse Margaret, that my insurance pays for a private room."

She smiled tolerantly. "There are no private rooms in the Care Unit, Mr. Locke—in fact, this is the last space available. I want you to meet your roommate, Mr. Ripperda. He's recovering from a stroke."

"Beg your pardon. Mr. **who**?"

"Mr. Ed Ripperda…a very nice gentleman. He used to be a coach—correct, Mr. Ripperda? A football coach…"

The old man's head came up. He laughed with surprising heartiness and then began to cough.

Barton was aghast. "This isn't funny! Please get him out of here! "

Ripperda continued to brighten. "Hilarious!" He turned to Nurse Martha. "It's my old pal Barton Locke." His face now was glowing. "You know what's wrong with him? He's mad because I used to beat him up when were kids. Once I even broke his violin." He laughed with unexpected energy. "This is a hoot."

Nurse Martha looked worried. "So you know each other?"

"I'm married to his ex wife," Mr. Ripperda said, grinning.

"Oh…good heavens…"

Barton calmed himself. "You can see, Nurse Margaret, that this simply isn't going to work."

"I'm Nurse Martha, Mr. Locke. The problem is we're—"

Barton smiled stiffly. "Please see what you can do. The arrangement obviously won't be good for either of us." He turned his wheelchair and rolled out of the room after her. He followed her all the way to the Nurse's Station. "You can't put a well man in with a vegetable. I swear I'll get a lawyer."

"I can't do a thing today, Mr. Locke. But I promise I'll be working on it ASAP." She glanced back down the hall. Her eyes widened. "Mr. Locke, you might want to sit in the Lounge for a bit. Mr. Ripperda's wife just went in to see him."

"Angela?" He sat in place contemplating this as Nurse Martha hurried off in the opposite direction. Hesitantly, he turned his wheelchair and began slowly moving it toward his room. As he rolled by the open door, he saw Angela—Angela Ripperda, once Angela Locke, born Angela O'Neil—sitting in a chair near the window, busily filling out forms attached to a clipboard. She was just Barton's age, but looked younger. It thrilled him that she was still attractive, even though the strain of the present situation showed in her face. He gathered resolve, moved to go in, and then lost courage and abruptly backed his wheelchair out of her view.

As he sat alone in the hall, he thought of Ripperda's derisive words, remembered that Catholic school playground so many years ago. He'd been playing a jig on his violin for some girls in his class, one of them Angela, who danced like an Irish sprite. A smiling nun stood watching them. Nearby, two older boys tossed a football back and forth. One ran straight toward the fiddler. His buddy threw the ball, and as he reached for it, he plowed into Barton, sending him sprawling.

The nun rushed forward."Edward Ripperda! Get to the office this minute! Father Owens will deal with you!"

"But it was an accident, sister."

Barton got to his feet. He held up his violin, the neck of which had snapped.

"He broke it," Angela said.

Swiping at tears, Barton said, "He's an idiot."

Ripperda glowered at him. "You baby. You showoff. You think you're Mozart or somebody."

"You **are** an idiot, Rip," Angela said.

The nun snatched his arm and led him off toward school. He glanced back at Angela with bewilderment.

Barton was nudged from this ancient dream by Angela exiting the room. He spun his chair before she noticed him and tried to escape toward the Nurse's Station. Yet she walked in the same direction.

She called out, "Barton!"

He stopped and slowly turned. "Oh, hello, Angela."

She moved close, standing over him. She wore a black skirt and green cashmere sweater, looking soft and tempting. Her red hair was still thick and youthful and largely absent of grey. Her eyes were older, but her presence never failed to inspire him. "Rip told me you were his roommate. How strange is that?"

"A nasty quirk of fate—I'm not the least bit happy."

"I can imagine." She looked into his eyes, and then away—tried sounding chipper. "Well! So here we are again. We've aged a bit. What has it been—ten years?"

"Thirteen this October. I've moved back to town, by the way." He stared at her. "I'm the one who's aged—you haven't."

"You're a liar, Barton—but always a charming one." She flashed a bright smile, her cheeks soft circles of pink. "How are you?"

"I'm fine—except for the fact that they've stuck me in this old folks' purgatory for physical therapy. Had a little bike accident. I'll be out of here as soon as my leg mends."

"Good for you. I don't think Rip'll be that lucky."

"Oh…sorry."

"I just can't take care of him any more. I can't lift him. He's pretty helpless."

He snorted. "Rip Ripperda helpless? Are you kidding?"

She gave him an unbelieving look. "Why would I be kidding?"

"Hmmm…what an odd situation."

She leaned in the direction of the entry doors. "Well…"

"Wait a minute, Angela. Don't go yet. How are your kids doing?"

"My kids?" She looked puzzled. "Fine, I guess. All grown up. We have three grandchildren now."

Barton's wheelchair began to pinch him. "Good Lord—don't tell me stuff like that."

"Life goes on, Barton."

He straightened himself in the chair. "Hey, what do I know?" He looked warmly at her, reached and touched her arm. The cashmere was deliciously soft. "I do know you look terrific, Angela—not like any damn grandmother."

"Honestly. You never change."

"I mean it."

"You've always had…well, a way with women." She smiled and turned toward the entrance. "Sorry, but I have to go. I'll probably see you again—at least if you stay in the room with Rip." She patted his hand, the one touching her sweater, and then walked briskly away.

He stared as she went through the door. Yes, a way with women—and what the hell to show for it?

Barton sat outdoors in the courtyard reading, avoiding his room for the next couple of hours. Angela's presence in this place had undone him. Nurses came and went, sometimes sitting down to eat lunch from sacks. Most Care Unit old folks stayed inside despite the sunshine and mild September weather. By mid afternoon, with a sun now the size of a tennis ball, Barton made his way back in. He rolled the long hallway, hearing outbursts of laughter from his room, the unmistakable sound of jocks.

He entered to find a visitor, a barrel-chested, aging black man with a sandpaper voice. The man ignored Barton and went on talking to Rip, who now lay propped up in bed. "Nothin's the same at East Catholic, Rip. You and me, we were on the same wave length about defense. This guy plays by the book—too predictable. You and me always kept 'em guessing. I'm thinking about getting out. It ain't the same."

"You're right, Big Dog, nothing's the same."

"No, something's the same."

"What's that?"

"You're still ugly."

"Yeah, and you're still dumb."

They both laughed, but Rip was working at it, running on empty.

"Dumb and Ugly," Barton said. "Lovely pair." He rolled to his bed and set his book on the nightstand.

"Keep it to yourself, Mozart," Rip grumbled.

Barton found it curious that he was able to inspire sudden surges of energy in his old archenemy.

The man named Big Dog scratched his fuzzy head, looking puzzled. "Mozart?"

"Yeah, sometimes I call him that. I call him Lockjaw, too. Or Locknut. He's some kind of musical genius. Plays a dozen instruments." His voice grew louder. "You were a child prodigy once, right, Mozart?"

"Sure. And you were the second coming of Knute Rockne."

Rip grinned. "You got that right."

Big Dog stuck out a heavy paw and shook Barton's hand. "Bobby Wheeler. He calls me Big Dog."

"I'm Barton Locke. He calls me whatever he feels like."

A CMA entered the room—broad, muscular, rugged good looks, tattoos on both arms and a ring in one ear. His nametag identified him as CARLTON. "Which one of you is Mr. Ripperda?"

Big Dog pointed to Rip.

"I'm here to take you to physical therapy."

Rip pointed at Barton. "That's him over there."

"I don't think so," Barton replied. "Your turn in the torture chamber, Ripperda."

Big Dog stood staring at Carlton. "Don't I know you?"

"Yeah."

Rip took another look. "Well, whatta you know…Miller or something. Yeah, Carlton Miller. Twelve, thirteen years ago, right? Fullback with some real speed. We went to state finals that year."

Carlton shrugged. "I didn't play much."

"Now I remember," Big Dog said. "Sure, Carlton Miller."

"You know what your problem was, Miller?" Rip asked him.

In a flat voice, Carlton replied, "No what was my problem, Coach?"

"You knew it all. You didn't need a coach. You wanted to be a star—never learned to be a team man."

"You gotta be a team man," Big Dog chimed in.

"You go to college?" Rip asked.

"Never got there. I was hoping football would be my ticket. So—here I am in this place."

Rip stared at him in disbelief. "How the hell can you stand it? It's full of old people. I hate being around old people."

Barton laughed. "In case you haven't noticed, you're one of them, Ripperda."

"Like hell I am." He looked to Carlton. "Hope you've learned your lesson, Miller."

Carlton turned sullen. "Learned a lot of lessons, Coach. Come on, let's get you in the wheelchair." Carlton went to him, pulled him upright, and lifted him into the chair.

In pain, Rip said, "God, be careful. I'm not a frickin football."

Carlton strapped him in, giving an overly aggressive tug in doing it. Rip cried out. "Sorry there, Coach." He wheeled him out of the room with Big Dog following after.

Several days passed without progress on a room change. Barton sat in his wheelchair reading the *New York Times*. Rip sat nearby in his wheelchair, slumped over to the right, watching Sports Center at high volume. Barton lowered his *Times*.

"Are you going deaf, Ripperda?"

"What?"

"Obviously you are."

"You got a problem?"

"TURN THE DAMNED THING DOWN!"

"Jesus, take it easy. I just want the baseball scores."

"They scroll them at the bottom of the screen. You can read them without listening to those loud-mouth, mesomorphic meatheads."

"That was a mouthful, Locknut. You always had a big vocabulary."

A young, attractive nurse with blonde hair gathered up

neatly at the back of her neck entered the room carrying a small tray. Her nametag read BETSY and her smile transformed Barton into something not unlike the tapioca pudding on her tray. Rip caught sight of her and muted the sound.

"Hello there!" she chirruped. "I'm going to be your day nurse for the next two weeks. My name is Betsy."

Barton's mood continued brightening. "Where is Nurse Margaret?"

"You mean Nurse Martha? She's on vacation—didn't she tell you?"

Barton offered up his warmest smile. "She might have. Whatever. Well—this certainly is an upgrade. I thought I was in purgatory until you walked in."

"Are you Mr. Locke? Martha mentioned you wanted to be moved."

"He doesn't like me," Rip said.

"I've changed my mind."

"Oh, how nice," she said. "I know it's been several days. We're still waiting for an opening."

Rip laughed. "She means waiting for somebody to die. Need a volunteer?"

"No, Mr. Ripperda. You're not about to die on my watch."

In a voice flatly ironic, he said, "Wonderful news."

She replied in her charming, enthusiastic way, "I have some tapioca pudding for you!" She went to Rip, pulled his rolling bed tray in front of him, and set down the dish of pudding. "I've brought your meds, too. Do you need some help?"

He answered with an emphatic no.

Barton, on the other hand, felt more solicitous about her services. "Nurse Betsy, while you're here, may I ask a small favor?"

"Of course!"

"I have something in my eye. Could you look at it?"

She smiled innocently. "I'd be glad to. Which one?"

"The left."

She moved to the side of his chair, leaned over him, and separated his left lids. The position was awkward, and she lost her balance. He took hold of her waist and steadied her. Her body brushed against his.

"Oh, sorry. Thanks for catching me. I don't see anything."

"It's under the upper lid. If you'd bend a little closer… Hmmm. Is that Giorgio you're wearing?"

"How did you know?"

"I've had some experience with it…very nice…very passionate."

Nurse Betsy pulled back. "Am I wearing too much?"

"No, no. It just tells me that you're…you're passionate about your work."

She bent closer to him but finally had to stand up. He held her waist for a second longer than necessary, and then finally let go. "I'm sorry, Mr. Locke. I can't seem to see it."

"Actually, I don't feel it any more. I think you got it."

Carlton came in and grinned at Betsy, who seemed to light up in his presence. "Time for PT, Coach."

"Could I have a few more minutes, Carlton?" Betsy was smiling. "I need some vitals from Mr. Ripperda."

"Sure thing, I'll be back."

Her eyes lingered on him as he went out.

"You like Carlton?" Barton asked.

"I think he's the nicest of our the med assistants." She wrapped Rip's arm with a blood pressure cuff and inflated it.

"And the hottest?" Barton asked.

She smiled, blushing deeply. "Well…that, too. I think you're a bit naughty, Mr. Locke."

"He's a dirty old man," Rip said.

"Not so—I'm an angel. I can't help it if your presence, Nurse Betsy, affects me like…like a breath of fresh ocean breeze."

Rip stared at him. "And yours is like a hot wind off a landfill."

"Shut up, Ripperda. You'll never understand poetry."

Nurse Betsy released the air from the cuff and unwrapped Rip's arm. "Nearly normal. Well, good luck in therapy, Mr. Ripperda." She put away the equipment and went out.

"Nice moves there, Locke. What a spectacle. Nothing sadder than a worn out Romeo still trying his old lines. Words don't turn her on—Carlton and his muscles do. She's looking right through you—or didn't you notice?"

Barton grumbled and raised his newspaper. "Would you turn up that sound again?"

Rip began trying to eat his tapioca pudding with his left hand. The first spoonful plopped onto his lap. "Dammit!"

"Trouble chewing your pudding?"

"My right hand doesn't work. My left hand is just stupid. Always has been."

"Want me to feed you? I'm always glad to help a helpless fellow human being."

Rip held out his left fist. "I may not be able to eat with this hand, but I could still kill you with it."

Barton set his newspaper in his lap. "Good grief. Vintage Ripperda." He laughed happily. "You threatened to kill me once in tenth grade—you the big senior jock—if I didn't give you the answers on a government test."

"Yeah, well, I ended up teaching government."

"There's a sad commentary on American education." Barton shook his head, sat thinking for a moment. "Hey— here's an idea. You always wanted to arm wrestle me in front of Angela. Why not now? How about it, Rip—you old warrior?"

"I'd still crush you, Lockjaw." He raised the remote, changed his mind, and sat in silence scraping the pudding off his lap with a napkin. He tried the spoon with his left hand again and clumsily managed a bite. At that moment, Carlton came back and rolled him away.

Barton had no idea how long he'd slept when an unnervingly familiar female voice cried out, "OH, BARTON!" He nearly jumped out of his chair. At the door stood a pillowy, pleasant-looking woman of about 60 in a flouncy summer dress.

"Good grief, Rosalinde, you scared the liver out of me."

She went to him and stood with her hands folded at her breast. "Oh, I'm sorry, I'm just so thrilled to see you! Why didn't you tell me this had happened? I found it out from my ex-husband, of all people." She sat down on the arm of his wheelchair so she could press her cheek to his. Her soft arms half smothered him. "My poor Barton. It's terrible to see you without your…vitality."

Barton looked up to see Angela entering, pushing Rip in his wheelchair. Rip appeared spent, but he perked up quickly. Angela looked in shock at Barton, who struggled for composure with this woman wrapped about him.

"Goodness! Excuse us!" Angela exclaimed. "Would you two like some privacy?"

With a Herculean effort, Barton pushed Rosalinde to her feet. Out of breath, exasperated, he cried, "No! Come in, for heaven's sake. It's your room, too."

Angela hesitantly rolled Rip over to the side of his bed.

"Um, I'd like you two to meet an acquaintance of mine. Rosalinde Fishburn, this is Angela and Ed Ripperda."

"Pleased to meet you," Rosalinde said cheerfully. "Have you known Barton long?"

Angela glanced at Barton. "Well…yes, as a matter of fact. I'm his ex-wife."

Rosalinde's face went through a number of odd contortions. "Barton and your husband are staying in the same room?"

Angela smiled. "It is quite a coincidence."

"More fate than coincidence," Barton replied.

"Don't go and get deep on us," Rip grumbled.

"Rosalinde, why don't we go down to the Lounge? There's a piano there. Maybe I'll play you something." Barton glanced at Angela, but her attention was on Rip.

"Oh, wonderful!" Rosalinde gushed.

The Lounge was empty except for them. Worn easy chairs and lumpy, flowered couches lined the walls. A fish tank was prominent in the center of the room. Barton rolled his wheelchair to the keyboard of a battered upright piano, pushing aside the bench. Rosalinde folded her arms on top of the piano and rested her chin on them with a dreamy look. The piano was not quite as bad as he'd expected. Someone had apparently tuned it within the last five years. He began playing *Clair de Lune.*

As he knew it would, the music transported him to a time in the late 70s, to a graduate student named Julie from his piano performance class—a girl moderately talented, bountifully endowed, and temporarily infatuated. They were alone in the small auditorium. She was playing *Clair de Lune* competently but without the impressionistic wash of sound

Debussy wanted. Barton demonstrated the difference, leaving her flushed and happy, grateful. She was 23, as he recalled—he was about ten years older with a mane of dark hair. They tried a four handed Spanish piece, *Andalucia*. He remembered telling her, "It's passionate…it's a folding together of four hands into one, a single vision, a single being—almost like making love. Do you understand?" It was a killer line.

"I really think I do," she'd said. Her face aglow, she nodded three times, and they leapt in. Their shoulders met and separated, their hands moved and crossed and touched in swift and breathless ways. The piece built like the accelerating heels of Flamenco dancers, backed off into something light and flowing, then began to crash toward a crescendo.

Barton suddenly stopped playing and faced her. "My God, Julie…"

Her face was deeply flushed. "Barton?" She'd always called him Dr. Locke.

They came together, mouths open wide. Their lips met in a crush. Their arms grasped and grappled. Barton accidentally hit several keys with an elbow, and they rang discordantly.

The music secretary, as fate would have it, had forgotten to tell him that his wife would be waiting in the back of the auditorium.

Barton glanced up just in time to see Angela fly out of the room. He jumped to his feet, rushed several steps in her direction, but was of course too late. She was gone, and this time for good.

Both men lay in bed. Rip had an oxygen tube in his nose. Barton lay with his hands behind his head, not sleeping. After a moment, he got up on one elbow, staring into the darkness. Then he fell back into the pillows.

"You awake, Lockjaw?" Rip asked.

It startled Barton. "Yeah, I thought you were sleeping… or dead."

"Can't sleep."

"Neither can I. My brain won't shut down tonight."

There was a pause. "Sounds like the weight of sin," Rip said. "My priest is coming tomorrow. I'll send him over."

"Thoughtful of you, but I'd hate to overwork the guy."

He yawned heavily. "I'm…just thinking about the past."

"The past," Rip said bitterly. "The past is all I got now. It ain't much, believe me."

"You forgot something."

"Huh?"

"You've got Angela."

"Oh, yeah…Angela. She's a good wife, but I'm not exactly making her life easy."

Barton's voice dropped low. "Neither did I." He went silent, struggling with his thoughts. "Hey, Ripperda, you seem to have insights into people. You know me pretty well. Remember you told Carlton what was wrong with him? What's wrong with me?"

He could see Rip smile in the semi dark. "The same thing."

"What's that?"

"You're in love with yourself. You've been calling attention to yourself ever since you were a kid. You're not a team man, even in a relationship. You always put yourself first."

Barton felt himself fill with resentment. "Thanks for that analysis, Coach."

"If you don't want to hear it, don't ask. Anyway, most of us have that character flaw."

"Good night, Ripperda. Jesus…"

At daybreak Barton was awakened by the sound of someone in the room. In the semi-dark, he saw Carlton bending down and crimping Rip's oxygen tube until Rip began to grunt and move about. Then a warning buzzer went off on the oxygen concentrator. Barton sat up, startled. "What the hell is going on?"

Carlton dropped the tube and the buzzer stopped. "It's just his oxygen machine. No problem."

"Why did you crimp that tube?"

"Just checking the alarm."

Carlton set things in order and moved toward the door, staring at Barton as if meaning to intimidate him.

Rip began making gutteral, irritating wake-up noises. "Whus all the racket?" he slurred.

Barton hesitated, wondering if he should say anything. "Not sure. But I'd keep an eye on Carlton."

Rip cleared his throat. "I got better things to do with my time."

"I don't think he likes you."

"What else is new?"

"Just give it some thought, Ripperda."

"Thanks, Lockjaw. I just did."

By week's end, Barton was up and practicing with crutches. A wooden cane, his next goal, leaned beside his bed. He thumped into the hallway, passed a Nurse's Station where Nurse Betsy and Carlton were chatting. Carlton leaned on the handle of a wheelchair in which a very old woman was sleeping. He was showing Betsy a tattoo on his forearm. As Barton shuffled by, he listened to their conversation.

"The sun means fertility and passion. And courage, too, I think," Carlton told her.

She smiled innocently. "That's interesting."

"You ought to get a tattoo. They're very sexy."

"I don't think I'd dare." She lowered her voice. "What'll they look like when you're old like her?" She pointed to the old woman sleeping in the wheelchair. "Do they sag and wrinkle up?"

Barton was amused by the thought and took a chair just down the hall from them.

Carlton pulled up the short sleeve of his white tee shirt, revealing a chain tattooed around his bicep. He raised his arm, flexing the muscle, stretching out the chain. "No sagging there."

Betsy reddened, embarrassed. "I can see that."

"Maybe we should go out some time," Carlton said, looking at her.

Barton sighed heavily and closed his eyes. How crude and graceless this generation was. In only a moment, Barton fell into a half sleep, his imagination lifting into flight.

A distinguished-looking man in his 30s appeared suddenly in the hallway and approached Nurse Betsy and Carlton.

"Excuse me," he said, reading her nametag. "Nurse Betsy?"

She nodded, offered him a smile.

"I have a question." He stared a bit too long at her. "Funny, you remind me of someone I know."

"That's odd," she replied. "You do, too. But I'm not sure who it is." Her smile warmed. "How can I help you?"

"I'm looking for a med assistant named Carlton."

"That's me," Carlton said with a smirk.

"You're wanted in Hallway B at the very end. Someone spilled a bedpan."

Wary, Carlton asked, "Who wants me?"

"The head nurse, Mrs. Madison. Hey, interesting tattoos. Are they real?"

Surly now, Carlton glared at him. "Are you here for somebody?"

"I'm visiting Barton Locke."

"Yeah, that makes sense." His voice was impassive; he glanced impatiently at Betsy, and then went off down the hall, pushing the old woman.

"Barton Locke—that's who you remind me of. Are you his son?"

"No, I'm not his son. We're related, though."

"I can see that. He's an interesting man. It would've been fun to know him when he was younger."

"Oh…women were quite taken by him."

Her smile broadened. "I'm not surprised at all."

"Are you married? I don't see a ring."

Betsy glanced down at her hand. "Oh…no, I'm not."

"I'm not either. I mean I was, but now I'm not."

"Oh."

"Was that med assistant flexing his muscles for you?"

She took a deep breath. "I was surprised…actually a little embarrassed."

"Kind of immature, don't you think?"

"Yes. Although he's usually very nice."

"Well…"

She stood silent a moment. "Mr. Locke is probably waiting for you."

He touched her forearm. "Now that I know you're here, I believe I'll come every day." He gently squeezed her forearm. "Listen, it's almost noon. Barton can wait awhile. Are you doing anything for lunch?"

Betsy dropped her eyes, blushing. "I was planning to run home to eat. I just live a few blocks from here."

"Oh."

"I have a stew in a crock pot. It's nearly ready."

"Oh, well. Maybe another time."

Betsy brightened. "I have enough for two. Would you like to come over?"

"Are you sure? I'd love a chance to get to know you better."

Happy now, she chirped, "My shift ends in ten minutes. I'll meet you at the front door." She moved away from the Nurse's stand, then turned back to him. "Wait. This is crazy. I don't even know your name."

He smiled. "Barton Locke."

"Ohmigosh! Another one?"

Barton, still half asleep in the hallway chair, smiled blissfully. His eyes opened. Betsy was writing something on a chart. Carlton hadn't moved—was still looming over the old woman sleeping in her wheelchair.

Friday arrived but seemed the same as every other day. Barton sat at the upright Lounge piano, his crutches leaning against it, fiddling with a tune he was inventing. A small, pretty, red-haired girl of about ten, dressed in a Catholic school uniform, entered and stood listening to him. When he noticed her, he did a stunned double take.

"Hello," she said.

"Hello."

She moved closer. "What are you playing?"

"Oh, I'm just making up a song."

"Play it for me."

He shrugged and continued playing. "It's not done yet."

"When you finish can I can hear it?"

"Maybe."

She took a cell phone from a pocket of her plaid skirt and began texting.

He stopped playing and turned on the bench to face her. "Are you visiting someone here?"

"Uh-huh."

"By any chance, is your grandma Angela Ripperda?"

The girl put her phone away, surprised. "How did you know?"

Barton hesitated. "You look just like she did a long time ago."

This brought a smile to her face. "Really? Are you a friend of hers?"

"Oh…I am. A very old friend. I met her in fifth grade."

She laughed. "Are you kidding? It's hard to picture Grandma in fifth grade. Was she pretty?"

"The prettiest girl in the school."

Pleased, she said. "She looked like me?"

"Exactly like you."

"Wow."

"What's your name?"

"Lucy Michaels."

"I'm Barton."

"Is that your first name or your last?"

He grinned, charmed. "I actually have two last names: Barton Locke."

"Should I call you Mr. Locke?"

"That would be polite. But I'd prefer Barton."

"Okay, Barton." She went back to texting, and he watched her.

"That's a very fancy phone."

"I got it for my tenth birthday. Do you have one?"

"Not like that. Mine has big numbers, and you can only make phone calls and text on it. It's not a very smart phone."

She continued her text as she talked. "That doesn't sound too interesting. Mine is really smart—a computer and a camera and a recorder. And you can play games and take videos with it, too."

"I'd be scared to try a phone like that."

"Oh, it's easy. I could show you how it works in about two minutes." She continued clicking keys as he watched her, fascinated.

"You must be smart. I'll bet you love school."

"No."

Barton laughed at her candor. "Well…do you have brothers and sisters?"

"Two brothers. I'm in the middle."

"I was an only child. You're lucky. Are they fun?"

Lucy stopped texting and gave him a vexed look. "No. We're not a very close family right now. I have to go to their sports all the time. Have you ever watched boys play football? They think it's some big heroic thing, but it's so boring I feel like I'm going to die from it. I really do. Grandma comes and gets me a lot so we can do something different. She has to drive a whole hour, but she doesn't mind."

"She's a very nice person."

"She's my favorite."

"What about your Grandpa?"

She shrugged and took a deep breath. "He's nice enough. But I think he likes boys best. He's very sick, you know."

Barton nodded. He turned back to the keys and played the tune he'd been working on. For her sake, he made it bouncy and funny.

Lucy clapped her hands and giggled, delighted. "That's a silly song."

"I'll call it *Lucy's Song*."

Behind Barton, someone cleared a throat. They both looked up to find Angela standing in the doorway. "Excuse me. May I join the party?" She entered the room and set her purse in a chair. "Have you made a friend?" she asked Lucy.

"Uh-huh. But he's really your friend."

Angela looked at Barton and frowned. "I hope you didn't—"

"—of course not. Lucy and I have just been getting to know each other. And talking about when you and I were in the fifth grade."

"He said you were the prettiest girl of all—and you looked just like me."

"It's uncanny," Barton said. "She's the image of you."

"That's what people say. I guess I can't see it."

They turned as a spare, athletic-looking woman with short, mannish hair came bursting into the room. "Oh, here you are. We were walking Dad outside, but then this med assistant came and took him away to therapy. We thought we'd go out to lunch. Want to go, Mom?"

"I think I'd better stick around." The daughter was staring at Barton. "Oh, Maggie, I'd like you to meet—" hesitating, "Barton Locke. Barton, this is my daughter, Maggie Michaels."

The daughter's face seemed to turn to stone. "Uh…hello." She glanced at her mother. "Are you kidding me?"

Angela stayed composed. "He shares a room with your Dad. Quite a coincidence, isn't it?"

In a guarded tone, Maggie said, "Good Lord. How is that going?"

Barton entered the conversation. "We're doing fine. I don't like him. He doesn't like me."

To her mother, Maggie said, "Should I be doing something about this?"

"No, dear."

Maggie shook her head as if to clear it. "Well…whatever you think. Come on, Lucy. Your dad is waiting in the car."

"But I'm not hungry."

"Lucy—"

Looking miffed, Lucy packed her cell phone into a pocket and followed her mother out of the room. Barton and Angela watched them in silence. She lifted her purse and sat down.

"Well…what did you think of my granddaughter?"

"I'm trying to recover. She's a delight. But meeting her was…I don't know…unsettling."

Angela looked puzzled. "Do you mean the way she lives on that cell phone? I don't even own one. She's way too young as far as I'm concerned."

"No, not that. Funny, Angela, I've never given much thought to kids…or grandkids. Well, except on holidays. I have no family left—no parents, no siblings. No male heir to carry on the family name…"

"I wouldn't worry about the Locke name dying out. Now, Ripperda might be a cause for concern."

Barton was too involved in his thoughts to be amused. "When I look at Lucy, I realize there's a sort of immortality in having offspring. She's you all over again."

"You're serious, aren't you? She isn't really. Lucy is my good pal, but she's no reincarnation of me." Her eyes became more animated. "I suspect she was quite taken by you. She usually isn't that outgoing."

"She has your spirit."

"I don't know about that, Barton. Don't make too much of it. Lucy is Lucy."

"Well…I'd like a Lucy myself."

She gave him a mystified look. "Odd time to be thinking about that."

It was late afternoon. Barton breezed into the room puffing after a brisk jaunt on his crutches. Rip lay rigidly on his bed with a blanket pulled up to his ears as Carlton folded up his wheelchair and leaned it against a wall. Rip raised his head a little. "Hey, Miller, I need another blanket. I'm freezing."

"It's seventy degrees outside, man. You can't be freezing."

He fell back into his pillow. "I don't know what's wrong. My blood is thin or something. I need a blanket."

"No, you don't," Carlton grumbled.

Rip got up on an elbow. "Where's Nurse Betsy?"

"The nurses are all in a staff meeting."

"At least help me to the bathroom."

"Don't bug me, Coach. I got a lot to do."

Rip stared at him. "Miller, I always liked it when my players called me Coach. With you, I don't like it."

Carlton snorted. "Get used to it."

A flash of anger crossed Rip's face. "There was a time you wouldn't have had the guts to talk like that."

"Yeah? Well that time is gone. You got no power any more, Coach. You're useless, man."

Rip glared at him. "You'll see, Miller."

"That's not what I'm told."

Barton could hold his tongue no longer. "You're way out of line, Carlton."

Carlton fixed him with cold eyes. "Mind your own business, Mr. Locke."

"You can't pull this kind of crap."

Carlton laughed. "I'm not pulling anything. The patients here are always complaining about the nurses and med assistants, even when there's no reason. Head nurse takes it with a grain of salt. Just try telling her—if you got the balls." He stared Barton down and then meandered out. The two were silent for several moments.

"Delightful guy," Barton said.

"Okay, okay…so he's mean as a snake. But I don't need you coming to my rescue."

Barton rolled his eyes, deeply irritated. "Who's coming to your rescue? I don't like you any more than he does. Hell, I should be the one getting even here, not Carlton."

Rip grinned. "That's more like it, Lockjaw. Keep your edge." As usual, he seemed to perk up at any sign of friction between them. "Hey," he continued, "did I ever tell you about the big Catholic wedding Angela and I had? Hundred and eighty people at Flanagan's for the reception? Boy, did I make Angela's parents happy."

"Not a story I'm dying to hear, Ripperda."

"Old man O'Neil put an Irish curse on you for eloping with his daughter. It took a few years, but it sure worked." He laughed merrily. "Funny, I thought your divorce would be a problem for us, but it wasn't. Declaration of Nullity based on Lack of Cannonical Form, they called it. In the eyes of the church, you were never married in the first place."

Barton glared at him, at the frail neck he would love to twist. "You're an idiot, Ripperda. I'll bet you've been waiting years to make that speech."

"Yeah, I admit it's kind of fun having you around." His face screwed itself into a grimace. "I gotta get to the bathroom. Dammit, go check and see if the nurses are back."

Barton turned on his crutches and moved toward the door. "You've got a call button. Handle it yourself, Coach."

Barton entered the Golden Sunset dining room—two dozen tables with some residents in chairs and wheelchairs having lunch. He was surprised to see Angela at a table by herself looking at a menu. He made his way over and stood leaning on his crutches. The air was heavy with the smell of fish and overcooked vegetables. "Mind if I join you, miss?"

She looked up and smiled. "Of course not."

"Who'd have guessed I'd one day be having lunch with you at the Golden Sunset Nursing Home?"

"It is a little weird," she said.

"Yeah—but I'm trying to look at it philosophically." He took a seat next to her. Her eyes were as blue and intense as the color of her silk scarf. "I figure, why not just enjoy each other's company while we can? I mean…assuming you're enjoying my company."

"Yes, surprisingly I am."

A teenager in hot pink tennis shoes came to the table, filled their water glasses, and took their order—they both chose the tuna burger, tropical mixed fruit, and broccoli raisin salad.

"Rip hates the food here," she said, pushing back her red hair in a way that tantalized him.

He unrolled the napkin from his silverware, checked to see if the fork was clean. "It's the one thing he and I agree on. Otherwise, we thrive on insults. It's fairly invigorating."

She smiled, crinkling the corners of her eyes. "I've noticed."

He carefully laid out his silverware and took a sip of water. "Angela—I don't get it. I never did. What the hell do you two have in common? There must be more to Ripperda than meets the eye. But it's a mystery to me."

She shrugged and gave it several moments' thought. "I think you know the story—I finished my degree and was hired to teach art at my old high school. Rip was the football coach. He showed interest…my parents were pleased about it. In a way he and I made more sense than you and I did. I was back in a familiar world that valued me—back in my own church."

"But he's such a meathead. How has it lasted so long?"

She let out a long breath, as if it was a difficult question. "How can you explain a marriage? Kids have helped. So have grandkids. It hasn't been a bed of roses. But Rip is a good man in a lot of ways. His bark is worse than his bite."

"Yeah, the bark is still formidable."

"He's a very religious man—never misses mass."

"Some of the world's worst people have been religious men."

"He's not one of those, believe me. He works with disadvantaged kids. He always has made sure his players succeeded at school…"

Barton interrupted her. "Has he been faithful?"

"That's an odd question to ask, Barton. Yes, he has. But I guess there are different kinds of mistresses. His was football. He's a man's man. He spent more time with his teams and coaches than he ever did with me. I always went to his games—at least the big ones. But we've led pretty separate lives. He's a very large presence—but then so were you. Wonder what that says about me?" She laughed.

Barton touched her arm. She didn't speak—seemed to be waiting for something from him.

"I don't know, Angela. I…I certainly was no bargain."

"Oh, Barton…" she sighed and then said in a voice so low

he could hardly hear, "I've only had one great love in my life." She began unwrapping her silverware. "But—"

"But what?"

"But I wasn't the one great love for him." She smiled at him serenely.

Barton stared at the table as the tuna burgers arrived. They smelled and looked like nursing home food. His mood darkened as his thoughts took him places he didn't want to go. She was always so perceptive, so on target. She knew very well there was another he had loved better. And her meathead husband knew it, too.

That evening in the room, Rip lay in bed, silent, staring at the ceiling. Barton sat in his wheelchair, hands folded in front of him, deep in thought. After a bit, the unnatural silence began to get to him.

"Are you okay, Ripperda?"

"Of course I'm okay. What's **your** problem?"

"You're not as loud as usual."

Rip raised his voice. "You want me to be loud?" Then louder, "**I'll be glad to be loud!**"

Barton yawned and stretched. "I've just come to expect a certain level of insult from you. I was missing it."

"Sorry. You usually inspire me, Lockjaw. I'm a little off my game."

"So am I." He brushed crumbs off the lap of his robe. "By the way, your pet names for me were amusing for awhile, but they're getting old. How about just calling me Locke? After all, we've lived together almost two weeks now without killing each other."

"Whatever. Two weeks? Really?" He took a remote and raised his bed to a sitting position. "You know what I've noticed about you in two weeks?"

Barton shook his head, not anxious for the answer. "No, what have you noticed?"

"You're a lonely old man. Who visits you besides an occasional floozy?"

"For your information, I haven't advertised my presence here. It's an embarrassment. And I'm not lonely. I make friends easily."

"No wife, no kids, no grandkids."

"You're more company than I need, Ripperda."

"You flirt with a nurse who humors you but doesn't even see you. You're an invisible man, Locke. So am I."

"What a curious delusion." On one leg, Barton pivoted from the wheelchair to his bed. With an effort, he got himself situated and pulled the covers around him.

Rip turned out his bed light. "Good night, Locke."

Barton turned out his light. In the semi-dark, he said, "Sweet dreams, Ripperda."

They lay in silence. Then low, out of the dark bed, "Hey, Locke. I gotta tell you something."

"What's that?"

"Carlton's doing a number on me. Big time."

Barton was stunned. "You're kidding. No—you're not kidding." Silence again. "What do you want me to do?"

He heard Rip take a deep breath. "I don't know…don't tell Angela…just watch him. Be careful."

In a low half-whisper Barton said, "I promise I will. That scumbag."

Barton sat in his wheelchair trying to ignore a family gathering around Rip's bed. Angela, Maggie, and Lucy watched the aging patriarch with concern. He seemed to be in and out of sleep.

"Dad," Maggie said. "Dave and the boys had to go back for a football game. But Lucy and I can stay through Monday."

Rip just nodded, saying nothing. His silence was disconcerting.

Barton found his crutches and pried himself out of the wheelchair. "I'll give you folks some privacy. I'll be in the Lounge."

Lucy brightened. "Mom, can I go, too?"

Maggie firmly shook her head. "You stay with us, Lucy. Mr. Locke didn't ask for company."

"Actually, I'd enjoy it," Barton said.

"No, Lucy."

Barton nodded and made his way out, listening as he did.

"I don't think it would hurt, Maggie," Angela said. "They've gotten quite friendly."

"Mom, he's your ex-husband!"

"He is?" Lucy sounded shocked.

"Oh, for heaven's sake, Maggie, did you need to do that?"

Defensively, Maggie snapped, "Why shouldn't she know?"

"Then he's sort of my grampa?"

Hearing that, Barton stopped walking.

"Heavens no," Maggie answered. "He's no relation. **None.**"

"Well, I like him. He made up a song for me."

"Let her go, for heavens sake," Rip growled. "He's not a child molester."

Chastened, Maggie said, "Honestly! Go ahead. Just go."

Lucy scampered from the room, catching up with Barton in the hallway.

"Skipping school on Monday, huh?"

"Yup," she said with a smile.

As usual, the Lounge was empty. He took a seat on a couch, and she plopped down beside him. She was in jeans today and pink blouse, her strawberry hair pulled back in a ponytail, her presence captivating.

"I have a favor to ask you," he said. "Would you show me how your cell phone works?"

She seemed pleased. She crossed her skinny legs, calling his attention to her pink canvas sandals with blue parrots on them. "Of course I will. But can I ask you something first? Were you really married to my Grandma?"

Taken aback, Barton hesitated. "Uhh, well. It was a long, long time ago."

Lucy smiled. "Wow. Did you love her?"

"Ohmigosh." Barton laughed. "Yes, Lucy, I loved her very much."

"Do you still love her?"

He stopped laughing and looked her in the eye. "You ask tough questions, young lady."

Innocently, she said, "That's not tough."

Barton thought about it. "Will this conversation be our secret?"

Lucy nodded. "I'm extremely trustworthy. My brothers aren't, but I am."

He took a deep breath and exhaled. "Okay. The answer is, yes, I still love her. She's wonderful."

Lucy's look bordered on the indignant. "Then why did you break up?"

Barton shrugged, looking away from her. "Because I was a fool."

"Oh. It was your fault?"

"Yes, it was."

She sighed. "Well, at least you admit it."

"For me, that's a big step."

This seemed to satisfy her. "Okay, now I'll show you my cell phone. What do you want to know?" She struggled to pull the phone from a jeans pocket and moved closer to him.

"You said it could do things like take videos and record sound. How does that work?"

She carefully showed him and had him try it. Before they were done, he asked another even bigger favor of her. She hesitated until he explained it was all intended to help her grandfather.

Late that afternoon Barton saw Nurse Betsy passing by as he did a circuit of the halls. She looked elated. "Hello, Betsy," he said. "Why so happy?"

Her face flushed a bit. "Well…I'm going out with Carlton tonight. He asked me."

Barton's spirits tumbled. "You're joking. Umm, I'm not trying to sound fatherly, but I'd advise against it. There are things about Carlton that…that aren't very likeable."

Betsy became mildly defensive. "I'm not sure what you're talking about. He seems a kind and caring person to me. I know sometimes he gets abrupt with patients, but he has to."

Barton instantly backed off. "Forgive me, my dear. It's none of my business. I guess I'm a little jealous. I'd like to be the one going out with you."

She smiled, softening. "Oh, Mr. Locke. I wish I'd known you when you were my age."

Barton sighed deeply, agreeing.

On Sunday morning, Barton watched Rip's family clean him up for a church service in the Golden Sunset chapel. He wore a white dress shirt and dark slacks, sat limply in his wheelchair, shaved and grimly presentable. Angela, wiping shaving cream from his ear, asked Barton to go with them, but he declined.

"You won't be missing a damned thing," Rip said. "It's

not Catholic. They told me it's all faiths. That ought to be interesting. The preacher's a woman. Catholics don't make those Protestant kind of mistakes."

Barton rolled his eyes. "Ripperda, have you been living in a cave?"

"Paul said women ought to be silent in church."

"That's ridiculous, grampa," Lucy said.

"Pay no attention," Angela said. "He's just pushing our buttons."

"He's outnumbered," Maggie said impatiently, leaning into the handles of his wheelchair. "Let's go."

Nurse Betsy had Sunday off, so Barton had no chance to ask how things had gone with the beast. He was worried. He spent much of the day on a bench in the courtyard with the Sunday *New York Times*. The fragrance of autumn clematis, heavy with snowy blooms, stirred memories of women he'd known. As if beckoned by his thoughts, Angela appeared. The sky was turning violet. Still in her church clothes, she sat down beside him on the bench. She told him she was concerned about Rip. Something was bothering him, she said, but she didn't know what. Barton was tempted to tell her, but he kept his word to Rip.

This nursing home experience, he knew all too well, would end for him on Tuesday: he was being sent home. He looked at Angela and wanted more. How could he not see Lucy again? He would actually miss the meathead. Barton closed his eyes, drifting with these thoughts, and without meaning to, fell asleep. When he awoke, Angela was gone. Good God, he thought, was he really getting so old he'd fall asleep with a woman beside him?

In the half-light of Monday dawn, Barton heard a faint sound and opened his eyes. Carlton was in the room prowling like a rat. Barton raised his head a bit, quickly lowered it. He slipped his hand under the pillow, touching Lucy's cell phone. Rip moaned in his sleep. At one point he cried out, "Fall on the ball! Jesus!" Carlton glided silently to his bedside and shook him.

"Hey, Coach. Wake up, man, you're having a bad dream."

Rip slowly came to, lifted his head, and stared at Carlton.

"Yeah…a bad dream. And I'm still looking at it."

Low and nasty, Carlton whispered, "You keep messing with me, old man, and I'm gonna be your worst nightmare."

"Come closer. I can't hear you."

Carlton bent close to Rip's face, hissing, "I said don't mess with me any more, Coach. You'll be sorry you ever saw my face." He grinned. "You'll wish you were dead. Hear me now?"

Ripperda's left hand struck like a snake and locked tight to Carlton's throat. Barton sat bolt upright in shock. Carlton seemed for several moments to be paralyzed by the power in Rip's hand. His face reddened and strangled sounds leaked from his throat.

Then began a slow turnabout. Both of Carlton's hands clamped on Rip's wrist and slowly, with a massive effort, pressed it down.

"Good Lord…Rip!" Barton cried out.

Rip's strength slowly diminished as his hand came loose from the throat and Carlton forced it downward toward the bed. Suddenly, all strength left him; the arm died and a deep moan wrenched from his lungs. Carlton, flushed and furious now, crushed the arm and pressed his face nearly into Rip's.

Barton rose from bed, the cell phone in his hand. He grabbed the cane leaning beside his bed and made his way toward Carlton.

"Nice try, Coach," Carlton said, breathing heavily. "But now you're gonna pay."

Barton came near the two. "Let go, Carlton!" He slipped the cell phone into a pajama pocket. "Damn you, let him go!"

When Carlton refused to respond, Barton raised the cane and brought it down hard across his back. Carlton suddenly released Rip, stood upright, and turned to Barton, who held the cane high; he was breathless but ready to strike again.

With a calm, murderous smile, Carlton said, "You look scared, Mr. Locke."

"You're the one who should be. Ripperda almost took you down. And I just witnessed what you did to deserve it."

With icy calm, Carlton said, "You just saw a confused old man attack me. You saw me defending myself." He moved close to Barton, got right in his face. "If you say otherwise, I'll hurt you. That is a guarantee. The other leg won't be hard to break." He wrenched Barton's cane away and snapped it in half. "Just like that."

"Impressive. I'm sure that's just how it would be."

Carlton nodded, stared menacingly at him, then turned and went out.

Barton rushed to Rip, who lay unmoving on his rumpled bed. "Ripperda. For God's sake, are you all right?" When there was no response, Barton pressed an ear to his chest. "No way this is going to happen. No way." He began doing rapid chest compressions. He took a deep breath to steel his resolve, then lowered his mouth toward Rip's.

"Try it, Locke, and I'll tear your lips off." The voice was like air leaking from a tire.

Barton jerked back as if a ghost had spoken. That moment, a CMA and several nurses came rushing in, led by Carlton. Barton backed away as they circled and began to work on Rip, who appeared to have lost consciousness again.

"It might have been a seizure," Carlton said. "He grabbed me by the neck and held on. Then he went completely limp."

An older nurse, taking charge, said, "We need an ambulance right now. You make the call, Carlton. I'll phone emergency downtown and let them know he's coming."

Carlton, all business, hustled out. Barton, stunned and helpless, watched him go.

Interminable hours later, Barton sat on the edge of his bed, dressed now, staring at Rip's neatly made bed. He took Lucy's cell phone out of his pocket, looked at it, and then put it back. He reached for his call button and pressed it several times.

Nurse Martha appeared at the door. "Hello, Mr. Locke. Remember me?"

"Where's Nurse Betsy?"

"She was just filling in. Do you need something?"

Worried now, Barton said, "I have to see her. I have something important to give her."

"There's no reason you can't do it. She's just in the next wing."

"Thank goodness. Which way do I go?"

"You don't want to walk it, Mr. Locke—it's quite a hike.

I'll call someone to wheel you down. Wait, I see Carlton right there…"

"No, it's okay. I can do it myself."

She leaned out the door and signaled. Carlton stepped inside. "Take Mr. Locke down to Nurse Betsy's station, would you, Carlton? He has something to give her."

Carlton smiled benignly. There were bruises on his throat. "Be glad to. Climb aboard, Mr. Locke."

Barton reluctantly got into his wheelchair, and Carlton rolled him into the hall and slowly toward the other wing, navigating through people inching along with their walkers.

"What have you got for Nurse Betsy?" His voice was bland, emotionless.

"Something to show my appreciation. I leave tomorrow."

"Yeah? What is it?"

Thinking fast, he pointed to a book in the arm bag on his chair. "It's a book I think she'll like."

"What's the title?"

Barton hesitated. *"Crime and Punishment."*

"Sounds heavy."

"Great book. Dostoevsky."

Carlton snorted. I'm not sure she has the brains for it."

"Oh, she'll manage just fine. I have faith in Nurse Betsy."

To Barton's relief, Betsy was working at the station. As they approached her, Carlton said, "Mr. Locke has something for you, Betsy…"

She gave Carlton a cold look, but smiled at Barton. "Hello, Mr. Locke. I was worried I wouldn't get a chance to see you again."

"That's why I came."

"He has a present for you," Carlton said.

"You don't have to stay, Carlton. I'll get myself back."

"That's my job. Mr. Locke."

In a chilly voice, she said, "It's okay, Carlton, I'll take him back."

Carlton shrugged, looked her up and down, and left.

Betsy shook her head. "You were right about him. What was I even thinking?"

"I've made my own mistakes, my dear." He folded his hands in his lap. "I had this sinking feeling I'd missed you."

She smiled, and her warmth returned.

"Have you heard anything about Ripperda?" he asked.

"Nothing yet. I've been praying for him."

Barton took a deep breath and touched her hand. "There's something I want you to do before I go home. It's important." He took the cell phone from his pocket. "Watch the video on this, and then show it to no one but your head nurse. Toward the end you'll see a shot of the inside of my pocket, but there'll be sound. Listen to it carefully."

Hesitantly, she said, "All right."

"I need the phone back. It belongs to Ripperda's granddaughter. She loaned it to me."

"I can load the video on my computer and give the phone back right now."

"You're an angel, Betsy." He squeezed her hand. "Here's a going away present." He handed her the book.

"*Crime and Punishment*?" She looked puzzled. "Well…I'll try to think of you whenever I read it."

He laughed. "I'll miss you," he said sincerely.

She attached a USB cord from the phone to her computer. "Will you come back and see us?"

Barton's voice was firm. "Not if I can help it."

Early that evening, back in the room, Barton sat on the bed where his suitcase lay open. He gripped Lucy's cell phone. "Video…delete…" he muttered, touching the phone with a fingertip. "There, finally." He slid the phone into a pocket and resumed packing his few things.

Maggie Michaels wandered in looking blank and weary.

"Hello, Maggie."

She nodded. "Sorry to bother you. I'll just be a few minutes."

Her presence made him uneasy. "How is your father?"

Trying to steady her voice, she said, "He died about eleven this morning. I'm here to get his things."

Barton sat in shock. "Good God." He held his head with both hands. "That's impossible."

"No, it isn't." Tears filled her eyes. "No one seems to understand what happened to him. I'd certainly like to know."

He wondered what to tell her…some edited version.

So he said, "It was right at dawn. I woke up to a room full of staff people all yelling directions. The place was crazy."

"It was probably another stroke."

Barton stood up but felt unsteady. "I can't believe he's dead. Jesus, I thought he was impervious. The man was strong as a bull." He put a hand to the back of his neck. "We got to be friends." He saw her incredulous look. "—I mean, in an odd sort of way."

"It must've been odd," she said without expression.

He sat down again. "How's your mother? How's Lucy?"

"My mom is not doing so well. She went home to rest. Lucy seems to be handling things for now."

"Any…you know, dates or plans yet?"

"No." She hesitated. "I'm not sure it would be appropriate for you to be there anyway, Mr. Locke."

Barton nodded in spite of the pain this caused. "I have something for you." He took Lucy's phone from his pocket. "It's Lucy's. She was showing me how it worked and then… sort of left it with me."

"I'm surprised. She's never without it." She took it. "If you'll excuse me, I have to get his stuff and get back to mom." She went to the closet and pulled out Rip's suitcase.

"I'll give you some space," he said.

"That would be nice."

Barton lifted his crutches and left the room.

The following noon, the day of his leaving, he received a visit from Mrs. Madison, head of nursing care, not long before the Golden Sunset van was to take him home. A dark brown, copper-haired woman with a no-nonsense demeanor entered his room, closed the door, and took a seat in the visitor's chair. She cleared her throat and introduced herself.

"Before you leave Golden Sunset, Mr. Locke," she said, "I want to thank you personally for bringing the Carlton Miller business to our attention. He honestly seemed to be a good employee, but sometimes it's hard to tell what's under the surface."

"Isn't it, though?"

"I thought you'd want to know he is no longer in our employ. There don't appear to be grounds for criminal charges, since Mr. Ripperda clearly assaulted him, but the verbal abuse you and Mr. Ripperda suffered was very evident. We haven't shared your findings with the family, by the way, but we will if you feel we should."

"No, they don't need that pain."

"Good. I agree. We're deeply sorry. And if there is anything we can do to rectify things…"

"I'm not going to sue you, if that's your concern. A place that would hire Nurse Betsy has to be more good than bad. She has a wonderful heart."

Mrs. Madison seemed greatly relieved. "Thank you, Mr. Locke. You may want to know that we have done one thing for you. Carlton Miller has been warned that if he is a threat to you in any way, we'll pursue charges against him."

"Thanks."

Mrs. Madison nodded with dignified authority and went out. It was only a moment before Nurse Martha stuck her head in.

"All packed, Mr. Locke? The van driver is here."

The driver was older than Barton—a volunteer who yammered about his grandchildren all the way to the condominium complex. Barton managed the conversation in monosyllables. It didn't seem to matter. The man carried Barton's crutches and suitcase to the door. The Golden Sunset had provided him a metal cane.

After being uninhabited for more than three weeks, his home was airless and stale. Mail was heaped inside the front door, most of it junk. He opened some blinds and took solace in the black gleam of his grand piano. He'd inadvertently left his cell phone on the charger, so he unplugged it and checked. It still worked. There were four texts from Rosalinde that he'd get to when he had the stamina. There was a request to play a wedding, a query from a student about her lessons starting up again, a message from Walgreen's about a prescription, assorted spam gibberish. All were indicators of a thin and brittle life—like the skin on the back of his hands.

He looked through his cupboards, phoned a local store and ordered groceries. The place was expensive but they delivered. He checked the liquor cabinet, relieved to find a full bottle of brandy. Though he could probably drive now, he felt like holing up, going nowhere. He sat down at the piano and began to play, relieved to hear such a bright sound. Yet what he played was solemn and plaintive, a song he'd written years before about the shadow show of memory, of love lost.

Barton stopped playing, struggling with emotions. He went back to the liquor cabinet and poured a brandy even though it was too early in the day.

Wednesday came and went, dragging its way. He ordered Thai food from a take out/delivery restaurant, but ate only a quarter of it. He packed the white cartons into the refrigerator for another day. He read newspapers and poured several brandies. Thursday morning he finally took a shower with his cast wrapped in a plastic bag. He shaved his gaunt, haggard-looking face. He knew he needed a shower seat, but that would mean going out to buy it. The thought of a medical appliance in his tub depressed him deeply.

When he heard his phone's ringtone for the first time on Thursday evening, he felt no motivation to read the text. Yet passing across the room for another brandy, and despite his lassitude, he lifted the phone. A message came up that said simply, "Grampa's funeral is Friday 4 pm at St. Patricks. Grandma and me would like you to come if you can. Love, Lucy."

Barton sat down, stared at this small piece of grace, and wept like a blubbering fool.

LIMBO

"It's final. We're all leaving late afternoon tomorrow," Benny said to her. His two teammates had gone out on the back porch to drink a beer. "You'll have the house to yourself. What a relief, huh?" He was grinning, only half meaning it.

Fay kept doing dishes, clearing them from the worn linoleum countertop. "It could have been worse." Her voice was low, impassive. "Jake at least helps once in a while."

"Come out with us when you're done."

"I don't talk baseball."

"Come on, Fay, it's our last night."

She sighed and nodded.

The house, part of an old Polish neighborhood, now belonged half to Benny and half to her. Their father, the West High football coach, had lingered five years after his stroke, and she had been his caregiver. With Benny still in high school and their mother long dead, Fay could see few options. She'd found a part time job scheduling medical appointments from home, so she was with him most of the time. He'd been a robust, athletic man, and the paralysis made him sullen and angry. She loved him—they'd been close when she was younger—but he was not an easy patient.

His pension from the state had kept them solvent but had ended when he'd died in February. His care had eaten up most of his savings. The house, at least, was paid for. She had turned 30 in May, and in many ways her life seemed over.

Her brother Benny was 22 now, a promising infielder with a double A affiliate of the Oakland Athletics. He was a big, personable boy (forever a boy), drafted after his second college season with a modest bonus. In a piece of luck that seemed to be sticking with him, he'd been promoted to double A after a year, and by good fortune the team headquartered in their city. So he played and lived at home. And he'd talked her into taking in two of his teammates who needed a place to live. They each paid her $350 a month out of their meager salaries, and she bought and cooked meals, kept the house cleaned, and endured endless hours of baseball prattle.

The minor league season had ended, and though Benny's plan had been to deliver beer and live at home, the Athletics had tagged him for Arizona fall ball, reserved for top prospects. His luck was holding. She would be alone in the house for the first time. The thought of it troubled her.

The three of them sat sprawled on the back porch in plastic chairs, their cans of Coors on the railing. Benny had his feet up on a post, looking pleased with himself. Both Rocco, a squat, muscular Italian kid from Cleveland, and Jake, the minor league veteran (something no one wanted to be) from Milwaukee, looked less carefree than Benny. Jake stood when she appeared, and pulled a chair over to the rail for her. They said hi to her, but she sat down without responding.

"Anyways," Rocco said. "I think I had a solid season except I still can't hit breaking shit, and every pitcher knows it."

Jake smiled. "So that's what you do this winter."

Benny took a swallow of beer, growing effusive "Man, you both were solid. Jake, another season above .280. And, what?—second in RBIs?"

"Yeah, second. You were first—too modest to mention it. Trouble is, I'm 28, and you're 16."

Benny laughed. "22, dumbass."

"I was talking maturity. Anyway, you're the golden boy. You're headed for fall ball. I bet you show up on the A's spring training roster."

"Jeez, how cool would that be?"

"Hell, I'm only 20," Rocco said.

"You're in the chute, Rock. How many catchers have a damn bazooka for an arm? How many can call a game like he's Buster Posey?" Benny was full of good cheer.

"And get in a hitter's head talking Italian," Jake added.

Rocco grinned, showing lots of teeth. "Yeah, it's true, but I still can't hit a goddam breaking ball."

There was a small cooler of beer on the floor, and Rocco and Benny popped two more.

"Would you like a beer, Fay?" Jake asked.

"No thanks." She glanced at him, and then turned away. He was a big man with powerful shoulders, yet he was gentle, more aware in ways than the other two. His skin was a soft caramel color that she sometimes found herself staring at.

"Fascinating conversation, huh?" Jake said to her.

"I'm used to it."

He leaned back in the chair, looking deep in thought. "You've been great to put up with us all season. We take some work. You're a patient woman."

She looked at him, surprised. "I am? I haven't felt…quite myself this summer."

"You've been like a mother," Rocco said to her seriously.

"Not quite how I'd put it," Jake said. He turned his chair a little to face her. "What are your plans once we're gone?"

The question unsettled her. "Plans? Oh, well…"

She said no more, and he laughed in a self-effacing way. "You sound like me."

"How do you mean?"

"Life in limbo."

She nodded. "Oh…I see."

She went inside shortly after that, but they stayed up drinking beer until well after she was in bed. She read for a long time, heard them each making noise in the bathroom and then falling into bed. Like boys, they were asleep within minutes. One of them, Rocco she thought, snored softly. She may have fallen off for an hour or two somewhere near morning, but she couldn't remember. The weight of a formless anxiety, a dark paralysis of will gripped her and worked to destroy sleep. Her job, she knew, wasn't enough to live on. It was necessary to find another to survive—but doing what? The house was falling down around her. Where was she to start? The past five years had been like a long hibernation during which her few relationships had grown distant. Except for Benny's occasional comings and goings, she was alone.

All three players slept in until nearly eleven; she summoned the strength to fry up a platter of bacon and eggs, something substantial to send them off, and then they spent the early afternoon stuffing clothes and equipment into suitcases. Jake had an old, once-luxurious Grand Prix, the only one of the three with a car. He had driven them all summer so

Fay's car (her father's Chevy) could be available to her.

Benny and Rocco had booked flights close to the same time, so Jake would drive them to the airport and then head off on the long trek home to Milwaukee. Benny suggested Jake bunk at the house for one more night so he could start fresh in the morning. Fay stayed quiet, not objecting, but Jake seemed hesitant, doubting the need unless there were flight delays. He watched her carefully as he spoke.

****

Benny's plane west got off on time, but Rocco's flight east was twice delayed, the first time for an hour and then for two more as another plane was rolled out and made ready. Rocco paced about, a nervous wreck—still such a kid that Jake hung with him until he knew he was safely on his way to Cleveland. By then it was ten and rain was falling steadily. The thought of the long drive made him wearier than he already was.

He rang Fay's number on his cell phone but got no answer. She was likely asleep. He knew something was pulling him back that had nothing to do with a night's sleep, and he feared its power over him. He knew it would snarl up his life. He knew he had carefully avoided it all the months he'd lived in her house. Still he could not resist it, and he drove through the dark, wet streets toward her.

He parked in the street in front and saw the kitchen lights. She was apparently still awake. The front porch light was on. He knocked at the door several times, but she didn't appear. He found the key at the top of a window frame and let himself in.

"Fay," he called quietly. "It's Jake. Are you here?" He went into the kitchen. On the table he saw a water glass and an empty pint bottle of Southern Comfort. Because he knew she rarely drank, he felt a moment of panic that someone else was here with her, but he listened and heard nothing. Full of misgivings, he walked the dark hallway and swiftly ascended the stairs. Her bedroom door was open. "Fay?" in a half whisper. He looked in and saw that the bed was undisturbed.

On the back porch empty Coors cans still stood on the

rail. The rain had finally stopped. He turned on the yard light and thought he heard a car engine running. The single stall garage at the back of the yard was a quarter open. The one-piece manual garage door had long been a problem, swinging back down if not pushed all the way to the top.

"Fay!" he yelled and vaulted over the porch rail to the grass. He heaved up the garage door, and exhaust fumes rolled out. Not until he tore open the driver's door could he see her. She lay sideways on the seat, apparently unconscious. He leaned in, coughing, trying not to breathe, and turned off the engine. He took hold of one of her wrists, yanked her upright, and dragged her into his arms. When she suddenly mumbled something, his heart began beating again. She was a tall, big-boned girl, and a dead weight. He backed out of the garage, dragging her. Her legs began to work a little.

"Whatizzit? Whattaya dune?" she slurred.

"For God's sake, Fay! We're going to a hospital."

"I jus need more SoCo. Jus goin' for more SoCo. Take me inna house. S'okay now. Needa bathroom…"

Jake stopped and looked in her face. She was drunk, ghostly pale. He had no idea how much of it was monoxide poisoning. Her face fell onto his chest as he struggled toward his car, his arms clamped around her. Finally, he got an arm under her knees and lifted her, lurching across the wet grass. Just as he reached his car, she moaned and vomited down the front of him and herself. The rank, sour, curdled mess brought him close to doing the same.

"Oh, Jesus…" he muttered. He held her slightly away from him and shook the worst of it to the ground.

"Jussa bathroom," she pleaded.

"Yeah, okay."

So he hauled her up the front steps and into the house. The full bathroom, thankfully, was off a small first floor bedroom, now her home office. He got her in front of the toilet, lifted the seat, and settled her limply against it. As he pulled off his shirt and began rinsing it in the bathtub, she threw up again, mostly dry heaves now, and then she lay down on floor.

"Get you out of these things," he said, pulling her sweater up over her head and tossing it in the tub. Vomit had plastered her hair to her cheek, and her jeans were a mess. She curled up on the floor, but he managed to drag her jeans off her an inch at a time. Her legs were well shaped, thick as his own. Her breasts were small under the lacy bra, her hips narrow and boyish in white cotton underpants. She kept nodding off, yet he didn't dare let her sleep. He quickly rinsed out her clothes and then somehow got her into the tub. She'd have to sit for a shower since standing wasn't an option.

"What're you doing to me?" her voice now more coherent.

"Cleaning you up. You're a disaster." He ran the water to the right temperature, and then pulled the shower lever. She screamed in shock as it cascaded over her. He knelt beside the tub, squeezed shampoo on her head, and began lathering. When he saw he was flooding the floor, he yanked off his jeans, got in the tub with her in just his boxers and pulled the shower curtain shut. He scrubbed her dark hair and her body except the private places, and then did quick work of himself. He knelt in front of her, letting the warm water pour over them until the soap was gone from her hair and the mess cleared from the tub.

Though she jerked down the shower curtain getting out, she'd begun to recover some awareness. She stood unsteadily as he dried her off, taking time on her hair, a jumble of loose curls, and then dried himself as best he could with the same towel.

"How can you stand me?" she asked in a low voice.

"Rocco's plane was late. I came back to stay the night."

"I'm a disaster. How can you stand me?"

"Don't say that. I didn't mean it. I'll get you a nightgown." He rushed up the stairs and found a blue cotton nightgown in the first drawer he opened. When he returned moments later, she was asleep on the bathroom floor, pale as ivory, breathing evenly. He undid her wet bra and pulled off her panties, glancing once at the silken nest between her legs. He quickly dried these intimate places, moved her to a sitting position to pull the nightgown on, and then half-carried her up the stairs and into bed.

What were the protocols for monoxide poisoning? He didn't know. He'd have to stay with her. A worn lounge chair stood near the bed. There, he'd spend the night. In Benny's bedroom he found an old bathing suit and a West High football tee shirt. These would have to do. He found a blanket in her closet and wrapped himself up in the chair, his senses alive to her powerful, vulnerable presence.

Some time later, he heard her say, "Where are you?"

"I'm here, Fay."

She rose on an elbow and saw him in the dark. "Come here with me. It's so dark. I feel lost."

"In bed with you?"

"Yes."

He stood and slipped into bed beside her, instantly feeling the soft warmth of her hip against his. She turned on her side, away from him, yet took his hand and pulled his arm around her, fitting him into the curves of her body. In just that way they slept—and awoke to daylight, hours later, in the same position.

"I need water," she whispered. "My mouth is horrid." She rose from bed more briskly than he expected. He heard water running, heard her brushing and brushing her teeth, and then, still very pale, she was back in bed beside him, looking away. "You saw my weird body," she said.

"It's beautiful."

"Did you save my life?"

Still facing the back of her head, he said, "I guess I did."

She lay silent for a while. "I'm sorry. I don't know why it happened. I think it was an accident. I hope it was. I know I wouldn't screw up Benny's life just because mine is hopeless."

"Yours isn't hopeless."

"I couldn't stop crying. I drank my father's crappy Southern Comfort till it was gone. I was going out for more, but then everything went haywire."

"Fay, listen. I'm here, and maybe it's for a reason. All summer I've thought about it."

"Don't think about it. I'm a disaster."

"No. Stop saying it."

She rolled over to face him, eyes passionate, pleading, fearful. "Your skin, Jake…your skin is so beautiful."

Her voice was hypnotic; her eyes possessed him. He sensed the fraying, fading baseball dream drifting away behind him, his life now in the hands of a woman he desperately loved and hardly knew.

BACK TO EARTH

Hannah sometimes felt that her parents and their close friends, who were all in their mid to late 30s, were more children to be watched after than their children were. Three couples, the O'Conners, the Posts, and her parents, the Jordans, had gotten to know each other well at the Presbyterian mega-church they all attended. Their behavior, when they gathered socially these days (nearly every week, it seemed) was not very churchy but more like a second go-round of college life. They tailgated at Big Ten football games. They drank wine like soda pop (the quantity of empty bottles in the Jordan's recycling bin was sometimes embarrassing to her; it was her job to roll the bin to the curb). They danced like dervishes to rock music that predated them by decades. And all three families spent numerous summer weekends together at the Post's old, rambling Victorian cottage on Lake Michigan—body surfing, sailing the catamaran, tearing about on jet skis, playing ferocious games of beach volleyball, climbing dunes, and sunning luxuriously. The children played a part, but the time was clearly adult-focused. They were having most of the fun, and something seemed wrong about that.

The O'Conners, Grace and Dick, were childless except for a 10-year-old daughter from Dick's first marriage; she lived with her mother in Colorado and showed up only two or three times a year. Bill and Lexi Post had two boys, Ezra who was 16, a year older than Hannah, and Barry, his irritating 10-year-old brother. Hannah had twin sisters, Lucy and Lilly, who were 8 and still fairly charming. When the families were together, Ezra and Hannah, because of their seniority, were assigned babysitting duties much more than they cared to be. The single consolation for Hannah was that she felt a strong, secret attraction to Ezra, a brainy eccentric who was popular at school for his shaggy good looks, his unpredictability, and his abilities in science and math. Through the summer at the cottage, he had launched a half dozen model rockets he'd built himself. They'd disappeared high into the summer sky and then come floating on parachutes back to earth. Occasionally, he lost one in the lake. Hannah had offered to swim out for them, but he'd waved her off, not at all concerned. She was looking for ways to please him. That summer he had taught her to play chess, but she was so unseasoned they usually settled for Cribbage.

The Posts were the wealthiest by far (Bill was a partner in a law firm) and his wife Lexi the sexiest, with the body and looks of a model. She did freelance interior decorating as a way of keeping occupied. The O'Conners, she guessed, were the brainiest, though they often didn't act it. They taught at the same college: Grace some foreign language and Dick comparative religions or something. Hannah, though, felt her parents were by far the coolest and most creative. Her father, Thorn, was an artist who marketed his own works, both originals and prints, and sold them in other clever and lucrative forms, like note cards, calendars, and coffee mugs. Her mother Maggie was a master gardener who wrote gardening books.

Hannah, herself, planned to be a mystery writer or a heart surgeon. She was very good at English, but hopeless at math. She struggled so with algebra that when school started, her parents hired Ezra to tutor her in the subject. For once, a shortcoming had paid off. And he actually was helping her.

It was a balmy Friday in late September, the last gathering at the cottage for the year. The plan was to watch the Michigan State-Notre Dame game at noon on the huge, flat-screen TV, enjoy the rest of Saturday on the beach, then move boats, jet skis, and a load of other equipment up into the boathouse. They'd pick up the church service by live stream on Sunday, have a final burger cookout, and then head for home. There was one hitch in the plan: the O'Conners had tickets to the game and would be leaving for South Bend early Saturday morning, missing the final gathering and, of course, all the work. Hannah had noticed this self-centeredness about them at times in the past, probably the result of not having to factor in children. Children certainly helped the other adults stay grounded, or so it seemed to her.

Since they were late arriving at the cottage from work

and school, Bill called ahead for pizzas for dinner, and Dick O'Conner and he drove into town to get them. Ezra disappeared upstairs to his room at the top of the cottage, third floor. The twins began a game of Sorry, which Barry sulkily joined only because there was no WiFi at the cottage. Grace O'Conner decided on a quick walk on the beach to stretch her legs, and Hannah's mother went along. Her father and Lexi Post stayed to toss together a salad before the pizza arrived, so Hannah began to feel a bit grumpy and left out. Then she remembered there'd be a bonfire later, so she slipped past the salad makers and out the kitchen door at the back and into the nearby woods to gather kindling.

She quickly found enough for two fires and dumped the sticks beside the stone fire pit. The late-September sun was dropping low already, and the back of the cottage was deep in shadows. As Hannah put a foot onto the first step of the kitchen porch, she saw her father with a glass of red wine in his hand and Mrs. Post, her back to him, cutting lettuce on a board. Her father was a big man, barrel-chested with long, dark hair pulled back and tied, and the rugged face of a boxer. Women always seemed drawn to him. He set down the wine glass, moved against the back of her, leaned over and kissed the tanned curve of her neck. His hands went around her and cupped her breasts. Hannah heard her say, "Oh, God," in a breathless whisper, saw her push his hands away, yet then she turned and kissed him heatedly on the lips. The next instant they were innocently making salad again.

Hannah took a step backwards off the porch and slipped into the shadows. A steel band tightened around her chest as she considered the sudden precariousness of all she took for granted, all that made her life stable and secure. Her mother, whom she admired more than any other woman, was being tossed over for a shallow, sexy interior decorator. Her father, whom she loved dearly, had turned into a scoundrel. It was the worst discovery of her life. She went back to the fire pit and sat down in a low, uncomfortable Adirondack chair. She hated Adirondack chairs, but all the people they knew owned them. She hated the casual recklessness of adults, especially when she considered the probable consequences of this treachery. It made her sick to her stomach, and when the pizza arrived, she couldn't eat a bite. She sat silent in a dark and murderous mood, but they all seemed too preoccupied to take any notice.

There was always a period before being excused from the table that the children sat enduring their parents' passionate thoughts on some complicated subject, this time the church, inevitably involving their aging and mildly conservative senior pastor who needed to retire. Hannah actually liked the man for being willing to listen, year after year, to a large congregation of nattering adults with strong and conflicting opinions.

"He'll never officiate at a same sex marriage," Bill Post said. "The church will simply not commit on the issue until he's gone."

"I'm not so sure he's wrong," Dick O'Conner said. Hannah had noticed an annoying kind of loftiness in Dick, the religion scholar. "I believe in inclusion. But marriage— that's quite a different matter."

"I agree," his wife said. "*Quite* a different matter."

Her father pounced on that. Her parents and the Posts were relentlessly liberal. "What if one of our kids was gay?" he nearly shouted. He looked at the kids at the table, including Hannah. "Are any of you kids gay?"

The question was meant to be outrageous, and the adults laughed, joined uncertainly by the younger kids, but Hannah didn't. She was finding her father intolerable. Ezra didn't exactly laugh, but he smiled.

Her father went on. "Strangers are free to rent our church and our pastors for hetero weddings. But if gay kids of ours— if we had them—wanted to marry a partner, they'd be denied a church wedding in the very place they'd been raised and nurtured from infancy."

"It's wrong, absolutely," her mother said.

Hannah wasn't much concerned about her sexuality. She sometimes wondered about Ezra, though, who'd never shown much interest in girls. Still, whenever she saw his tight, wiry body in a bathing suit, and his glossy, flying long hair, she wondered less. She had girlfriends who thought (fashionably) they might be bisexual, though the notion struck her as their way of appearing complicated and chic.

No, she had few serious doubts about her own orientation, but had lots of doubts about her body, which had recently begun to get lumpier in spite of her efforts to stay trim. She wore bathing suits that covered as much as possible. Thankfully, part of the lumpiness was breasts that had gone through a sudden growth spurt—which she found both a relief and an embarrassment. Her bras didn't fit well now so she sometimes went without. She wished her mother paid more attention to such things, especially with two more daughters yet to navigate adolescence.

Dick O'Conner would never gracefully yield a point, so he hammered on. "I don't know of any world religions that have ever condoned same sex marriage. But some have been more welcoming to varied sexual orientations than others. Some medieval Hindu temples clearly depict male homosexuality and lesbianism in carvings, suggesting a society and religion more tolerant than now. But marriage was a different matter."

"Honestly, Dick," her mother said, "where do you get such arcane crap? Do you make it up?"

The adults, even Dick, chuckled at this. And they thankfully dropped the subject.

But her father abruptly opened another that tightened the band about Hannah's chest. Her father wondered—and he seemed serious—if either of the two wives (not his own) would ever consider sitting for one of his paintings? The little kids took that as a cue to disappear from the table.

"In the nude?" Grace O'Conner asked with a sly grin.

"Your call," he said. "It's always the option I'd prefer."

"Well, Thorn, I find that rather tantalizing," she said. "What do you think, Dick?"

"Not crazy about the idea, even in the interests of art," he said.

"You are a Philistine," her father said, and they all chortled again, a very jovial bunch, but Hannah was not in a jovial mood. Somehow her father's question hadn't come round to Lexi Post, who suddenly stood and began clearing the table. Hannah suspected he'd already asked her. Her mother rose from her chair, cheerful and oblivious, blind as a bat, and began boxing up the remaining pizza.

Ezra and Hannah helped with the table as her sisters

and Barry set up another game of Sorry in the sunroom. Bill Post opened two more bottles of wine, and Lexi found some vintage Aerosmith on her tablet. The adults set to dancing, even while they were cleaning up. As wine began to flow, Ezra looked at her and rolled his eyes. "Did you bring your algebra?"

She nodded, greatly relieved.

"Good. Let's do some tutoring. We won't hear much noise in my room."

Hannah told her mother their plans. "It's the weekend, honey," she replied, yet she seemed pleased with their industriousness. "Go to it, then. But save time for a little fun."

The third floor was a climb, the final staircase steep and narrow. She'd never been up here before. His room was a reconfigured attic, a little musty, with slanted ceilings and two dormer windows looking away from the lake toward the woods. His single bed was loosely covered with a comforter. Rocket equipment cluttered a makeshift desk between the windows. The walls were bare knotty pine, a bit depressing. The cottage bedroom she shared with the twins was far more cheerful. Walls were blue with white canopy beds and several bright paintings, one a landscape done by her father.

"This is an odd little room. I mean, I like it, but doesn't it get hot?"

"Sometimes. I have a way of dealing with it, though. I just like being apart from the thundering herd."

"Parents, you mean."

"Yeah. Do you want the desk chair or the bed?"

She sat down on the bed and drew in a long, anxious breath. "Before we start algebra, I need to talk to you about something."

"Sounds serious," he said. "I hope it's not same sex marriage."

That made her smile a little. "No. But it is serious. I don't even like to think about it, let alone talk." She took in another long breath. "Anyway, I was out in the woods earlier getting kindling for a bonfire…and it was getting quite dark, see… and I happened to look into the kitchen where my father and your mother were making a salad…"

"Yeah?"

"Well, he kissed her on the back of the neck, and then she turned and kissed him." She couldn't bring herself to tell him the breast part.

"So? They're both big flirts. They're always doing stuff like that."

"I saw the kiss. It wasn't just flirting, Ezra. It was passionate, like in a movie."

Instead of sitting in his desk chair, he flopped down on the bed beside her. "Really?"

"It made me feel so lousy, I couldn't even eat. I don't know what to do."

"Jesus, I wish our parents would grow up."

"No kidding."

"Listen, how can we say anything about just a kiss?" he asked after a thoughtful silence. "It's not convincing. We need more evidence."

"Okay. Well then, let's get it. Let's watch every move they make." It occurred to her that the mystery novel she would write someday might just have its genesis in this family betrayal.

He stood and began to pace like Sherlock Holmes. "I have an idea. Come across the hall. I want to show you something."

She followed him out of the room and across the hall to a narrow plywood door on hinges. He opened it and moved into an attic stacked with boxes of children's toys and sports equipment. A thin, striped, camp-style mattress lay on the floor with a blanket draped across it and a lumpy pillow at its head. It rested directly in front of a large, octagonal gable window that looked out over the lake, the beach, and the dunes below.

"I sleep here whenever it's hot, and I love watching wild storms on the lake. The window opens out six inches at the bottom. The wind comes through and the lightning is spectacular. Look—you can see the whole beach and hidden spots in the dunes where people go to do…whatever. It's the best place in the house for the view, but my parents use it as an attic. So it's my secret spot. It's like the crow's nest in a ship where you watch for whales. Your dad walks early in the morning. I see him sometimes. If he goes out tomorrow, you sneak up here, and we'll see if my mom has the same idea."

Ezra's reasoned support took the edge off her anger that evening. Their parents gave up dancing early and started a bonfire before the little kids went to bed. Everyone sang, and the parents slowed down on wine and gave up on socializing by midnight, early for them.

At 7 a.m., she heard the door to her parents' bedroom open and close quietly as her father went out for his walk. Her mother, never a morning person, would sleep until 9:30 or 10—plenty of time for him to carry out his plans. She quickly pulled off her pajamas and got into shorts and a tee shirt. She stopped in the second floor bathroom briefly, then slipped up the narrow stairs in bare feet, trying not to make a sound. She went into Ezra's room without knocking. He was still asleep.

"Ezra," she whispered. "It's time."

He woke up instantly, shot out of bed in just his pajama bottoms. His long hair was a jumble, but he didn't seem to care. He led her across the hall, opened the plywood door, pushed her inside ahead of him, and pulled the door shut with only the faintest of squeaks. He knelt on the mattress, and she got down beside him.

They could see her father already on the beach out front, dallying there as if looking for Petoskey stones. He wore a bathing suit with an unbuttoned flannel shirt. His large, hairy chest looked obscene to her. Only moments later, Lexi Post appeared, also in a bathing suit with a short, pink beach cover over it. Her legs were tan and disturbingly gorgeous. They chatted a bit, things neither Hannah nor Ezra could hear. They set off up the beach together. The bluffs were only a moderate height in this area, but they cast shadows on the two.

"They're taking the path to the grotto," Ezra whispered.

"What's the grotto?"

"The hidden place where we keep our canoes."

"Will we be able to see?"

"Maybe. It depends on what they do."

It took only moments to find out. In the grotto, the two began groping at each other, kissing with ravenous mouths. Ezra groaned. "Jesus…"

She was about to say, "There, it's true," when the two dropped out of sight.

"Now I can't see them," he said. "Maybe…maybe it's not what we think."

"But probably it is."

"How will we know for sure?"

She looked into his troubled eyes. "I didn't tell you everything about last night, Ezra. When my father was kissing the back of your mother's neck, he was also…also touching her breasts."

He exhaled a deep, rattling sigh. "God, those idiots are risking everything. They make me sick."

She didn't know what to do or say, so she touched his arm. "Can you see anything now?"

"No, but I can certainly imagine…"

"Do you really think they're doing it?"

"Isn't that the point when you have an affair?"

"I just can't picture our parents doing it together." And she added as a guileless afterthought, "Have you ever done it?"

The question made him visibly uncomfortable. He didn't answer for a moment. "Well…you know, some here and there, but not all the way. I don't need to get a girl pregnant right now. What a disaster." He paused and glanced at her. "Have you?"

"No," she said.

"I wasn't sure. You're quite well developed for your age."

Hannah looked down at her breasts. "You think so?"

"Very well developed." Then, in a nervous voice, "May I see?"

She looked into his curious and innocent eyes. She was puzzled at what to do, and then hesitantly pulled up her tee shirt. At the cottage, she never wore a bra. He stared, his mouth slightly agape, and then he reached and touched her right breast gently. She found herself trembling inside, fearful of revealing her imperfect body, yet swooning with a pleasure she'd never felt in her life. He touched her other breast and then unbuttoned her shorts. As she stood and pulled them down for him, he switched on a reading lamp.

"I want to see you," he said, running his fingers along her hips, over her slight paunch and into her small triangle of pubic hair. His eyes pored over her; he studied her body with a scientific fascination. He pulled her to her knees and kissed her with his mouth open, her first kiss ever, and touched his tongue to hers, scorching her.

Alarmed suddenly, he groaned and switched off the light again. "What the hell am I doing? If they see the light, they can see us, too."

"We're just doing what they're doing."

"Yeah, but we aren't married to someone else. It's different. And I promise I won't go all the way like them."

She was glad. That thought frightened her, and these preliminaries were almost too much pleasure to bear. The front of his pajamas had grown distorted. She reached and pulled the drawstring. It was immediately clear that though they both had youthful, adolescent bodies, parts were already very grown up.

In this breathless exploration (she nearly sick with desire to know the whole of it), time passed dreamily by, neither knew how much, and all at once Ezra's mother came bursting through the attic door, winded and puffing like an engine. The two of them lay naked as babies, still rubbing this and that together, discovering how it felt. Hannah turned toward the sound, shocked at the intrusion and then frightened at the berserk look in Mrs. Post's eyes. They scuttled away from each other and covered up as best they could.

Mrs. Post tried hard to calm herself. "Good God in heaven," she said in a half whisper. "I don't believe this. You both are children!" She turned her eyes full on Hannah. "Young lady, what are you thinking of?"

Hannah, seeing something uncertain, something like fear in Mrs. Post's eyes, said, "Mrs. Post, what are *you* thinking of?"

"Yeah, mom," Ezra added with surprising calm. "You probably shouldn't preach to us right now."

Inexplicably, Lexi Post burst into tears—quiet, sorrowful tears. After some sniffling and Kleenex work, when she'd calmed herself a bit, she managed to say in a low, unsteady voice, "Get dressed and come down to breakfast. We won't mention this. Just stop doing it, please. There's lots and lots going on today. Things will be okay." She turned slowly, shut the door behind her, and left them there together.

The day went pretty much as planned. Notre Dame won the game, though Hannah wasn't interested and spent most of it playing Cribbage with Ezra. There seemed to be an unspoken bond between them now—she was sure he felt it, too. They were far older and wiser than they'd been when the weekend began, though she wasn't sure she preferred it to her younger, clueless self.

Before they began packing the Post's stuff away for the season, Hannah's father asked her if she'd take a stroll with him on the beach. She went, not wanting to. He talked lightly about the game, and she replied in monosyllables. When they were well out of range of the cottage, he put an arm around her shoulder. She wanted to squirm away but didn't.

"I hear you were kicking up your heels a little this morning," he said.

She heard her own voice, flat and unamused, say, "Yeah. You, too."

That made him uneasy. "Hmmmm. Are you going to be mean about it?"

"Yes."

"Well, you shouldn't worry. It was nothing. Nothing at all."

"Then why'd you do it?"

He hesitated. "Curiosity, I guess—same as you."

"It's not the same."

They walked a bit farther in silence. She had to keep telling herself this man was her father and not just some sleazy womanizer.

"We need to make a pact, honey," he said. "We need to forget this—as if none of it happened. For all our sakes."

Not looking at him, deeply unhappy and untrusting, she nodded.

He exhaled, relieved, rubbed her head, and turned back toward the cottage. Her father knew her too well. She didn't want marital breakups, didn't want the dreary shuffling about of parents and children, and certainly didn't want Ezra as a stepbrother. She'd never be able to look him in the eye.

That winter, her parents' tailgate party life began to wane. The following summer, the Posts moved to the east side of the state where the firm was opening a new office. They kept the cottage, of course, with promises of continued gatherings. But they all got together only once, in the early fall, and Ezra, who was involved in lighting for the high school play, stayed home.

Hannah now saw there were distinct passages in adult lives, just as there were in children's. For the present she was done with sex. It seemed to cause more trouble than it was worth.

And yet there were balmy fall days in math class when she found herself daydreaming of Ezra setting off his rockets on the beach, blasting them up into the blue and endless sky. She could imagine herself riding one of them into the upper atmosphere, into the clouds, and then slowing, turning, the parachute opening, bearing her gently back to earth.

A CHANGE IN THE HOUSE

Joey Kovacs' mother Rita was an emergency room nurse for St. Anthony's, the town's Catholic hospital. Before that she'd worked only now and then as a home care nurse, wanting quality time with her two little boys. When Joey was six and Stephen two, their father had died in some faraway land called Afghanistan, bringing much of that quality time to an end.

Rita Kovacs was a tall, good-looking woman (too good-looking for a mother, Joey thought), whose competence made him wonder where his lack of it came from. He was 14 now, young for a freshman. He dreamed of making his mark as a hard-hitting outfielder for the school baseball team. He could field and throw, thanks to the backyard help of his mother, a softball star in high school, but his lanky, stork-like build made him an easy target for pitchers, and when he did hit, he usually dribbled singles through the infield. He had other problems he didn't care to think about, like his physics grade, which had the potential to keep him off the team.

The main affliction of his life, however, was a more recent one. His grandfather, Jozsef Kodaly, for whom he was named, had moved in with them in October almost a year after his wife (Rita's mother) had died of cancer. He was a moody old man in his late 70s who now occupied Joey's room, forcing him to share a bedroom with his 10-year-old brother. Joey's mother had shamed Joey into the change, but he didn't pretend to be happy about it.

The old man rarely spoke to any of them, sounded a little like Count Dracula when he did. Joey wasn't sure what was ailing him, but he took a large assortment of pills that Rita kept organized. He left his stale pipes lying around the house, and at night he kept his false teeth in a cup at Joey's former bedside. Jozsef had been an important man, his mother said, a geologist who travelled the world for environmental companies. Now he spent much of every day reading newspapers and books, listening to classical music, burning holes in his sweaters with smoldering tobacco, and never watching television except for the playoffs and World Series.

The most aggravating part of the arrangement was that Joey could no longer steal looks into the bedroom of Betty Herman, the hottest junior at East Catholic. His little brother's room faced the opposite way, toward the piano store. Not that he'd ever seen much. Mostly she sat on the bed doing her homework or texting on her cell phone. Once he'd seen her walking around in shorty pajamas, but then she'd closed the blinds, which she always did when she changed clothes. Still, he had hopes—until the old man arrived.

"Why'd you get a paper route?" Stephen asked him one evening as they sat doing homework. They were trapped together because the old man was downstairs listening to the *Hungarian Rhapsody* on the stereo. His little brother irritated him in a hundred ways. He hogged the laptop for math games, got better grades than Joey, read more books, went to confession (Joey never did), had the makings of the athletic build Joey wanted, and (this drove him insane) was always making Joey's bed and straightening up his homework. Their one connection was their father's throwback music—Pink Floyd, the Beatles, the Rolling Stones, David Bowie. They had all their father's cd's, but Rita made them listen with headsets because the music brought back too much she was trying to forget.

"I'm doing it for money," Joey grunted.

"Whatta you need money for?"

"A cell phone, dope. Mom says she won't pay for it."

" Why does a kid like you need a cell phone?"

"To communicate with people. Why else? Aren't you supposed to be the smart kid in the family?"

"I don't need a cell phone. I talk to people in person."

"You're ten. You don't know anything about the world."

"Yeah, well, I think it's dumb to walk all over town in rain and snow delivering papers when you could just walk over to somebody's house and talk."

He had a point, but Joey wasn't about to admit it. It was November, and the winter part of the job was already starting to worry him.

Baseball in Michigan ended or was forced indoors for more than a third of the year, with the season ordinarily opening on a month of cold, soggy spring misery. Joey had rigged a net in the back yard and daily hit baseballs into it off an adjustable tee. He planned to keep doing it until snow began piling up. Some days he saw his grandfather nursing a glass of brandy, watching him through the kitchen window. The old man made him self-conscious and threw off his timing, but he kept swinging anyway.

The freshmen at East Catholic were sequestered in a wing of their own, apparently to keep them innocent for a little longer. Joey had chosen physics in the fall because he needed a physical science credit, and Mr. Benjamin was supposed to be the easiest of the choices. He was new at the school, young and fairly friendly, but he seemed to have no clue about how to make physics interesting. Joey had him first hour, and it was agony. Second hour he had Mr. Kowalski for phys ed. Mike Kowalski was also the freshman baseball coach, so Joey busted his tail to impress him. They'd just finished a unit on volleyball; now it was weight training. Joey was intent on developing muscle everywhere he could, but it wasn't easy when even Kowalski called him No-pack Kovacs.

In the first week of class, Joey twanged something in his left shoulder trying to bench press the same amount as the kid before him. The pain was sharp and scary. Kowalski was concerned and phoned Rita, who hurried over from the hospital still in her green scrubs. Even in those, she looked terrific. She pushed back her dark, curly hair and carefully examined the shoulder, moving his arm in slow circles as he winced.

"He's strained it. How much was he lifting?" she asked Kowalski, whose whole demeanor had transformed in her presence. Joey had seen it before with male teachers. She gave him an edge he wasn't sure he wanted. Kowalski was a big guy, a little younger than she was, and split from his wife for quite a while.

"I told him to start with 40 pounds."

"How much was it, Joey?" she asked.

"Same as Jake White. He's an outfielder, too."

Kowalski checked the bar. "80 pounds."

Rita's eyes sparked with anger. "You trying to end your baseball career before it starts, Joey? Honest to God, you need to be careful with weights."

"That's what I tell them, Mrs. Kovacs."

"Sorry, mom. It's really not that bad." It was killing him. "Honest. I'll be okay in a few days."

"A few weeks, if you're lucky. At least it's the left shoulder."

Kowalski brightened. "Got an idea. Joey, how about you do second hour in my office making up a training schedule that fits you as a baseball player? I'll help when you need it. Then when you're better, you can train the intelligent way— all the way to try-outs, if you want."

Rita smiled at that, and Kowalski basked in the glow. Joey knew his chances of making the team had just taken a giant leap forward, but it wasn't exactly the way he wanted to do it.

Though the shoulder healed in a few weeks, he wasn't able to swing a bat at all during that time, and now it was December and well into crummy weather. The newspaper (*The Drumbeat*) he delivered was more shopping news than real news, serving the suburbs and full of bland community interest stories and advertising. Thank goodness it was a weekly. On Saturday, he delivered it to every house in a six-block area, his tender shoulder forcing him to pull Stephen's Radio Flyer wagon from porch to porch instead of using the shoulder bag. When it was raining, he put the papers in mailboxes or inside storm doors. For that he made $15 a week, $60 a month, enough to get a cheap phone plan, if he didn't spend it on anything else.

On the second Saturday in December, a black mass of clouds rolled toward them from the west, looking ugly. He put on a Tigers cap and pulled a cotton hoodie over it. Grabbing a raincoat from a hook near the back door, he noticed his grandfather watching him.

"Storm is coming," the old man said.

"Yeah, Papa. Looks like it. Gotta run."

And run he did. Snagging the handle of the Radio Flyer, he raced to the corner where his bundle of papers lay stuffed in a plastic bag. He had his own delivery system: he worked the west edge of the route first, making his way quickly to the houses farthest out, then he'd wind his way back from street to street and home again, two hours on a good day.

He was two-thirds done when the black sky turned day into night, and the trees began twisting crazily. In the next moment, hard freezing rain came slashing down on the slant of a mean west wind. "Perfect," he muttered, hurriedly trying to cover his papers with the plastic bag. By the next block his head was soaked, his nose dripping cold rain, his tennis shoes and socks soggy and freezing. The sidewalk hadn't turned to ice just yet, but he could feel it coming.

Ahead, he saw a large, indefinite object moving toward him. In the downpour it looked like a big balloon with sections of orange and white. It came closer—pushing against the wind. Joey ran to another porch and shoved a wet paper in the storm door. As he returned, he saw feet beneath the orange and white balloon. Now he saw it was no balloon but a huge golf umbrella from his dad's old set of clubs.

"Mom!" he shouted above the wind. "You shouldn't be out in this. I can handle it."

"It's not Mom," he heard a male voice say. "Get under the umbrella and wait. Things will change soon."

"Papa?" Joey was disbelieving. "What are you doing, for Pete's sake?" He saw Jozsef's weathered face, his ancient eyes—eyes dark and small and set deep in nests of wrinkles and puffy sacks. He'd never really looked at those eyes before.

"Get under with me and stand here a minute. A change is coming."

Joey got under the umbrella and pressed close to his grandfather, the only time he remembered touching him. The next moment something momentous happened. A pale, phosphorescent glow burst through the darkness. The wind died, the rain stopped stinging the side of his face and turned into feathery snowflakes drifting in a slow, random dance. The leaden sky split apart, and a beam of sun set the wet street on fire. The strange light dazzled and half blinded him. And then, a few seconds later, it vanished. Snow continued flying about, sticking to his eyelashes.

"Wow, what just happened?"

"A scientific thing, but more like poetry. The surface was cooling fast. It first turned snow to freezing rain, but cold came and turned it back to snow. It's quite dramatic."

Joey nodded, and rain dripped from the bill of his cap. "You shouldn't be out here, Papa. You'll get sick."

"I'm dry," he said. "You're wet. I'll help with the rest."

And the old man wouldn't go home until the route was done.

During Christmas break, Joey plagued his mother with questions about hitting a baseball. She told him she didn't know…the softball swing was just different enough. He needed to talk to Mike Kowalski, she said, so Joey bugged her until she called Kowalski, who was there (big surprise) within an hour. There was a foot of snow on the ground, so Kowalski had to demonstrate on the front porch with Joey's metal bat that looked like a matchstick in his massive hands.

Kowalski grinned at Rita and said, "Well, a little heavier bat would help, Joey." Then he broke down the swing in slow motion. "You hit against a firm front side, see. Keep your head on the ball. Hands are always palm up, palm down. Head in the middle of your feet. Stay back. Follow through with your back foot on its toe…" He took a mighty swing to show how it all came together, and his follow through sent their snow shovel flying across the porch.

He stayed for a beer (another big surprise), which he drank with Rita at the kitchen table. Joey went into the living room, where his grandfather sat with his glass of brandy, smoking his pipe. Joey glanced at him for some kind of reaction, but the old man just shook his head.

"He knows some things. Physics he doesn't know."

"Physics? It's just a baseball swing."

"Physics," Jozsef said, pulling on his pipe and blowing out a small cloud.

If hitting a baseball depended on physics, Joey was in trouble. Fall semester would be over in less than a month, and his physics grades were now disrupting his sleep. One night before dinner, his mother opened a letter, read it with a deepening frown, and marched Joey into the living room. His grandfather was in a far corner reading his newspaper and listening to Franz Liszt's "Piano Sonata in B Minor." Joey knew the piece by now, even the title, because the old man announced it each time it played. "Apotheosis of Hungarian music," he quietly proclaimed to himself. Joey caught himself humming bits of it at times, which unnerved him.

"This is from Mr. Benjamin. Honestly, Joey, what the hell is going on? You're close to failing physics. He says the final project will make or break your grade. Have you started it yet?"

"Ummm…well, it's still sort of in the planning stages."

"In other words, you haven't done anything."

She had him, but he wasn't about to admit it. "I… well…was getting sort of interested in the physics of the baseball swing." It was desperate, the first thing that popped into his head.

He surprised her. She thought for a moment, nodded, and smiled. "Very interesting. Sorry for doubting you. I like it. It has some personal relevance." She paced about the room, thinking. "Your Papa knows about stuff like that. He helped me back when I played—taught me about swing plane. In fast pitch, see, the softball usually drops a little as it comes at you. It comes so quick from so close you need super fast hands and an upward swing plane. Baseball is different, but you'll have to ask him about it. He really loves baseball."

They both glanced over at Jozsef, who was off somewhere, eyes closed and head bobbing, adrift in Liszt's piano music. Joey, who had saved face for the moment, felt a strong premonition of doom.

He'd never admit it to his mother, but he was afraid to talk physics to the old man for fear of revealing his stupidity. So he stalled, and valuable days went flying by.

His mother was worried about her father, Joey could tell. She knew how to cook for him—goulash, stuffed cabbage, plenty of paprika. But he nibbled at food now and didn't sleep well. He was listless. He dozed in his chair at night, and she would get him up, lead him upstairs, and gently put him to bed.

Kowalski called to ask her to a New Year's Eve party, but she told him her father wasn't doing well—she needed to stay home. It wasn't a lie. Joey stayed up through the dopey

Times Square show on television, gave his mother a New Year's kiss, then hauled himself up to bed where Stephen had been asleep for hours. He could hear the old man coughing, his mother going in to check on him, and then leaving. Much later, Joey was awakened by a low, eerie moan. It stopped, but came again a few minutes later. He got up, slipped into the hallway and groped through the darkness to his grandfather's open door.

"Papa?" he asked. "Are you all right?"

There was a long pause. "Maybe you get me a drink of water."

In the bathroom Joey could find only small paper cups, so he filled two of them and went back. His grandfather was sitting on the edge of the bed now, his arms bracing him. He slowly drank one small cup, then part of the other. "I have bad dreams," he mumbled, and then more clearly, "Always the same—about Budapest, 1956. I was a boy and saw my father killed in the streets by the Russians. He was fighting for our freedom—now he dies over and over in my dreams. You are a lucky boy. Free to go to school, to play baseball, to become what you want to be. A person never really knows what it means to be free until he isn't free any more." Tears began running down his cheeks. He turned away and wiped them with the sheet. "One letter from your father I've read. Rita showed me. Your father had one dream all the time— getting home to you boys and her. He said it was a nightmare there—the Afghan people suffering like he's never seen. There was no freedom, only fear. Like my father, he died, too. I'm sorry for both of us."

Joey watched his grandfather, waiting for the old man's emotion to pass, feeling pain of his own. "More water, Papa?"

"Not water—brandy. It's on the shelf beside the stove."

Joey hurried downstairs, guided by a nightlight his mother kept on near the phone. He pulled his grandfather's snifter from the dish drainer and poured it half full. He heard a familiar squeak in the floor, looked up to see his mother standing in a robe. "It's for Papa," he said.

She nodded. "Thank you."

Back in the bedroom, he watched his grandfather taste the gleaming caramel liquid, cough a little, follow it with some water.

Joey suddenly blurted out, "Help me with a physics project, Papa? I really need your help."

His grandfather looked up, taken by surprise. "My help? Well…maybe so. Maybe I can help you understand some things, but the doing will be up to you."

"That's what I mean."

The old man stared for a few moments as if thinking. He nodded, and handed the snifter to Joey. "Try it."

Joey hesitated, but took the glass and lifted it for a small sip. It burned in his throat but warmed the rest of him, leaving a faintly sweet aftertaste.

"Don't tell your mother."

Joey laughed. His grandfather took the glass back and drank a little more, nodding again as if to seal something between them.

Their collaboration began with a physics formula, which Joey initially found disheartening. He sat beside Jozsef at the kitchen table. With a dark pencil, the old man wrote the formula in large, bold print:

$KE = \frac{1}{2}\, mv^2$

"Kinetic energy, Joey, is ½ times the mass of the baseball bat times the velocity of the swing squared."

"I don't understand. How do you know that?"

"A physicist figured it out. Newton, I think."

"Yeah, but what did he know about baseball?"

"Nothing. It's a law, Joey. It works the same with everything."

"I don't get what it means."

"In baseball, it means the heavier the bat, the farther the ball travels. But then, what does a heavy bat do to your swing?"

Joey thought about it. "Slows it down."

"That's right. Suppose, then, instead of a heavier bat, you choose to increase bat speed?"

"The ball will go farther, too."

"Yes, but which is best?"

"I don't know."

"Then figure it out with physics, Joey. We'll make it simple. You have a 32 ounce bat—that is 2 pounds—and a 50 feet per second swing which is slower than yours, but this is just for easy math. Go ahead, do the formula."

Joey sighed and scratched his head. "Okay, 1/2 times 2 pounds times 50 feet per second squared. That's simple— the answer is 2500. 2500 what?"

"Units of energy applied to the ball. Now, just for fun, double the weight of the bat."

Joey did it in his head. "That makes 5000 units of energy."

"Good boy. So a heavier bat helps, but it slows down the swing. Instead of increasing your bat weight, try doubling the speed of your swing to 100 feet per second."

Joey worked it out, stared at his answer, and looked at his grandfather. "That's 10,000 units of energy. It's way better to increase your bat speed! I can't believe it!"

"Baseball is physics, Joey."

It **was** physics—he could see it. How brainlessly resistant he'd been. Maybe science wasn't something separate from life after all.

"Wait, Papa. How am I supposed to increase bat speed?"

"Forearm and hand exercises, legs and core work," he said, "not muscle man bench presses."

Joey grumbled, knowing he'd have to rewrite the training schedule he was doing for Kowalski.

In the next few days, the old man went on to show him what swing plane meant in baseball. While a softball usually dropped a little in flight, a baseball dropped more. He said that a slightly upward swing plane was best to match the drop. Breaking balls dropped a lot. Joey needed to learn to spot the curveball. At high school level, pitchers nearly always gave it away—a change in the windup, a different arm slot or delivery speed. He explained the physics of a curveball: friction between the sideways spinning ball and the air caused air molecules on one side of the ball to move faster than on the other. Uneven air pressure pushed the ball toward the side of lower air pressure, and the ball curved. A batter had to stay back and wait on a curveball. Commit too early, and you were done for.

The B+ Joey got on the physics project earned him a C for a final grade. He spent his paper route money on batting machines, not a cell phone. Instead of a six pack, he developed fairly impressive forearms—Kowalski amused himself by calling him Popeye now. In March, he made the team legitimately, had to trade off playing time because of five outfielders, yet he managed to bat .270 with no home runs. He instead found satisfaction in a half dozen roped doubles, two of them off the fence. His grandfather showed up for all his home games, sometimes with his mother and little brother with him.

One night in the summer, he saw the old man and Stephen up on the flat roof above the back porch, looking at constellations and planets through a telescope. He found to his surprise that he liked the wildness of Bartòk's *Concerto for Orchestra*.

His mother went out with Mike Kowalski a couple of times, but not until the baseball season was over to avoid a conflict of interest. Later, when Joey asked how it was going, she said simply, "Nice guy but all jock—not really smart enough, if you know what I mean."

He did know. Already, he was aware of becoming smarter himself, better at school. He still loved baseball, but no longer did he consider it his life's work. In August they celebrated his grandfather's 80th birthday. Joey paid his mother to buy a bottle of brandy, which he tied with a ribbon. Stephen made him a model of the solar system out of Styrofoam balls glued to a cardboard chart of orbits. Both gifts seemed to please him.

The old man's eyesight was dimming, but he still saw in ways Joey had never seen. As they ate cake and listened to Bartòk on the stereo, Joey knew there was something altered in the house, and he dreaded a time when there'd be only them again.

MESSAGES IN PINK

Jonah went to his locker in the Walmart employee area to get the bagged lunch his mother had made him. He spun the dial of his padlock, and as the door swung open, a folded pink note dropped to his feet from one of the metal slots at the top of the door. He picked it up. The hand-printed message read, "Jonah. I watch you every day. I think you are the best worker here. I like you. S."

He'd been at the job only a month, and it had already begun to feel like a prison sentence. But this message created an odd excitement, a fluttering in his chest, the first stimulation he'd felt in this place. Was S a woman, an admirer? What else could it be? Though this seemed a strange way to communicate, he was intrigued—and his job for the rest of the day became an enticing kind of mystery story. Who in the world was S, and what was she thinking? He'd avoided socializing with fellow employees, except in the most superficial ways, and ate lunch in his car. He was certainly not "the best worker here." He didn't know many names yet (didn't really want to), and everyone masked, so it was hard even to recognize people. No one he knew had a name starting with S except his department manager, Steve, who was male, middle-aged, bald, a Walmart devotee, and an unlikely note writer, especially on pink paper.

Jonah's life happened to be at its lowest ebb. Even though he'd attended a local community college for two years to save money, his degree from the nearby state university had put him $30,000 in debt. The BA degree, supposedly his golden ticket, had landed him a job in the call center of the local symphony at $10 an hour. His payment on his student loan was $348 a month.

He'd found a downtown studio apartment, just slightly larger than a dorm room, but rent had been raised in January from $700 to $850 a month. Next, the pandemic hit the world, the symphony shut down, and he found himself jobless, isolated, and feeling buried alive. He collected unemployment and his stimulus checks (for some reason significantly more than he'd earned), endured lockdown and masking for months, began drinking too much and watching hours of inane television and YouTube videos. He was a reader and a neophyte writer, but he lacked the concentration to stay with anything literary. Depressed, unkempt, living mostly in his pajamas, he at last went to his parents and, in desperation, asked to be with human beings again.

So they helped move him out of the apartment and into their walkout basement. He looked for jobs that paid more than the government was giving him, but they didn't exist. Most available work was low paid and hazardous because of the rapid spread of the virus. So he sat and waited. Both his parents worked online from home now, so (ironically) privacy became an issue for him. Even their church services met on Zoom. He took long walks, watching people and their dogs move to the other side of the street rather than pass close to him. He understood their caution yet felt like a leper, felt as if all sociability had disappeared from existence. His parents were understanding and patient, but who wanted to live with parents at his age? How could he take out a girl during a pandemic, and where could he take her?

At last, his parents qualified for the COVID-19 vaccine, and shortly after, Jonah did as well. Life began to relax a little. His unemployment checks ended, but his uncle used a business connection to get him a job in retail sales at a local Walmart store, $13.50 an hour. Though it felt like a giant step into purgatory, it was at least movement in some direction.

For several days, Jonah studied nametags, time cards, and employee lists. There were at least ten employees with first names starting with S, and eight of them were female. The note had said she watched him every day, so he concentrated on sales personnel in nearby departments. He worked in Menswear mostly refolding clothing people had tried on or simply messed up. Across the aisle were Womenswear and Jewelry, likely places to start, and entirely staffed by females. In Womenswear he had found a Susan and a Sophie. Susan kept to herself and was older, around 40 maybe, but Sophie appeared to be friendlier, in her 20s and fairly pleasant-looking, at least in a mask.

His hopes, though, lay in Jewelry, where a flashy brunette named Serena worked the counter. She looked to be Hispanic with dark satiny skin, dramatic eye makeup, and a small butterfly tattoo on the outside of her left ankle. Even her facemasks were sexy: black with a variety of red hearts or bright birds. He watched her for several days but never caught her looking his way. He saw she was consistently cheerful and vivacious with customers. Just watching her lifted his spirits and made him examine his own glum semi-presence at his job. Toward the end of the week, he saw her as he was punching out and followed her into the parking lot. She removed her mask with relief the moment she was outside. She wore deep red lipstick even though no one saw it. The fact exhilarated him, as did the view of her whole face, a very pleasant face though a bit older than he'd expected—maybe 30. As she was unlocking an old Dodge van, he passed close to her and stopped.

"Excuse me," he said. "I'm Jonah from Menswear. I just want to tell you how terrific you are with customers. I watch you sometimes just to give me a lift. If I ever bought jewelry, I'd want to buy it from you." This was the most assertive he'd ever been with a woman he didn't know. But he had a feeling she'd be receptive. Sure enough, she broke into a broad smile.

"Wow, I don't believe you said that." Her voice quivered a little with emotion. "I mean staying cheerful takes every ounce of my energy. I'm thankful somebody notices. I'm telling my husband what you said." She opened the van door and got in, still beaming. "See you tomorrow, Jonah. That was really sweet."

As she drove off, she waved to him. The encounter left him feeling the best he had in weeks except for one thing: she clearly wasn't S. It was too bad, because he'd really wanted her to be.

Life in the world began loosening up a bit. The YMCA downtown opened again, though masking was required. A high school buddy, Phil, began meeting him there for pickup basketball; they regularly got whipped by guys twenty years older, but it was fun, and Jonah, an inch at a time, began coming out of the shadows. Phil was jobless but looking into getting a real estate license to cash in on the wildly inflated sellers' market. Jonah's Walmart job was a source of great amusement to Phil, especially with the college degree he'd paid a small fortune to get. Phil himself had bailed out of community college after two semesters and as a result was debt-free. Jonah, calmly enduring his humor, told Phil the job was temporary desperation. He planned to quit soon and was almost convinced he meant it.

The next day, though, a second note appeared in his locker.

"Jonah. I think you are just what I need. Maybe you will feel that way, too. S."

The printing was the same, the same folded pink paper. The message stunned him. He didn't have to read deeply to see an undercurrent of middle school infatuation. Still, he was fascinated. The long months of forced celibacy had created in him some of the urgency he sensed in the note.

Serena now looked his way every day, and though she was masked, she smiled with her eyes and sometimes waved. How beautiful and bright her presence was! He tried mimicking her amiability with customers, who acted pleased and startled that someone would be offering unsolicited help in a big-box store. He caught Steve watching him at times, his look more curious than critical.

Sophie in Womenswear was a redhead with very fair skin and a rash of freckles on her forehead and (he assumed) across her nose. Jonah had a soft spot for redheads and liked the name Sophie. So he watched her as she worked. After several days, she noticed and came over to him as he rearranged a rack of men's belts.

"Hi," she said, and glanced at his nametag. "Uh, Jonah, is it? Did you want something?"

"Hey, Sophie—sorry. I don't mean to be so conspicuous about watching you, but you're really good at your job. I'm trying to learn a few things. I'm pretty new at retail."

This surprised her, and once again, a woman smiled at him with her eyes. "Honestly? You think so? I'm actually bored out of my mind, but I try hard not to show it."

"Believe me, you don't show it."

"Well, thanks. I'll be glad to tell you what I know about retail any time. I worked at Macy's before this, but…then the pandemic hit. You seem pretty good at it already. I've been watching you."

"You have?" Something like a hummingbird began fluttering in his stomach. "Hey, I'm eating lunch in my car today. Want to join me? My break is at 12:30."

"Mine, too. Sure. Meet you at the front door."

Lunchtime came, and she kept her mask on outdoors, so he did as well. His battered Dodge Stratus was an embarrassment, but he kept the inside looking respectable, since he dined there often. He opened the passenger door for her—she carried her lunch in a plastic Ziploc with a blue freezer pack. She slipped in nimbly, pulling her full skirt after her. He caught sight of a plump, attractive thigh before he lightly shut the door.

Once in the driver's seat, he watched as she removed her mask, revealing lots more freckles, a wholesome kind of sweetness in her smile, and very white, overly large teeth. They upset the symmetry of her face, but it was something he thought he could get used to. He removed his mask, and she looked at him with interest.

"You're nice looking," she said. "Too bad we all have to hide behind a mask."

"You are, too. I've always had a thing for red hair and freckles."

She rolled her eyes. "I wish I did. I'm always under an umbrella at the beach. I get fried in no time."

"Well, my mother deep-tans, and she's turning to leather. You'll stay young and milky white."

She smiled at that and opened her Ziploc bag. "Mine's a cold BLT. What are you having?"

He opened his brown lunch bag and took out a sandwich wrapped in wax paper. "Looks like peanut butter and jelly. My mother made it. I've living with my parents right now until I can afford an apartment again. Want half?"

"I'm living with mine, too. I had a roommate in an apartment, but he lost his job because of COVID. Then I lost mine, too."

"You lived with a guy?"

She shrugged and passed him half of her cold BLT. He handed her half of his PBJ. "He was gay. It worked out pretty well. He had great decorating ideas. I went to a few drag shows with him. Weird but fun."

"So you're not seeing anyone?"

"I am. But it's not working out too well. COVID kind of kills intimacy, you know what I mean?"

"Yeah, do I ever."

She sighed and munched on his PBJ. "I should be talking about retail sales."

"It's okay. I learn just from watching you. It's nice to see somebody who's so good at it." His praise was exaggerated—she was no Serena. But her face lit up instantly. In spite of it, he sensed from her casual presence that she was not the S of the messages.

At the end of the week, Menswear ran a sale on shoes, and Jonah was working the department alone. The place was mayhem, yet when she could, Sophie slipped across the aisle to help him sort and rebox the heaps of sneakers, work boots, and old man slippers scattered in the aisles. Sophie's fellow worker Susan watched with a flat, impassive look. For the first time, he noticed her worn-at-the-edges attractiveness. Though her eyes seemed hard, the rest of her was soft and abundant, especially in the yellow cotton dress she wore.

It was a curious coincidence that after work that same afternoon, as he was getting into his car, he noticed Susan sitting at the nearby bus stop. He walked over to her. "Hi. I'm Jonah from Menswear. Susan, right?"

She wasn't wearing a mask. Her face was pretty but fading a bit, her eyes the oldest part of her. "Hi. Sure, I know you."

"Give you a lift?"

Her face reddened slightly. "No, it's all right. The bus goes near my place."

"Where's your place?"

"Hillside Apartments on College."

"I go right by there. Come on. It's no problem."

Her glazed-looking eyes brightened. "Are you sure? It would really be a help. My 12-year-old is by herself all day doing school online. I hope she's back in class soon. My neighbor checks in on her and makes her lunch. I honestly can't tell if she's learning anything. She's the kind of kid who needs a teacher and a bunch of classmates around her."

"Yeah, these are weird times," he said, surprised to hear so much personal stuff pouring out of her. As they moved toward his car, he wondered about a husband and guessed there wasn't one.

From that point on, when their work schedules coincided—most of the time—Jonah drove her to work and home again. On a couple of occasions she invited him in for a beer. Her daughter Maggie was skinny as a stick and mostly silent in his presence. She seemed moody and a worry to her mother. Susan's husband, he soon learned, had disappeared when Maggie was six weeks old. Things weren't easy, especially without a car, but Susan did little complaining. Jonah looked forward to their time together, and Susan now was noticeably friendlier at work, though she revealed no romantic leanings toward him at all. They'd had opportunities when Maggie was away at her grandma's, but Susan gave him no signs. If she had, Jonah would have gladly cooperated.

Near Halloween, he found a third pink note on the inside of his locker. It read, "Jonah. You can't imagine the things I could do for you. S."

This was a new tone, more assertive, more suggestive. He was obviously missing something in plain sight.

He'd found another S who worked as a stocker, sometimes in his department. Her name was Stella, and she was big and somewhat horsy-looking, with hair cropped close like a man's. She was brash and edgy, a little scary. That fall he'd seen her speeding around on a forklift in the Patio and Garden Department. It would be just his luck.

Out of curiosity, one day in the employee lunch area he took a seat across a table from her. The weather was colder now, and eating in his car was not a comfortable option. He was mildly astonished to find himself still working at Walmart after nearly four months, but the messages had drawn him back a day at a time as had several of the people working there. Stella's red handkerchief mask was on the table; her nose looked as if it'd been broken more than once. *Harley-Davidson* stretched across the hills and valleys of her chest. She glanced at his nametag.

"How'd you get a name like Jonah? You running away from God?" Her laugh was like clearing her throat.

Taken aback, he could only smile self-consciously. "Maybe.

Probably. It's my grandfather's name. You're Stella?"

"Yup. Hey, I got the deli pulled pork today, and it's way too sweet. What are you having?"

"Egg salad sandwich. Want half? I'll take some of your pulled pork."

"Yeah, I can do that. I like egg salad if it's not made with Miracle Whip."

"Nah, it's mayo and onions."

She cut her bun in half and shoved it to him on a napkin. He handed over half his sandwich. She took a large bite and nodded. "You make this?"

"My mother did. I'm living at home right now."

"Too bad."

"It's okay. I lived alone during the lockdown. Went a little crazy, I think."

"Yeah, that can happen. I live alone, and I'm crazy."

He glanced at her and laughed a little. She smiled. Her teeth were straighter than her nose.

"I'm named after somebody, like you are—Stella in *Streetcar Named Desire*. You know that play?"

"Of course. **Stelllllla!**" he yelled, turning heads all around the room.

She grinned. "I can't believe a Walmart stiff knows something literary."

"Yeah, I read. I even write a little."

"Why are you working in this dump?"

"Because I got a degree in English."

This seemed to break her up. "Me, too. So now I'm qualified to drive a forklift. Hey—I just reminded myself of a line: 'What a dump.' Who said that?"

Jonah smiled. "Ummm—Martha in that crazy Albee play? *Who's Afraid of Virginia Wolfe?*"

She clapped noisily. "Good! But there's more to it— mouthy Martha was quoting somebody else. Who was it?"

"You got me."

"Bette Davis in *Beyond the Forest*."

He shrugged. "Way before my time."

"I'm only 25, smartass. Don't you watch Turner Classic Movies?"

"My mother likes Hallmark movies. The tv belongs to her."

She took another bite of his sandwich. "Well…at least she makes good egg salad."

Before she left to go back to work, she told him, "In case you're thinking about hitting on me, you should know I've got a girlfriend."

The way she said it sounded humorous. He snickered. "Lucky you. Since the pandemic, I've been considering the priesthood."

She walked away nodding, amused.

He worked Black Friday after Thanksgiving—a nightmare except for Stella coming by with a utility cart loaded with boxes and handing him a book. It was a thick volume of the short stories of D. H. Lawrence.

"Here's something to help get you through COVID. Very passionate."

Jonah knew a little about D. H. Lawrence. He'd read a couple of stories and *Lady Chatterley's Lover*. "What's the occasion?"

"It's a loan, not a present. I thought we could trade books once in a while since we're literary types." With that, she wheeled away, scattering customers.

"Hey, thanks!" he yelled after her.

Two weeks later he brought her a copy of *Slaughterhouse Five*, since she'd mentioned she'd never read Vonnegut. She returned in to him in two days, now a passionate Vonnegut fan.

Christmas and the New Year came and went. Jonah worked Christmas Eve and New Year's Eve, in part so Serena and Susan could stay home. He kept hauling Susan back and forth to work, her presence often the best part of his day. In late January, on the way home in the dark, Susan had news for him.

"I've heard some scuttlebutt that Steve is about to offer you a promotion."

"Can't be true. I haven't even been there six months."

"Yeah, but you're terrific with people, great for morale. Steve tries to hold onto promising young guys, but they don't stay."

"Believe me, Susan, I have no plans of climbing the corporate ladder at Walmart."

"It's $3.50 more an hour."

He thought about that for a moment, and then dismissed it. "Want to know why I've stayed this long? It's the people I work with—like you. How long have you been there?"

"A little over four years."

"Have you been promoted?"

"A couple of raises, but no promotions. I wouldn't mind one."

"I don't want it. I don't deserve it. I'm staying where I am. I hope you get it."

She smiled. "I think Steve's being pressured to find a guy. This store is mostly run by women."

"More power to them."

He dropped her at the front door of her complex and drove home.

In the kitchen his mom was stirring a pot of chili. He kissed her on the back of the head as he passed. "Smells like heaven, ma."

"It needs an hour yet."

He grabbed a beer as he passed the refrigerator. "You're asking a lot."

"Get out of here." But she was smiling.

Jonah went to the basement and into his bedroom. He closed the door, popped open the beer, and opened the top drawer of his dresser. Susan's news was gnawing at him in a strange way. Under a pair of socks lay the pink messages. He sat down on the bed, opened them out on the spread, and read them aloud.

"Jonah. I watch you every day. I think you are the best worker here. I like you. S."

"Jonah. I think you are just what I need. I think you will feel that way, too. S."

"Jonah. You can't imagine the things I could do for you. S."

It struck him—like a two-by-four to the back of the head— how easily he could have misconstrued every one of the messages, how much of his own needs he'd read into them. But then he thought: no, impossible, Steve isn't anywhere near clever enough.

It remained, though, that months of searching had failed to turn up the identity of S. The mystery perplexed him.

There were days when he wondered if the messages had been some sort of divine intervention, especially considering the road he'd travelled from misanthropic hermit to now. S had shown interest in him, so he'd returned it, and everything had changed. It was the kind of transformation angels were known to make in people.

Steve did offer him the promotion, and, true to his word, Jonah turned it down, saying he didn't feel as qualified as someone like Susan. So the job was offered to her, and she took it. Within a couple of months she bought a car (something Jonah regretted, though he was happy for her).

There were no more pink notes. Jonah stayed almost two years at Walmart, more than he'd ever dreamed of doing, appreciating his friends and hence the job. Finally, when Serena left for a real jewelry store, Sophie announced her engagement, and Stella took off for the west coast on a motorcycle, Jonah made the decision to quit, to live for a while on the money he'd saved, and to try writing a story about the enigmatic nature of life.

DUMB DOG

Barney had been gone for three nights, and Will figured it was the end of him. Yet here he was on the couch again, seeming none the worse for wear except for a missing collar and tags. Will had walked and driven the neighborhood daily hoping to catch a glimpse of him or to hear his irritating, seal-like bark. He'd apparently found a family for a brief reprieve, a vacation, before returning to the near-empty house. Like a bad penny he was back, and Will was relieved he didn't have to make phone calls explaining yet another loss.

Barney had mainly been Sam's dog. Sam, their oldest, had loved him unconditionally, forgiving him his heedless behavior more easily than they'd forgiven it in Sam. But from the start of high school, Sam had begun disappearing from the family scene whenever possible, and the dog suffered. Peggy, their precocious second child, had named him—after the dog in *Barney Beagle Plays Baseball,* her earliest and favorite chapter book. Their Barney, however, was not a beagle but a Daisy dog, lovable to look at but a shameless mess-maker.

Peggy was the dutiful child, and she struggled to keep the house spotless to mollify her mother who expected more of her than she did her son. Barney regularly left muddy paw prints on their cream-colored chairs—a fabric they'd chosen before a dog came into the house. If left alone at home, Barney would express his displeasure by peeing through the rungs of the open banister onto the walls and carpet below. At such times, Peggy would shriek with despair, and Will's thoughts turned murderous.

Peggy loved the dog, but he disrupted her measured life. He whined miserably when she ran the vacuum. He'd rumple her homework and curl up on school clothes she'd ironed and laid out. She was an overachiever, especially with softball. For years, Will pitched tennis balls to her baseball-style to sharpen her batting, and Barney delighted in chasing them down and tearing them apart, or he ran off with game balls, turning them slick with dog slime. He once chewed the thumb off her best infield glove, bringing her to tears.

And still—this puzzled Will—when Sam was gone, Barney slept tight to Peggy's back, and she'd pass the night without her usual bad dreams. The dog was a train wreck, but a part of them.

The day after the prodigal's return was a Saturday with no agenda. Will sat in the den sipping a beer, watching the Master's Tournament while admiring the azaleas ablaze on the fairways. Barney was tucked against his hip, staring up at him with those needy chocolate eyes. Will often wondered what, if anything, was actually going on in that small, dysfunctional brain.

"What's the problem, Barn?" he asked absently.

Barney uttered a whimpering sigh and settled his chin on Will's leg. This time, Will thought he understood: "So it's come down to this—I'm your dog now," was the gist of it.

When golf ended at six, Will turned on the oven to preheat it for a frozen pizza, unhooked the leash from the back of the door, prompting a burst of frenetic jubilation—their vet called it the zoomies—during which Barney, though twelve years old now (theirs for ten of them) tore around the circular track of the house like a drugged race horse. It took an effort for Will to restrain him long enough to snap on the leash. Once outside, Barney dragged Will forward like a water skier behind a power boat. The animal had never learned to heel or observe basic walking etiquette. Will blamed it on getting him as a grown dog—already beyond hope of meaningful training.

In truth, the dog had been his wife Ruth's idea at the urging of her friend Sally, whose hyperactive poodle passed their house daily on a leash. When Sally stopped to talk, the dog was all over his wife or him or one of the kids. Will was not even remotely a dog person, but Sally was convinced it was great for the kids, taught them responsibility, and helped bond the family. Ruth, who apparently felt the absence of some of those things, began quietly to work on him.

He told her if she could find a calm, intelligent, loving dog that didn't poop, he might come around. Instead, in their first browsing-only trip to the Animal Shelter, they happened upon a cream-colored Daisy dog who whimpered and begged and dragged his butt around the cage (a treatable anal gland problem, they were told) until they began to waffle and actually consider it. A sign on the cage read: "The sweet little Daisy dog is a mini-mix of all our favorite pint-size pooches. It brings the intelligent Poodle together with the curious Bichon Frise and the outgoing Shih Tzu for a fine family dog that loves to play, enjoys meeting new faces and seldom barks." Did such a singular creature (hardly pint-size) deserve the fate awaiting unwanted shelter animals?

"Sounds perfect," Ruth said with unnerving assurance.

When Will asked the reason the dog was in the Shelter, the young female attendant shrugged, guessing he'd been abandoned or picked up as a stray with no identifying tags.

On the way home, they stopped at a grocery store for basic dog supplies. The instant Ruth opened the car door, their new family member took a wild leap from her lap, raced across the parking lot and disappeared behind the building. Will went after him running, came upon a railroad track stretching west to the horizon. He could see the dog trotting down the middle of the track. Will took off after him. The dog, apparently thinking it a game, speeded up, stopped and glanced back, and then ran off again. It was utterly maddening.

Will, realizing his efforts were futile, threw up his hands and shouted "Suit yourself, you dumb, boneheaded dog!" and turned to retrace his steps to the car. By the time he reached the parking lot, the dog was at his side. Ruth opened the car door, and the Daisy, having made at least one crucial decision in his life, jumped onto her lap. "Maybe he's smarter than he looks," she said with a sigh. From then on, she left the responsibility of a dog to the rest of the family.

Will suspected Sam and Barney stuck close together as solace—ports in the all-too-frequent household storms. Will and Ruth had been married thirteen years when Barney arrived on the scene. Ruth was second generation Italian and possessed of a volatile temper and large emotions. She was also a model of competence when it came to running a household: a fastidious housekeeper, excellent cook, family bookkeeper, protective mother. From her father she'd learned basic plumbing and electrical skills, things Will admired and happily let her handle.

From her critical, controlling mother she had learned to doubt herself, and that seemed to color everything. She thought sometimes about going to college but lacked the confidence. She worked part time in a bakery deli, their most effective employee.

Will, on the other hand, lived in the limelight, director of the vocal jazz program at a nearby college, a musician applauded and admired by many. Self worth was not his problem. She bitterly complained that he was too self absorbed, too self contained. He didn't need them (as if they were a faction of three lined up in opposition). His agenda always came first. Students treated him like a minor deity, especially the females.

Her shrill accusations contained some truth, he knew, but she was wrong about his not needing them. A family was a messy, vital part of his existence.

Though their marriage had much to commend it, the two were gasoline and flame. The kids lived atop a volcano. Will had spent a fair amount of post-eruption time in local hotels.

He had grown up in a peaceful, supportive family—had needed years to learn to battle back. He'd noticed even before they'd married that her emotional upheavals were often wildly out of keeping with the situations provoking them. The firestorm would usually pass quickly for her but leave him shaken and confused, sometimes for days. If over the years he'd grown more combative and less sensitive to her feelings, it was the result of the thick, calloused skin grown round his heart.

Their kids each had unique gifts, though once Sam found his way into the dark side of high school, you wouldn't have known it. He was the one with undeniable musical talent, especially after years of piano lessons with fine teachers. But at sixteen he'd quit all of it and lost interest in school. He'd graduated thanks only to the worried concern of his teachers. He caused his parents many agonized and sleepless nights, followed up by angry confrontations, yet there remained a winning, loving side to him that bore no grudges. He seemed to have more friends than any of them and knew how to make people smile.

Peggy became so adept at fast pitch softball that in high school she was voted to the All-State team. She soloed in the church choir, wrote dark, obscure poems, started a mystery novel, earned all A's, bit her nails to the quick, and frequently covered for the bad behavior of her older brother.

The dog, Will soon discovered, had a curious ability he'd never seen in another. Only one day into dog ownership, he and Ruth were outside having lunch on the deck. Their back yard was spacious and tree lined, full of vegetable and flower gardens of Will's design, and wholly encompassed by chain link fence. While they sat enjoying the ambience, Will saw Barney (newly named) drop the first of many years of dog bombs (including those bright, foil-laced ones from ransacked Halloween candy). His eyes travelled with the dog as he scratched grass half-heartedly toward the pile, calmly went to the fence and stretched paw over paw into the diamond-shaped holes of the links, hauling himself to the top where he took an awkward tumble to the ground on the other side and disappeared into the wooded ravine and creek dividing developments.

"I don't believe it," Ruth said to him. "A Daisy dog can't do that."

In the distance they heard his strange, seal-like barking. He'd apparently picked up a scent.

"Damn," Will said in disbelief. "We don't even have tags on him yet."

Through the next week, Will fastened chicken wire, leaning inward, to the top of the chain link. It was unsightly but effective at thwarting the dog. Will was immensely pleased with himself. Yet when Sam went off for nine days of camp with friends, Barney, in misery, found a weak spot in the construction and was gone. Nothing, as it turned out, could contain him. Like Sam, he loved his family yet seemed driven to run from a spirit living in it.

They all learned it was no use chasing Barney down. By the following day or the one after, they'd get a call from some family he'd attached to. Their kids already loved him, Will was told, and they hated giving him up. Will was tempted each time to hand him over. But of course he didn't. Barney was theirs, signed on for life.

Once, the call had come from a neighbor down the street. The frantic woman told him his dog had been hit by a car and was lying on her front lawn. Will and Ruth rushed over. Barney lay on his side, unconscious but breathing. Will knelt down and gently touched his head.

"Oh, god," Ruth said. "How do we tell Sam?"

"I'll get a blanket and wrap him up."

The neighbor woman, wiping tears with a bunched-up Kleenex, said, "The driver barely braked before he hit him and then just drove off. The bastard! I saw it happen. The dog flew twenty feet—right to where he is now. The poor thing. I feel just terrible. Do you suppose he'll live?"

Will ran his hand gingerly down the dog's back, and then examined his legs. "I don't know."

As if on cue, Barney opened his eyes, got unsteadily to his feet, shook himself all over as if wet, and allowed Will to take him in his arms.

Except for bruises and a broken tooth, the vet found no serious damage. Sam had left work to be there. He was helping a friend paint houses at this point in his life. His fingers, coated with yellow latex paint, touched the place at the base of Barney's neck that only he could find. Barney closed his eyes and purred like a kitten. He'd made the same sound years earlier, curled under the piano bench as Sam played *Moonlight Sonata*.

In those happier days, Sam would haul his sled to the top of the steep embankment they called Breakneck Hill, set Barney on his lap, and push off, dog and boy flying down with the same wild-eyed, fearless look. In the summer they'd do the same but in the Radio Flyer wagon that Sam intentionally crashed and rolled at the bottom of the hill. They'd end up tied in knots, laughing and yipping crazily.

In high school, Sam, only eight months into his driver's license, wrapped Ruth's car around a tree, totaling it while somehow only spraining an ankle. He'd blown high enough on the breathalyzer for a DUI but got off with a stern warning from a cop who'd been his Little League coach. The second time, he was riding with a friend who'd driven his snowmobile over the ice of a nearby lake and broken through. Both were rescued, suffering from severe hypothermia. The friend received a DUI citation.

And so it went. Sam seemed charmed, watched over by a special angel, as his dog seemed to be. Yet one day he borrowed money to buy an old, overpowered BSA motorcycle from his painting friend, and Will began to have fears about the durability of the charm. On his first ride through the countryside on a chilly March day, Sam lost control of the bike going 80 on a winding road. He had on leather and a new helmet, but it cracked like an eggshell on a stump seventy feet off the pavement.

They'd put the dog in a kennel for three days to get him out from under foot.

The three of them made their way dazed and ghost-like through the formalities of the funeral. Sam's friends—some they'd never seen before—showed up in droves.

Except for Barney (and Peggy coming home on breaks), they were now alone together—much as they had been when they first married. A twenty-three year run was laudable, but life and loss had worn them down. The house had more space now, yet they seemed in each other's way. Ruth grew moodier by degrees, irritated with the way he talked to the dog or dabbled with tunes on the piano. Her vacuuming (why hadn't he noticed with Peggy?) drove him to distraction. She moved to another bedroom, claiming he snored. She spent more and more time at work.

Some months went by, and one day she hired a lawyer, gathered up what she wanted, and moved in with a man named Carl. Will, suspecting it but saying nothing, felt a powerful rush of relief accompanied by emptiness as deep as he saw in Barney's eyes.

Shortly after Ruth left, Peggy called him, pleading to come home and care for her Dad, but Will gently declined. He told her she was grad school material with amazing things ahead. They shared a laugh when he mentioned he had Barney for companionship. "That dumb dog," she said. "I'll bet he's suffering more than any of us."

Peggy was a starting shortstop as a sophomore in a Big Ten school two hours down the road. Will made it to every game he could. Ruth sometimes showed up, and Will sat with her. Talking was easy enough; it felt as if they'd spent five lifetimes together.

Carl was a printer with a business next door to the bakery deli. He'd come in for years to eat and chat with Ruth. Will and he had met there once or twice and even spoken. Carl had never been married and was at least ten years older than Ruth. He seemed a decent man. In Will's better moments, he wished them well.

Ruth's friend Sally had a different poodle now. She'd been divorced for several years and stopped often these days to ask gardening questions. Sometimes she brought brownies for him that couldn't touch Ruth's. Her yard was showing all the signs of family disruption. And the truth was, Will's gardens had gone a bit ragged, as well. A March storm had brought down the huge willow at the back of the yard. The mess was still waiting for a tree service to haul it off. He had, however, managed to remove the chicken wire from the chain link fence, eliminating that bit of cheesiness. But the signs of neglect were abundant enough.

Will's job required him to be at the college only three or four hours a day, so Barney didn't suffer long periods alone, and he stopped peeing in the house. There was a problem ahead, however, and Will wasn't sure how to solve it. In less than a month, he would be traveling with his vocal jazz ensemble to a competition on the West Coast. The event would take a week. They had placed Barney in a kennel just that once (through those terrible days before the funeral). The kennel owners thereafter refused to take him back—a permanent ban for impossible behavior.

Will tried asking Ruth to keep him for the week, but she wanted none of it.

Their walk wound down, Barney sniffing and sprinkling every tree and hydrant on their route. Will entered through the garage, hung up the leash on its hook, and baked the pizza, later slipping Barney a small slice. As he cleaned up his dishes, he heard Barney's nails clicking on the ceramic tiles of the hallway. Predictably, he heard him lapping water and crunching his dry food. It was Saturday night. They would again watch a movie together, their lives reduced to basic enduring.

Rousing himself, Will decided to run through some numbers for the upcoming competition, so he made his way into the living room where the grand piano stood in a bow window. To his surprise, Barney was stretched out under the piano bench, a place he hadn't occupied, to Will's knowledge, since Sam last played.

"Hey, Barn," he said, sliding onto the bench. "What's on your mind?"

Barney stayed silent, his chin on his paws.

Will ran a few scales to loosen up his hands, and then reached to a stack of music in a bookcase beside the piano. He found it quickly—Sam's student version of *Moonlight Sonata*. Curious, he opened it and began to play.

Barney heard but made no sound, not a purr, and never lifted his chin from his paws.

Oddly disheartened, Will moved on to other music. A few minutes passed, and Barney stood up and ambled away. He went to the patio door and began to whimper. Will heaved an impatient sigh, trudged to the door, and let him out.

An hour or more later, with *Ordinary People* just beginning, Will remembered the dog. His forgetfulness made him uneasy. Usually Barney scratched the glass to let him know he wanted in. Will went to the slider and walked out into the darkening yard.

He saw no sign of the dog, even among the fallen, dying branches of the willow, even in the lengthening shadows of the empty house. "Hey, Barn," he called. "Hey, boy, come on," as if the sound of his voice offered something to coax him home.

HOUSE OF ROCKS

There was an old man named Peter, a farmer, whose house and parts of his barn were full of rocks. His wife and close companion of many years (her name was Amber) had been dead nearly 18 months, a difficult loss for him. He wasn't sure of what to do with his life, let alone with the multitude of rocks, minerals, and fossils they'd collected over more than 40 years. She'd been a high school geology teacher and in her retirement a craft jeweler who'd sold her goods online and in craft shows around the state. Because he loved and admired her, he'd learned to share her enthusiasm for treasures from the earth. Their travel, even with friends, had been planned around rock hunting.

Much of their large collection they'd prepared and labeled and displayed in glass cabinets about the house, yet a large back room off the kitchen and several storage areas in the barn were filled with heavy clusters of amethyst crystals, uncracked geodes as big as bowling balls, chunks of quartz, topaz, celestine, and dozens of other trophies they'd never gotten around to breaking and cleaning for display. They were beyond him now. A sort of paralysis gripped him, leaving him unable to make decisions on such matters. His days were empty and solitary. At night he dreamt of rocks. He had a recurring nightmare of rocks bringing down everything—house and barn—all collapsing under the impossible weight.

Peter no longer kept livestock; he leased his hay fields to a neighbor and lived alone with a Labrador retriever named Opal, who loved the freedom of the farm and had never been chained. The farm, even with just a dog, was now a bit too much for him. He was managing daily chores, but slowly and mechanically. His youngest child, a daughter named Beryl, wanted him to sell the farm and live as a part of her family (husband and four hyperactive children) in a nearby city. But what would he do with the rocks—or with Opal? For the time being, he'd decided not to leave behind the farm and all the sweet and bittersweet reminders of his wife, at least until their possessions were taken care of in a satisfactory way, a way she would approve. He'd attended a nearby Lutheran church faithfully for most of his life. He wanted someone who knew him presiding at his funeral and burying him in the Lutheran cemetery beside Amber.

For several weeks Peter had faced another matter. A problem had arisen with the old Henderson farmhouse next door. The place had sat empty and for sale for several years without a buyer. It was a drafty, jerry-built house, with a large, sagging shed just behind it. No sane person would buy it for anything but demolition. Yet a family from the city, he learned, had negotiated to rent the place with an option to buy. The father of the family was large as a bear, heavily bearded, with a fixed scowl that softened only when his two young daughters or his wife were around. That softening was a relief to Peter, who was uneasy with his presence, even from a distance. The man drove a panel truck with painted letters on it that read ROCK, PAPER, SCISSORS – MOBILE SHREDDING. He left early most mornings and came back late, still scowling. He labored evenings trying to repair the countless household defects, but it was clear he lacked the equipment and skills and often lost his temper. Peter wondered if he should offer advice or help, but the man's sour aspect made him hesitant.

One day the man's wife appeared at Peter's porch with her daughters. She introduced them as the Scherers, and she spelled out her name, Charlee. He introduced himself and shook her outstretched hand. She seemed an irrepressibly chirpy, Pollyanna type to Peter; she was certainly neighborly—and very sweet to her two pretty little girls of 7 and 9. The three politely called him Mr. Felsen, carried home-baked cookies for him and sat on his front porch for a half hour or more, explaining that they were home-schooling, that they had left the city for a more wholesome country life, that they hoped to raise chickens and maybe horses, and to grow as much of their own natural organic food as they could.

"We already have a rabbit," Holly, the pig-tailed older girl, said. She had on jeans and blue cowgirl boots. "I show him in 4H."

"We'd rather show horses, though," April, the younger girl added, whistling through half-grown front teeth. "We've had two lessons. And we want to buy two horses for our farm."

The girls sat on the step with Opal, who nudged their hands whenever they stopped petting her.

"Horses take quite a bit of work," Peter said, knowing their place would never do. He'd raised and ridden horses for years—even competed in team penning in his younger days.

"Oh, work doesn't bother us. We plan to build animal care into our home schooling. Right girls?"

They both nodded and Peter nodded in return, not wishing to discourage them. He offered to help Charlee's husband with repairs, if he needed it.

"Zach is pretty good at that kind of stuff," she said. "But I'll certainly let him know you offered."

Zach, as far as he could see, knew as much about home repair as his wife knew about horses. He suspected the house might be unlivable when winter hit but hoped only the best for them and added the family to his daily prayers.

Within a week, the newcomers had acquired a dozen chickens that ran free all over their property and onto Peter's. Opal chased them off, chased them around the neighbor's house, barking with glee as they fluttered and clucked in panic. Peter tried to call her off, but Opal wouldn't listen.

That evening Peter noticed the sour-looking bear of a neighbor bearing down on his house. He met the man at his door.

"You must be Zach," Peter said.

"Yeah, I'm Zach, and I'm here to complain about that dog chasing our chickens."

"My dog? Well...do you plan to let those chickens run free?"

"Of course. We believe in free-range birds. They're healthier and their eggs are better."

"Free-range just means they have access to the outdoors. My dog isn't your problem. She just chases them. Leave those chickens out for a week and foxes and raccoons will get most of them. Hawks will take a few, too. "

"I haven't seen any foxes," he snarled. "Maybe if you kept your dog chained up like normal people do..."

Peter paused a moment, calming his temper. "Can't do that. Opal's a free-range dog. Always has been. You won't see the foxes or raccoons very often. But your chickens will."

"Isn't there an ordinance about not letting dogs run free?"

"Not out here."

"Well—there damn well oughtta be."

Peter looked into the man's narrow dark eyes and took a deep breath. "Your old shed is what those chickens need, with a little door to get to an outside run. I have some rolls of wire fencing in the barn. I know you've got lots of work to do on the house, so I'd be willing to build you a chicken run."

His sour look remained. "Hate to keep them cooped up. It don't seem right."

"The chickens will thank you for it."

"Maybe. I've heard they're dumb as rocks."

"I wouldn't put it that way—not fair to rocks. Truth is, chickens are fairly smart. They have personalities, and they respond to affection. I've even talked to a few in my time. They listen better than most people."

"You're messing with me now." He didn't smile. "But if you wouldn't mind doing that coop, then go ahead. I'll pay you for it."

"It's a housewarming gift."

"Well…whatever. Control that dog of yours, though. I'll file a complaint if I have to."

Charming man, Peter mused, as he watched him lumber back across the yard. This couple seemed a grievous mismatch. They puzzled him.

In a corner of his barn, he had an unused pile of round, 8 foot fence posts and four bundles of wire fencing, enough to do a pasture he'd never gotten around to. He started his tractor, hooked up his ancient flatbed hay trailer, and hauled the stuff over to the old Henderson place the very next morning, soon after Zach's truck was gone. Charlee and the girls came out to greet him and offered him coffee and cinnamon rolls.

Using the auger on his tractor, he had the posts set and a 24 x 24 foot fence with a wood-framed gate up by noon. Then with a drill and his reciprocating saw, he cut a small door that opened on hinges, a place for the chickens to enter and exit the shed. Charlee was full of praise and wonder. He explained to the girls that the chickens needed to be in the shed at night and the small door closed, and then let out in the morning. The run didn't have a top (he told her some netting would work, if they wanted), but the fence was 6 feet high, enough to keep most chickens in and most predators out. As a bonus, he put together a 2 x 4 x 8 rabbit hutch with a hinged top along the outside of the run. He cut a small hole in the fencing for the rabbit to enter and exit the run at will. Peter told them that rabbits and chickens could coexist, if you let them get used to each other. The hutch would allow the rabbit to escape the flock when he needed to.

When the work was done, Charlee, marveling at his efficiency, had him come in for more coffee—Holly poured and April served it to him. Charlee moved a children's Bible opened on the kitchen table, and he sat. The rabbit, a small white creature named Muffin with dark ears and feet, hopped about the room, tried squeezing behind the refrigerator and backed out, dust balls clinging to him. His wire cage sat open in a corner.

"We were just doing a Bible study," Charlee said. "The girls and I are Christians, and we're hoping Zach will become one someday, too. He has a world of cares on his shoulders, and he needs to give them to the Lord. He's got this new document-shredding business that isn't going as well as we'd hoped. Things keep breaking down. He worries about supporting us, but I tell him the Lord will take care of it. For one thing, we'll soon be eating the food we raise."

"Well, you'll be eating it late next summer," Peter said.

She seemed surprised. "I know it's August, but aren't there a few things we could plant now?"

"Afraid not. But I have two apple trees, a peach, and a pear. You're welcome to any fruit you'd like."

"See!" she exclaimed. "The Lord always provides! And we're already getting eggs!"

She invited him to dinner that evening, but he declined. He had things to do, he said. She hesitantly cautioned him that he might not hear from Zach about the work he'd done. Zach was very proud, she said, and hadn't learned to accept the help of others. "It's a character flaw he surely needs to work on."

Peter stood. "I've had plenty of thanks already," he told her. He went home tired—yet pleased with having actually accomplished a sizable task.

A couple of weeks went by. Peter stopped once to check on the run. All seemed well with the chickens, and Muffin was nosing around in the midst of them, nibbling on tufts of grass. Charlee walked with Peter outside the run while the girls scattered feed about on the inside.

"The chickens like their new space," she said. "We can find the eggs with no trouble now. You've been a good friend to us."

"Glad it's working. If there's anything else I can do, let me know." He glanced at the back of the house, the missing shingles, the half dozen or more cracked, single-pane windows, the curled, weather-beaten siding, the sagging wood porch on the verge of collapse, and he felt a wave of pity and exasperation at such blind optimism.

September brought heavy rains. Peter saw Zach trying to tie a tarp on a side roof above a bedroom. The wind was up and Zach couldn't hold down the plastic long enough to tie it. Peter put on his raingear and went over. Together they got the tarp secured.

"We're a sad lot," was all that Zach said, rain dripping from his nose. But Peter heard him mumble, "Thanks." The rain ended after another day, but the "temporary" tarp remained in place. The leaks, after all, had been stopped.

A week later, a dreadful thing happened. Peter had gone to the barn to hunt down a tool when Opal ambled in carrying some kind of critter in her mouth. She approached him and dropped it at his feet. It was a dirty, bedraggled, and very dead rabbit. Peter knelt beside it. He could see the truth immediately: it was Muffin, the girls' pet. That knowledge horrified him. "Oh, Opal, why would you? Oh, my God, you're a bad, bad dog." Opal looked confused and hurt, and she slunk away. Peter's heart rattled in his chest. He could barely breathe for a while and sat down on the ground beside the rabbit. He imagined Zach demanding the killer dog be put down or permanently chained.

"Dear God," he said. "We do need your help."

And as if in answer, a singular idea entered his head.

He lifted the stiff little body, got to his feet, and carried it to the house. In the kitchen, he set Muffin gently on the counter and filled the sink with warm water. Carefully, he washed the carcass with dishwashing soap. The hair turned white again, and he scrubbed the grime from the black ears. With a large bath towel, he dried the rabbit and fluffed up the matted fur with his wife's hair dryer. The faint smell of decay disappeared beneath the scent of lemon soap.

Late that night, when all the Scherer's lights were out, Peter shut Opal in the kitchen and went out carrying Muffin, wrapped up in a towel. The chickens stayed quiet inside the shed. He silently lifted the hinged top of the rabbit hutch and laid the immaculate rabbit inside.

The following day, a Sunday, was Beryl's birthday, so he phoned her after church and listened to her lengthy rationale for his move to the city. A knock at the door saved him, and he abruptly ended the call. To his great distress, a dark hulk loomed on the other side of the door—Zach come for some sort of reckoning.

Peter opened to him, not knowing what to expect but fearing an explosion. But Zach was subdued, no anger apparent in him. If anything, he looked troubled.

"Could I talk to you for a minute, Mr. Felsen?" he asked quietly.

Peter nodded, still on high alert. "Of course, Zach. Come in and have some coffee."

The big man followed Peter to the kitchen, glancing at glass cabinets of their rock collections as he went. "What are these?" he asked.

"Oh—my wife taught high school geology. We collected rocks and minerals for years—mostly semi-precious stuff. Maybe your girls would like some of these for home school. Amber—my wife—died 18 months ago. Now I'm left with more than I know what to do with."

They sat down at the kitchen table. Peter poured two coffees.

"I'm sorry to hear about your wife," Zach said. "We wondered." He went silent for a bit, seemingly in thought. "Sure, your rocks would be a help to us. I can't imagine how ignorant we must seem." He stared at his hands. "Charlee is the sweetest woman in the world, and I love her dearly, but she is dead set on living the country life and home schooling our girls. First off, neither one of us knows a thing about farms. The house is a wreck, and I don't have time to fix it because I'm trying to start a business. Then she wants horses, too! Jesus, some days I feel like I'm losing my mind."

Peter began dimly to comprehend the man's anger and frustration. "I could help you with the house part, if you'll let me. I'm not farming any more."

Zach shook his head, but without the usual stubbornness. "I have a hard time with that, since I got no way of paying you back, but maybe you could bring over your rocks some time and do a little science with the girls. That would help. Charlee got through eleventh grade but that's all. She can't do much math or spell very well. I just found out she can't even read a tape measure. She knows the Bible backwards and forwards, but that's about all the reading she does. I can't imagine what she'll do with science. I'm in a fix, Mr. Felsen. I want our girls to grow up smarter than us. They need to go to school. But I also want to give my wife the things she wants, and all my trying just seems to get us deeper in trouble."

Peter looked hard at the man and for the first time felt compassion. "Of course I'll do some science with your girls. I know enough, I think. Not like my wife, of course."

Zach sat silent, staring into his coffee. He looked as if he still had something to get out. It took some time, but finally he said, "I've really come here for another reason that has me about half crazy. I need to talk to somebody." Still staring at his coffee, he cleared emotion from his voice. "A couple of mornings ago, see, I found the girls' little rabbit dead in his cage—old age, I think—he was at least eight or nine. So I took him out in the woods and buried him before they got up and saw him. Well, they've been crying for two days because of it, and because we didn't have a burial service with some Christian words. I told them those words weren't meant to cover rabbits. Animals don't go to heaven as far as I know. Anyway, I tried and couldn't even find where I'd buried him. But just this morning I walked out by the hutch, and, good God in heaven, there was Muffin lying there fluffy and clean, white as snow, as if halfway to being an angel. It shook me so that I just backed away and left him lying there."

Peter listened in a daze.

"Are you a religious man, Mr. Felsen?"

Peter coughed and cleared his throat. "Yes, I'd say I am."

"What do you make of this?"

Peter thought about telling the truth, but for his dear dog's sake he decided never, ever to do it. "Well…you see…I think maybe you need to do a proper Christian burial. I think animals have souls. You've left important things unfinished."

Zach thought long about this and finally nodded. "It's surely a sign to me. Charlee has been praying for me from the time we first met. I think I've finally seen a glimpse of what she's been talking about."

"Yes, I think you have." Peter said, exhaling heavily and glancing at Opal asleep under a coffee table.

"Mr. Felsen, I'd appreciate it if you'd come along with us and say some words at the burial. Would you do that?"

Peter could hardly say no.

So that afternoon he said a few lines from Ecclesiastes about a time to be born and a time to die and then the Lord's Prayer over a small grave marked with a heavy chunk of amethyst crystals, noting Zach's bowed head and the tears in his eyes.

The next day was Monday, a school day, and Peter carried several boxed collections to the Scherer's place, all properly labeled, and gave them to the girls along with a handbook of rocks and minerals. Charlee was unusually quiet during his teaching, and once he'd done lessons on three occasions, she admitted to him she wasn't near smart enough to teach except for the Bible. It was a stunning bit of personal honesty.

She and Zach enrolled the girls in a public school. The girls caught the school bus out front and quickly made up the weeks they'd missed.

Peter had an idea and dug out Amber's jewelry-making tools and supplies and gave them to Charlee, who soon discovered a gift for such things and a way to help her family. He assured her of an unending flow of materials.

In the spring, at Peter's advice, the Scherers did not buy but leased two mild-mannered, aging horses from the friend who worked his hayfields and kept a small stable and outdoor arena nearby, a deal made only if Peter agreed to be with them to oversee and teach. This was miles beyond any commitment he wanted, but he couldn't find a way to say no, and in the end was pleased he hadn't.

Zach's business still scratched along, but began to pick up little by little, largely due to his personality change. He had become a more pleasant man, especially when Charlee's jewelry began bringing in enough to pay the utilities that winter.

Peter had never been a proselytizer. He didn't like telling people what to believe. But in the case of Zach, he took a certain pride in knowing that, at least once, he'd helped God work His mysterious ways.

UNDER THE PIANO

He was in a wilderness so deep that only threads of light came through the giant trees. He was drenched but not cold. His canoe and fishing equipment were gone—launched over a waterfall of maybe twelve feet where no waterfall had been before. He'd gone over with the canoe, but somehow saved himself by clinging to rocks and struggling to shore. The shoreline was overgrown and impossible to follow. So he took the only option and set off through the heavy trees, hoping to find his way out of this hinterland. He was bruised and shaken but not afraid, at least not yet. The woods were damp and fragrant, and a breeze made hushed music in the leaves and pine needles.

He walked for what seemed several hours until weariness crept into his legs. His clothes were dry now, but he felt an uneasy chill. He sat down to rest against an ancient, twisted cedar trunk and closed his eyes. Momentarily, he reopened them to see ahead of him a pool of sunlight, visible through the weave of limbs, a clearing of some sort. He stood and made his way toward it with a brisk step. He pushed through a thick stand of tamaracks to find himself gazing at a field of glimmering gold. It lay like soft quilting over acres of rolling hills, surrounding a farmhouse tucked in a valley with a large green barn and white silo. All of it was deeply familiar. He skirted the edge of the wheat with seed heads heavy and ready for harvest and found the tractor path that wound down to the barn.

Ahead on the path appeared a person obscured by sunlight. As they neared each other, he recognized her—a slender young woman in a blue summer dress, her long yellow hair tied in a blue bandana. She was unchanged in spite of all the years. Her beauty pierced him like a sword, and his heart filled to overflowing with sorrow and inexpressible loss.

She came to him and reached for his hand. "So here you are at long last." Her smile shone with love, her voice as pure and golden as her hair. "Where have you been, Danny?"

"Far away," he said aloud, startled at being lightly shaken by an old woman in the seat next to his.

"We're getting ready to land," she said. "Sorry to waken you. The seat belt sign is on."

He cleared his throat, hoping to clear his head as well. "Thank you," he told her. "I was having quite a dream."

"I thought as much. You were making odd sounds."

"Sorry."

"Oh, no bother. Are you from Detroit?"

"No. Traverse City. One more connection before I'm home. My mother is ill. I haven't been home for a long time."

"I'm sorry. Is it serious?"

He buckled his seatbelt as the flight attendant passed by. "Old age. Dementia. The usual. She was a marvelous pianist in her day."

"That's sad. I wish you well on your mission."

Their conversation ended. She stiffened and gripped her armrests as the plane descended. Was it indeed a mission he was on? He wasn't at all sure why he was going home. Variations of the dream had haunted him for months and seemed to be drawing him back to something hidden yet stirring in the shadows of his subconscious. Was it the girl, Elise, his first and sweetest love, whom he'd let slip away long ago? Or something else he'd valued and lost due to careless judgment? He was aware of personal losses, a fair number (his marriage, for instance), but had always been able to balance the ledger with successes. In his mind he had done well with his talent, though not as stunningly as he'd hoped. His was a second line success, but still more than most of his friends had achieved. In Traverse City he was Danny Ross, the celebrity, or so his family had told him.

His sister May met him at the small county airport. She was five years his senior, a first grade teacher whom he hadn't seen in at least a dozen years. Though she was in her early 50s now, her gaunt, aging face shocked him. She'd been married, and like himself childless, but her husband had left her several years ago for a much younger woman. Her once-soft smile now had a strain to it, but he embraced her warmly, meaning it.

"Hello, May. I've missed you."

She separated from him a bit. "We've missed you, too, Danny."

"How is mom?"

"I'm afraid you won't know her." She peered a bit too long into his eyes, as if to dramatize her meaning. This was a new, less comfortable sister than he'd left years before.

He located his single bag, and they headed to her car, a nondescript Ford sedan. In Los Angeles, he drove a BMW but owned an antique Jaguar as well. May drove carefully, hands tight on the wheel, winding around the south shoreline of Grand Traverse Bay, up into the west hills toward his childhood home. They made small talk about changes in the town.

Though there were new resorts and expensive homes on the bay, much seemed the same as when he'd left it. The familiar views, the fresh wind off the water, the gulls dipping and crying out, were like remembering music he'd loved but forgotten…his mother's music, especially. He was known to be a bit odd as a child (he loved church), with odd whims, one of which was lying under his mother's grand piano as she played. He could feel the hammers striking the strings, the vibrating soundboard exciting the air. He could *feel* the music in his skin and bones. It was palpable. He loved to watch her small right foot, often bare, on the damper pedal, sustaining the chords. Her thin forearms glided together like long-necked birds, and though he couldn't see her fingers from this vantage point, he had watched them many times from above, more nimble and athletic than his fingers would ever be. She had taught privately; he was one of her students as was May (far more disciplined), and he had learned to play respectably, though his gifts, he would find, lay elsewhere.

The house was a simple white farmhouse on four acres of land. From the upstairs windows, on a bright, clear day, he had always been able to see a tiny slice of the bay. As May parked by a side porch, he noticed immediately that the elaborate gardens his father had planned and planted were now mainly mowed grass with ragged, untrimmed edges. His father had died years before, moments after Danny had gotten off the bus from his second day of fourth grade. His father was kneeling, pulling weeds from the marigolds. He dropped his head as if in prayer, tilted sideways, and settled quietly into his flowers. Danny had watched, confused. He called to him but got no answer. When he found the courage to touch his father's face, it was still warm, but the half-shut eyes, unfocused and empty, told the truth.

His father had been a simple man, a carpenter and cabinetmaker who adored his young wife, spent most of the inheritance from his own father on her grand piano. His father's garden had been a place of peace and joy to Danny. He loved the solitude and beauty of it and of the nearby woods. He loved canoeing alone and fishing trout streams. His mother and he had kept up the garden until he'd gone off to college. By then, his sister had a degree, a local teaching job, and she took over his part of that grubby, rewarding work.

His mother had played with the Grand Rapids Symphony before she'd married and moved north. Once established in Traverse City, she was the first booked to accompany guest artists, both classical and jazz, who came through town. She'd played in restaurants and bars, was sought after for private lessons. She was admired if not famous. With her husband's death, life became more difficult, less joyfully simple, and Danny quietly resented it. Necessity pushed his mother into a music director's job at the Presbyterian Church where she'd dragged in her children to sing duets. Danny had a voice, they discovered. It would take him onto the stage and briefly into film where he became interested in writing and found his passion, found success.

May led him into the kitchen, had him sit down at the table, and poured two glasses of wine. "Mom's home care nurse took her to the neurologist. I usually would do it, but I was meeting you. I live here now."

"You sold your house?"

"I did, a few months ago. I thought I'd wait to tell you. She needs me here at this point. By the way, thanks for your help with her expenses."

He took a sip of wine. "I'm sorry, May. I've left you with a lot to handle. I didn't realize how involved it'd gotten."

"Well…we're in a sort of rhythm now. But it's hard. You'll

see." She smiled and touched her wine glass to his. "So here you are at long last. We've missed you, Danny. Our golden boy. Mom subscribes to *Variety*, so we get news of you fairly often. It sounds like an exciting life."

"It often is, yes. Too many cooks in the kitchen, though." In truth, the messy, collaborative nature of film work was weighing on him these days, though the enduring ease of the lifestyle did much to compensate for it.

"We've loved some of your films."

"Me, too. Some. "

"You should move back here and write a book."

He smiled at the thought. It was appealing. "I should. I know. Artistic freedom. Fresh air. Blue water. Six months of ice and snow."

She laughed. "Better for a writer, I'd think, than year-round swimming pools."

He sighed and nodded his agreement. From the kitchen window he could see one of several apple trees his father had planted. The leaves were brown-spotted and the small apples scabbed and misshapen.

"Do you remember Elise Brown?" he asked.

"How could I forget? I loved her. I thought you were an idiot to break up with her, Danny. Her parents still have the farm, but I hear they're going to sell. Elise is gone—married a minister and moved to Ohio...or maybe Iowa."

This news was curiously painful. "A minister? Good grief."

"We once thought you were headed in that direction."

"The ministry? Well...I was a pious child." His laugh was a bit thin. "It all made sense to me then."

"Mom still has your Sunday school attendance medals."

He smiled and rolled his eyes. "She was the music director. We *had* to go to church." He took a long swig of the wine—Riesling from a local vineyard. It was surprisingly good. Not Californian, but the old place seemed to be coming on in ways.

He remembered his last time with Elise. It was Thanksgiving break during his freshman year at the University of Michigan. He'd gone to her house for dessert after his own family gathering. Elise was in a nursing program at the local community college. They hadn't seen each other since late August. She seemed shy and in awe of his theater work at school. None of them—her parents or her—had heard of the Jacques Brel show he was doing. They listened to his explanations, but their questions seemed naïve and provincial. At Christmas he hadn't bothered calling her, and that was mostly the end of it.

May uncovered a cutting board of crackers and Brie and set it next to his wine glass. "Being sacked from the church was a blow to mom. But she was 73, and they called it a retirement. She'd already shown some memory problems, but the crux of it was a young new minister who wanted praise music—you know, electric guitars, keyboard, drums. The whole disaster."

"Good God."

"She still had some private students, thank goodness. But in a couple of years, she couldn't do it any more."

"Does she still play?"

"Not at all."

His chest felt heavy. "All the music, all the muscle memory. Jesus, May…"

"I know. She doesn't even know me half the time. But there are occasional good moments. Don't get your hopes too high, though, Danny. You've been away a long time."

The home care nurse, a young, attractive redhead who looked in her mid-20s, held his mother's arm as they entered the side door into the kitchen. Her name was Molly. May introduced them. His mother, blank and spectral, was an unearthly white—both skin and hair. The woman who had been their strength for years was now a haunted scarecrow. He took a deep breath and glanced at May. Molly led her to a chair beside Danny, and she sat down. Her physical movements, though slow, appeared moderately normal.

"Hello, mom," he said.

She looked at him without recognition.

"Danny's come home to visit," May said. "He's staying a few days with us."

His mother looked at him. "Hello," she said. "Are you visiting?"

"Yes, I'm visiting. May and I have been catching up and having something to eat."

"Is it time to eat?"

"Not yet, mom," May said. "I just picked up Danny at the airport. We're having a snack to tide him over."

"Are *you* visiting?"

"I live here, mom. I'm May, your daughter."

An awkward silence ensued, in the midst of which the young nurse asked, "Are you tired, Grace?"

"I think I'd like to lie down."

With gentleness and extreme patience, especially from someone so young, Molly helped her toward the bedroom.

"Molly's a gem," May said once the bedroom door had closed.

That evening, after a dinner his mother had eaten slowly and with odd, irritating difficulty, May ushered them into the living room and left Danny there with her, saying only "Give a shout if you need me." The two sat on either end of a worn leather couch. The grand piano stood across from them.

"Mom," he said with a bright, determined voice. "Would you play something? I love your playing."

She looked perplexed. "Why are you calling me mom?"

He reached across and touched her hand. She pulled away. "Sit at the piano with me a minute?"

"I don't think so."

"Dad bought it for you."

She sat, thinking. "Yes, he did." A moment of hesitation, and she stood and went to the bench. He rose and took a seat beside her. "I don't play," she insisted.

He carefully took her right hand and lifted it to the keys. "Just stretch out your fingers."

She shook her head but didn't seem upset. Her fingers rested in slight hollows she herself had worn over many years. She seemed to recognize the feel of them. She spread her fingers wider and tentatively pressed the keys—a B flat chord. Surprised, she moved her hand a bit and played a C chord. "You do remember," he said.

"I don't play."

She tentatively struck several more chords, put her left hand to the keys and began a halting tune. He recognized "This is My Father's World." She kept on as the music slowly came back to her. She closed her eyes. Without pause, she moved into "Morning Has Broken," but with more assurance.

On impulse, Danny slipped to the floor, stretching out under the piano. The strings and soundboard resonated through his body. He watched her small, slippered foot moving on the damper pedal.

"Danny," she said. "Stop being silly. You're too big to be doing that."

He was thrilled at hearing his name and the amused clarity of her voice. For a moment the years fell away. "I can feel the music here, mom."

She laughed and played on. He saw May standing in the kitchen doorway, observing with wide, unbelieving eyes. She moved toward the piano, piecing together the words to the hymn. Under the piano, he rose on an elbow and joined her. Thirty years, and they could still harmonize—they sang through all three verses, yet his mother played on. Tears brightened May's eyes. Emotional himself, Danny looked away from May and kept singing, returning to the words of the first verse. At the end of it, his mother took a deep breath and smiled. She stopped playing and lowered her hands to her lap. He felt heroic.

And then she spoke. "Some suffer. Some don't," his mother said, distress invading her voice. "Some care. Others won't. You learn it in Sunday school."

Coming out from under the piano, he watched as her eyes emptied. He got to his feet, distressed by this metamorphosis, by her enigmatic words. He'd worked a miracle a moment ago, and now it had evaporated.

"May?"

"She can still play. I'm amazed."

"I was betting she could. It's the magic of music."

"Such a wonderful, lucid moment." May smiled sadly. "You made it happen. It was you." She touched his shoulder. "How I wish it could last, but there's no fairytale fix, Danny." She helped her silent, vacant mother to her feet. "I'll get you settled in your room, mom." May gently led her away.

The moment *had* been magical, but not at all the sort of outcome he'd envisioned. This was bleak. A few moments of clarity had come of it—for his mother, at least, if not for him. Hope had soared sky high and then crashed to earth—dramatically wrong—yet the way things seemed to be in this place. Something vital was missing here, or perhaps missing in him.

Standing rigid, feeling inadequate and somehow bereft, he made the sudden, magnanimous decision to stay a week, not just three days, and help May with her loving, thankless labors. Danny could manage a week of it, he was almost certain. The fair Molly might even provide some pleasant company while May was teaching.

He sat in the kitchen for a while, drinking wine, waiting for May. From the bedroom he heard his mother shriek something forlorn and unintelligible. He heard May's voice calming her, calming her, and finally silence.

May appeared in the kitchen, shaking her head. "She gets upset with feeling lost," she explained. "She finds a moment of light and then it's gone." She looked bone weary, said no to the wine, but seemed gladdened at news of his new plans. She whispered goodnight, kissed his forehead and went upstairs. He now felt almost good about his impulsiveness.

Yet when he'd settled into his childhood bed for the night, staring out at the slice of moonlight on the bay, hearing the shriek of an owl (not unlike his mother's) in a nearby tree, he began to sense the disturbing barrenness of his own heart—like an impassable wasteland barring him from all that was once Danny Ross.

PIOUS LIES

The first fracture in my youthful sense of father's omnipotence came while I watched a television rerun of *Harry Potter and the Chamber of Secrets*. It happened at the moment I noticed that Dobby the house elf had a strange habit of referring to himself in the third person. "Dobby has come to protect Harry Potter," was the way Dobby spoke.

"That's the way my father talks!" I said aloud. I'd never considered the peculiarity of it before. If I would ask something like, "Want to try some of my carrot cake?" my father would reply, "No, Zoe, your father doesn't care for carrot cake." On the phone to a church secretary he'd tell her, "Pastor Ned has a doctor's appointment at 10 today. He won't be in until noon." He'd been doing it (on and off) for as long as I could remember, and after identifying the oddity, it began seriously grating on my nerves—in part because I was discovering it was not a trait unique to my father and Dobby. Reading and writing were my passions in high school, so I was paying attention to language, even getting picky about it. Donald Trump spoke of himself in third person all the time. A character in a *Seinfeld* episode did it. Some superstar sports heroes like LeBron James did it. Elmo, the furry red monster on *Sesame Street* did it, much in the fashion of Dobby. It was downright weird. What did it mean?

My father was a pastor, or more accurately, an interim pastor, a job for which he had been specially trained. He took over the leadership of churches seeking a new minister. He stayed at a church (except in unusual cases) a year or less, helping congregations through the transition, conducting services, advising the search committees about the protocol of the search, the interviews, the call, and so on. I knew he didn't make much money—we always seemed to be scraping by—but he drove a nice car and dressed in expensive dark suits, concerned always about his image. My mother, on the other hand, drove a twelve-year-old van and made most of her own clothing and some of mine. She earned extra money working as a teacher's aide in elementary and middle schools.

My father at times was hired by nearby churches, so then mother and I could attend his services. Much of the time, though, his job was halfway across the state, and we often saw him only once a week or less. Then we'd attend the Presbyterian church my mother had grown up in.

Even at a young age, I saw obvious advantages to the interim ministry. My father had a small library of sermons and favorite stories that he could recycle at each new place he went. His favorite sermon was one entitled "Arrows," based on a story he loved telling of his barnstorming great-grandfather who worked as an early airmail pilot, flying from New York to San Francisco and back in the 1920s, before planes had navigational systems. The U.S Postal Service developed a solution to navigation called the U.S Airmail Beacons System, involving 70 foot concrete arrows painted bright yellow and lighted by revolving beacons on 50 foot towers. These giant arrows and beacons were built 15 miles apart (less in the mountains) on air routes across the country. From 3000 feet, pilots could see from one arrow to the next the entire way from coast to coast. "A century later," my father would exclaim, "hundreds of these guiding arrows still exist, one on our family farm!"

I'd heard that sermon half a dozen times or more. It was his favorite, and it had, like all sermon stories, a spiritual point. He was blessed with something resembling the voice of God—deep, sonorous, and full of authority—and he seemed to love hearing the sound of it.

"How wonderful it would be," he would rhapsodize, his eyes raised, his bald head gleaming in the pulpit spotlights, "if the faith journey were so clearly marked. Pastor Ned has often lost sight of those arrows in fog, in clouds, in times of darkness—as he's sure every one of you has done at one time or another. But the arrows are there still, my friends— are there pointing to our destination. This holy book—" and he raised his leather Bible above his head—"this wonderful book…provides the surest arrows we will ever find."

I could have recited that last part by heart. The message seemed to move people. But the airmail history behind it was what fascinated me. Could my unremarkable family actually have raised up an adventurer with that kind of daring? The closest my father had ever gotten to a cockpit, as far as I knew, was his office chair.

Still, I had grown up thinking of him as formidable. He wasn't a warm man, yet people treated him with an overabundance of respect and went to him to solemnize their weddings and funerals, to grace the bedsides of their sick and dying. He was not at all like a regular father. My mother, younger, prettier and much nicer than I felt he deserved, was the one getting me places, talking me through problems, helping me with homework, and supporting me in sports. Father was forever working on church business and was not to be disturbed. Or he was off working in another town. He loved being a man of authority, and for a long time I feared him. His disapproval, which I'd suffered a number of times, was suffocating. My mother lived in his shadow, yet his power over her was limited in ways I didn't understand. In her quiet, unassuming manner, she exercised a measure of control, and he often bowed to her wishes. Their marriage was a mystery to me.

I was serious about school and sports (soccer and basketball) and tried to avoid boyfriends, fearing my father's disfavor. I'd been to a few dances, a church group hayride or two, but my romantic experiences were nothing to talk about. One boy, however, intrigued me—a Latvian student named Valdis Edgars who'd recently moved to America with his family and played soccer like no one else in school. Colleges were scouting him, and so was I in my timid way—a way so subtle he hardly noticed me. He wore his long dark hair tied back and a Latvian morning star (his teammate explained it to me) tattooed on his forearm. He spoke with a pleasant lilting accent and rode to school on an old British motorcycle. Though not very outgoing, he attracted admirers with his elegant ferocity on the soccer field.

I was among them. He seemed to have no weakness in soccer. He wrote left-handed in class, but I could not see the left dominance in his kicking. He could send a ball screaming into the goal with either foot. I was right dominant and struggled daily with a weak left side, forever trying to get it out of the way of my right. The problem was even worse in basketball. I felt as if a clumsy, inept version of myself occupied the left half of me. She couldn't kick, dribble, make shots, throw a ball, write in longhand, or even manage simple tasks like brushing teeth. She exasperated me because she seemed resistant to training.

Valdis Edgars and I happened to share the same English comp class in the spring of our junior year. Mr. Henry, my favorite English teacher, assigned us a research paper, a large portion of which was to be done with personal interviews as a resource. Though I hated research papers, I found myself growing excited because my subject already lay at my fingertips—my heroic great-great-grandfather, the U.S. Airmail Beacons System, and those giant arrows pointing the way across America. My father could serve as my chief resource, and possibly direct me to others who would help. Mr. Henry approved enthusiastically. That same day he caught me as I was leaving the building.

"Zoe, I need a favor. Valdis Edgars has never written an American-style research paper. You have a gift for such stuff. I've told him that I'd speak to you about helping him navigate the assignment." His bright, hopeful smile was flattering. "He means a lot to our soccer team, you know."

I was dazed. Nervously, I said, "That's nice of you to think of me, Mr. Henry. Are you sure I'm the right one? I don't really know him."

"He's quite friendly," he assured me. "An interesting young man. Yes, I'm certain you're the one to do it."

I nodded sheepishly. My sudden good fortune seemed almost more than my nervous system could handle.

At the time, my father was pastoring at a church two hours north, so he drove home after his service each Sunday and back mid-day on Tuesday. I caught him reading in his office on a Sunday evening and explained the research project I wanted to do. I expected his response to be enthusiastic, possibly even excited; instead he seemed perturbed.

"Zoe, dear," he said in an unnaturally controlled voice, "your father believes that it is his story to tell, not yours."

I was shocked. "But, dad, it's so interesting. My plan is to interview you about it. You'll be my primary resource. I can't think of anyone else who knows the details."

He pondered that for a moment, folded his hands and pressed two fingers to his lips. "That's probably true. But your father would prefer you didn't offer a private family story to the general public."

"But my English teacher will be the only one reading it."

"Well, you can't know that for sure." He smiled bleakly and turned back to his reading, ending our discussion. I drifted out of the room, confused at this incomprehensible reaction.

After school on Tuesday, knowing he was safely gone, I talked to my mother about the matter. She nodded as if not surprised.

"I say do it without your father. He can't control such things."

"But he's my main interview."

She had me sit down at the kitchen table while she poured me an orange juice. She got coffee for herself and sat down beside me. "Well, there is someone else in his family who might be able to help. We'd have to call her and see. You have a great-aunt who lives about four hours away in northern Illinois. Aunt Olive is her name—your father's aunt and your paternal grandfather's sister. She must be over 80 by now— the only one of that generation left."

I'd never heard of her. "If she's part of the family, why don't we ever see her?"

My mother took a sip of coffee. "She never cared much for your father. He doesn't say a word about her, so I guess the feeling is mutual. She still lives on the farm where one of those arrows is located. Her grandfather built the place. He was the man your father's story is about."

"Then she'll know the things I need!"

"If her memory is still good, I'm guessing she will. I have to warn you, she's a crusty old maid who speaks her mind. The few times we met, though, she and I did all right. Call it a mutual understanding of your father."

My hopes rose, and I agreed to make the trip and tell father nothing of it. My mother found her phone number in an old address book. After nine or ten rings, Aunt Olive answered the phone, seemed confused at first until she understood who mother was, then was pleased about the prospect of a visit from her grand-niece. I listened with my ear next to my mother's. "It'll be nice to meet the child once before I die," she said. "It'll be pleasant to see you, too, Alice."

I could see from mother's reaction that this was unexpected. But she quickly adapted, "Yes, it will, Aunt Olive. Ned won't be along, of course. He has a church up north to see to."

I was hugely relieved that the plot now involved the two of us. I'd only had my license a year and wasn't confident about the drive, and even less so about confronting Aunt Olive on my own. We made a plan. Weekend after next, the two of us would leave on Friday right after school, hope for the best with the van, stay overnight at the farm, and return before dark on Saturday. We'd share the driving and if father called (he rarely did), we'd have our cell phones. And unless the car broke down, he'd never know about our trip—that is, unless he read my research paper. The possibility didn't weigh heavily on me. At this point, he hadn't shown much interest in the things I wrote.

The next Monday I had my first meeting with Valdis Edgars after school in Mr. Henry's empty classroom. The room was my haven in high school. Posters of Mr. Henry's favorite books (*The Hobbit*, *The Book Thief*, *The Great Gatsby*, a dozen others) brightened the walls. A reading corner invited us with soft chairs and pots for tea and coffee. Student writing hung in display on the bulletin boards. The room was designed to make us feel like writers, and Mr. Henry insisted that we were. It was a warm day in early May, yet I sat trembling. Valdis appeared at the door, leaned in, and smiled.

"Zoe?" he asked. "Very good to meet you. You have a poem on the bulletin board. I like it." He came in briskly, loaded down with books. He set them on a chair and shook my hand. He wore a short-sleeved soccer jersey that had SKONTO RIGA printed on it.

I saw his tattoo and studied it a moment.

"Do you like tattoos?" he asked.

"Pretty well."

"Do you have one?"

"No. My father would have a heart attack."

He laughed. "My father has a larger tattoo than I do." He sat down beside me.

"What is SKONTO RIGA?"

"My father's football team in Latvia. He played, but now he's retired. Your General Electric Company hired him to design wind turbines."

"Did he teach you to play?"

"Of course. You play, too—I've seen you."

My face grew warm. "I was hoping you hadn't."

He smiled wryly. "You do pretty well."

For something to say, I told him about the inept person living in the left side of me. He thought it was very funny. "Mine lives on the right," he said.

"You don't have one. You're brilliant with both feet."

"It's an illusion. I'm never as good with my right. I never quite trust it. But I've trained that useless part of me so it usually does what I say. My father showed me how."

"Could you show someone else?"

"Do you mean you? Why not?"

We talked on and on—more than I'd ever talked to a boy. I glanced at the clock and was shocked to find it was five o'clock. The time had passed in a flash, yet in that space we'd found a subject for his research paper—training the non-dominant foot for soccer—and a primary resource, his father, a professional authority. We'd also found a little something more, I hoped, but was wary of getting ahead of myself.

A janitor came into the room, saw us, and went out again. We both laughed.

"I've kept you too long," he said. "How do you go home?"

"I walk."

"Come on, let's have a ride."

He had a helmet but made me wear it. I sat behind him on the motorcycle, my books in a backpack, wrapped my arms around him, and away we flew. His hair came untied and blew in my face. The engine screamed each time he accelerated. I was petrified and locked him in a death grip... rejoicing in the dizzying rush.

Father saw him through the front window—the tattoo, the wild hair, the battered motorcycle. I got off the bike windblown and flushed, pulled off the helmet, gave Valdis a quick hug, and waved as he roared away.

I said hello to my father as I went in.

His look was stern, but I barely glanced at him. "Who, may I ask, was that unruly-looking character?"

I hurried past. "A foreign student. I'm tutoring him in English."

I could feel him stiffen. "Well, what am I to think of that?" There it was—the leaden weight of his disapproval. It was no surprise. The surprise was that he had referred to himself in the first person rather than the third.

"I don't really know, father. You shouldn't think anything. He's very smart and very nice. He's from Latvia. I only met him today."

I went into the kitchen where my mother, lifting a casserole from the oven, flashed me an uncertain smile.

Valdis Edgars and I met twice more after school that week. Both times he took me by motorcycle to a park beside the wide river that meanders through the center of our town. Soccer and baseball fields were scattered along the shoreline. He showed me juggling drills for my left foot, dribbling drills, single leg balance exercises, single leg squats. We ran parallel to each other, passing and shooting using only our weak sides. After a half dozen tries, I managed to hit the goal with a strong left kick. He cheered and tumbled to the grass to rest. Elated, I flopped down beside him.

"You learn very fast," he said. "It helps me, too. It works well for practice—me being dominant left and you dominant right. If we could somehow be joined together—well, just imagine it. What a soccer player! It makes me think of a certain poem Mr. Henry read us. It was about marriage, I think, but it fits my thought: joined together we would be 'like an arch, two weaknesses leaning into a strength.' Remember?"

"Yes," I said, thrilled, knowing there was not another boy in the school or maybe the whole world who could quote John Ciardi. "It's beautiful."

He smiled and looked up at the blue sky. I stared at his face, the high cheek bones, the strong Roman nose, and felt myself free falling from a mountain top.

Of course, now I had no desire to leave town, but my mother and I were committed. Aunt Olive's farm was near LaSalle, Illinois, and surrounded by newly planted fields. The house was an old, well-kept rustic white farmhouse with a huge front porch. The large unpainted barn sagged along the center roof beam but was still in use. I could see stacked hay bales through the open barn doors. We'd arrived about seven in the evening and found that Aunt Olive, a spry, wiry, wisp of a woman with a loose bun of streaky gray hair, had waited dinner for us. We'd stopped at McDonalds an hour before but didn't tell her—so we slowly stuffed ourselves with fried chicken, biscuits and gravy, followed by rhubarb pie she'd baked that day.

As the sun dropped low in the sky, we went out to the porch with cups of tea and sat in white wicker chairs. Her plowed fields, flat as tabletops, stretched half a mile in each direction. She told us the farm was 160 acres and now mostly leased by neighbors for corn and soybeans.

She turned to me, looked me over, and then announced, "Well, Zoe, thank God you got your mother's fetching looks. You're not the least like Ned." She patted my mother's knee. "Alice, I could never figure out what you saw in that man."

My mother laughed and sipped her tea. "Oh, well, I was just a farm girl and he was older and educated and very sure of himself."

"Honestly, I could have warned you. He grew up just down the road—a damned nuisance as a boy, forever tattling on people, bragging about things he didn't do. He wasn't much liked by other kids...sort of a puffed up little weasel. You could tell he was an only child. My brother and his wife spoiled him rotten." She shook her head and stared out across the fields. Then she sighed heavily. "Of course I also know he ended up a pastor, so you must've had some sort of improving influence on him."

"I hope I did," my mother said, glancing uneasily at me.

"You still deserved better." She turned her deep-set eyes on me. "Oh, hell—forgive my sharp tongue, Zoe. Here I am telling stories about your father's disagreeable boyhood. I'm sure he's different now."

I had no idea what to say, so I smiled a little and stayed quiet. As the silence grew uncomfortable, my mother took the subject elsewhere. "Aunt Olive, I told you on the phone that Zoe's here to interview you for a school project. We could start now, if you'd like."

Aunt Olive nodded, her head bobbing loosely on her skinny neck. "Glad to help if I can. You want to know about that giant arrow out there in the west field." She pointed toward the sunset, and I could faintly make out light gleaming on what looked like a long concrete driveway. I asked her if I could record her voice on my cell phone, and she didn't mind. She sat back in her chair, looked out toward the west, and started her story. "Way back in the 1920s and 30s, before my time, those big arrows pointed the way east and west for mail planes. There used to be a tall steel tower with a beacon light on it right by our arrow, but they tore that down in the 40s to use for war materials. I've got a family album with some pictures of it as it once was. They used to keep emergency landing fields every 50 miles or so. Those pilots were crazy as loons, flying from coast to coast in all weather just to move the mail faster."

Fascinated, I leaned toward her. "Did your grandmother worry much about it?"

She looked puzzled. "About the mail getting here? I don't think so."

"No—about your grandfather flying across the country."

"Beg your pardon?"

I glanced at my mother who was now staring at the porch floor. I felt my face heat up. "I heard a story about your grandfather being one of those daredevil airmail pilots…"

She laughed. "You must be talking about a man over in Princeton. I think he flew for a couple of years. Don't recall his name. My grandfather was a farmer—never got off the ground in his whole life. Who told you he did?"

"We must have heard the story wrong," my mother said.

It only took Aunt Olive a second to understand some subtle thing that I didn't. "Damn, Zoe, I hope this won't spoil your project. I can still tell you all about how the airmail operated. And I've got lots of photographs. You could get a picture of that big arrow out in my field…"

She talked, and we toured through the whole next morning. I took multiple photos of the arrow—viewed best from the loft of the barn. Aunt Olive managed to find the name of the pilot from Princeton in an ancient news clipping saved in an album. I didn't leave empty-handed, thankfully, but it wasn't the story I'd come to write.

Heading home, my mother and I were quiet for the first few miles. She drove, and I stared out at the highway. At last she said, "She's quite a character, isn't she?"

I looked over at her, but her eyes didn't leave the road. "Yeah. She sure doesn't think much of dad. Tell me honestly, did he make up the story about his great-grandfather?"

We traveled another space in silence. Finally, she pulled into a rest area, stopped, turned off the engine, and slumped down in her seat.

"This was a long drive just to make a point, but I wanted you to find out for yourself, Zoe. Just telling you wasn't enough."

My insides felt hollow as a steel drum. "How many more of his stories are like that?"

"I don't know...most of them, I think. He tells me he's making them better from a spiritual perspective. Adding color to a story, according to him, is common practice in the ministry. Maybe it's like what a fiction writer does. Your father's usually the hero, of course. That bothers me a bit—but I've seen some of his stories turn out quite helpful to people. I guess I'd rather think of the good he's done than be bitter about his failings."

"But he's a liar, mom." My sense of my father was recalibrating so fast that I felt dizzy and nauseated.

She had her hands laced together, squeezing and squeezing. "Some time ago he showed me a quote from Martin Luther. It said, 'What harm if a man tells a strong lie for the sake of good?'"

"Martin Luther didn't say that."

"He did. I looked it up to be sure."

"That's terrible...that's saying the ends justify the means."

"I know, honey. Anyway, your father's nervous about you—afraid you're too smart...that you won't approve."

The thought was staggering—yet a moment later it was like a stuck window opening with a burst.

"The interim ministry is right for him," she went on. "He leaves before...well... let's just say God has discovered a way to use him."

"Mom, how do you stay with him?"

"Honey…I manage fine, especially with you around. He's gone a lot, and the truth is, after so many years, I do care for him."

Some hours later, we arrived safely home, though the house now had a strange feel to it, as if someone had rearranged furniture while we were gone.

Illeism. I discovered it online, from the Latin ille (he): a term for speaking of oneself in the third person. In my father's case, illeism seemed to be a way of distancing his public self from his private defects. After a bit I began to distance myself from them, too, and from his disapproving nature. I said nothing to him about my research paper or the visit to Aunt Olive. Still, he seemed to sense a change. I wondered sometimes if his peculiarity had some connection to the defective person living in my left side—but I wasn't curious enough to pursue it. I was much too busy discovering a new and improved self—on the back of a motorcycle.

HALLMARK LIFE

Jerry's mother was watching a Hallmark movie about Christmas, though it was only mid-October. She loved Hallmark movies because they always ended with the right people in the right relationships, the wrong people bowing out but not resentful—in all ways the opposite of her own experiences. Jerry would sit across the room, trying to read a magazine, but listening to the dialogue. Though he would never admit it to his mother, the Hallmark endings lifted his heart in a thrilling and tearful way. He half-believed the promises—a loving home, a meaningful career, a beautiful, gracious wife. Though he'd never seen it happen, he sensed it was possible if you tried hard enough to be a good person.

His mother had been married twice, both times to losers, one a trucker (his father), one a bread delivery man, who both regularly turned into mean drunks. They were gone now, thank goodness, but his mother had to work in a call center to make ends meet. He helped her out with money from his tire job, and together they'd paid off the mortgage on her house. He wanted to make her life easier, so he was good to her and patient in spite of her constant complaining about the people she ran into on the phone.

The Hallmark life existed, he was fairly sure; he just hadn't found it yet. He was 29 and had begun to notice that the women he knew were nearly all married. The playing field seemed to be narrowing daily. To broaden his scope, he took classes now and then at the local community college, subjects as diverse as auto repair and poetry (something he knew females cared about), but the college girls were mostly too young for him. His main hopes lay in the Steelhead Tavern, a roadhouse bar and restaurant on the outskirts of town, with a dance floor and live music on Friday nights. Jerry could dance—dance like nobody else. He was the best tire man at Discount Tire, but it was his dancing that set him apart from the mainstream of human life. His dancing was poetry.

And the women at the Steelhead noticed.

The movie ended, and his mother wiped her eyes and blew her nose on a Kleenex. "Are you going out tonight, Jerry?" she asked.

"It's Friday. I think maybe I'll go to the Steelhead and dance a little."

"Well, don't get drunk."

"Ma, I never get drunk."

"You drink some. I smell it on you."

"One beer. That's it. I go to dance."

"I know, son. I know you're a good boy."

"I'm 29, ma. Honest to Pete. You should trust me by now."

She smiled at him sheepishly, lovingly. "I guess I'll never stop being a mother."

He smiled back. "I know, ma. It's okay."

Jerry arrived at the Steelhead after the dinner crowd had cleared and the band was about to start playing. The place was a cement block bunker set in the middle of a field with a gravel parking lot. A big sign with a leaping steelhead gave some color and promise to the entrance. Jerry had on an outfit he regularly wore—more of a costume, really—a western shirt and fringed leather vest, skinny boot cut jeans and embroidered western boots. He carried his Cody James cowboy hat but put it on only to dance. He was known in the Steelhead as "Cowboy," and what he did, once he felt the spirit moving, was more like a show than a dance. And he danced alone, at least until the women in the crowd worked up some courage.

His usual booth across from the bar was empty so he took it, setting his hat on the table. Cleo, his favorite waitress, saw him and waved, drew a pint of Bud Lite, and walked it over. Cleo was the color of coffee with cream. He loved the warm glow of her skin. She was somewhere in her mid-30s, he guessed, a bit heavy in the hips, but with a sunny disposition and broad smile that always made him feel she was happy to see him.

"Hey, Cowboy," she said, setting down the beer. "Is that fringy vest new? You're looking just like Tim McGraw."

"I got it through Amazon. Like it?"

"It's baaad. Yeah, I like it." She lifted his glass and put a napkin under it. "I missed you last week. Hope you weren't sick or nothing."

"Nah—my mother's birthday."

"Well, good for you for staying home. Good for you, Cowboy."

The music started up. The band was a young cover band he'd heard a few times. Good guitars, good lead singer, and they'd play most anything you wanted. He sipped the beer, always waiting until it was halfway gone before he went to the dance floor. He never hurried it. It took a while to get in the mood.

There were several tables of women, most of them local wives escaping the house. He recognized all of them. They'd drink and get louder as the night went on, and then they'd hit the dance floor to do their usual moves with each other, or sometimes, when they were feeling crazy, with Cowboy who allowed them into the outskirts of his solo routine. A few of them could dance, but most were awkward as ducks on ice. He liked the women because they were fun, but there was no future in any of them. He wanted nothing to do with breaking up marriages.

It took him a good twenty minutes to hit the midpoint of his Bud Light, but by then his mind was right. Sitting in the booth, he did a kind of self-hypnosis with deep breathing and heavy exhalation. It drew the attention of nearby patrons who grinned in expectation. By the time he stood and put on his Cody James hat, he had reached the altered state he needed to perform. The band was playing "Love Shack," a perfect choice. He swaggered to the edge of the dance floor, hands stuffed in his jeans pockets.

Three women were doing clunky line dancing that didn't suit the music. Jerry, staring at the floor, began with nothing but a subtle, rhythmic bounce on one leg. Then it shifted to the other. One arm reached toward the ceiling, the other toward the floor. His hips began to move, then his feet just a little. He was like a robot suddenly switched on, coming to life as electricity coursed to his extremities. With a "Yee-haw!" he exploded in wild choreography, a cowboy Baryshnikov. The musicians watched as they played. The three women sat down. The room was spellbound. When "Love Shack" ended, he heard the burst of applause and merriment with quiet satisfaction. He went back to his booth and took a sip of beer. The next song, "Billie Jean," began at a run, so he couldn't stay down. For the rest of the night, except for breaks, he owned the place. Ladies drank and filled the dance floor and took turns trying to move with him. A few men got up, drunk enough to feel they could compete. It was no contest.

He stayed till the band was packed up and leaving. When he finally made his way to the parking lot, there was frost on the windows of his pickup—and here it was only mid-October. His mother's impatiens would be limp and shriveled by morning. It made him feel old. The summer had come and gone in the blink of an eye.

He looked up when he heard a car engine grinding away nearby, followed by a clicking that meant a dead battery. As he scraped his window with his plastic library card, he saw Cleo get out of the old Chevy, looking harried.

"Hey, Cleo," he yelled to her. "Got trouble?"

"You just heard it," she said. "Damn piece of junk."

"My jumper cables are home. I'll give you a lift and help start it up tomorrow."

"God, Cowboy, that's real nice. My kids are home with a sitter."

She climbed into his passenger seat, and he started his truck to get the heat going. Neither of them had known about a cold snap coming, so neither had a coat. She huddled up, her hands on the heater outlet. He finished scraping enough to see the road, and then got in beside her. Within a mile of the Steelhead, the windows had cleared.

"Where're we going?" he asked, glancing over at her. She had a pretty face that looked bone tired.

"York Apartments on Franklin."

"Sure. That's near where I work." He knew the place—a low cost housing complex in a seedy area maybe a mile from the tire store.

"Yeah? Where do you work?"

"Discount Tire."

"I pass by it. You a salesman?"

"Tire technician."

She smiled. "You about wore out your tires on the dance floor tonight."

"It was great."

"You keep them girls staying late and spending money. Mel oughta give you free beer, at least."

"You never charged me for my Bud Lite."

"Hell, you only drink about a nickel's worth. Mel pays the band. He oughta pay you for the show. Where'd a white boy learn to dance like you do?"

"From YouTube."

"You ever dance to jazz—like Ella Fitzgerald?"

"I dance to anything."

She patted him on the arm. "I just bet you do, Cowboy."

"My name is Jerry. I'm Cowboy just at the Steelhead."

"Well, I figured you had a name. Anyway, you look like a cowboy—tall and lean and sure of yourself." They went quiet for a moment, but then she was talking again in her easy way. "Speaking of names, I got twin daughters, just six years old. One is Ella, named for the singer I just said. The other is Nina, after Nina Simone. My mama named me Cleo after Cleo Laine. My mama was some sweet singer, but she never got a break. I had some hopes myself once, but life kinda gets in the way, know what I mean?"

"Yeah, I know. But I still have hopes."

"Good for you. Truth is, I never had what she had, so it's no big deal."

"I'd like to hear you sing."

"I don't sing to nobody but my girls. They think I'm fine, and it suits me. I'm happy with it."

Jerry drove past Discount Tire, and a few minutes down the road he turned onto Franklin. She pointed to an aging brick two storey apartment building that had the look of a 50s motel. The second floor was lined with balconies. She pointed him into a parking spot, his lights flashing on a picture window with curtains closed.

"Right there is my place, number 120." She reached over and put a hand on his arm. "Could I ask one more favor of you, Jerry? The twins' daddy is just out of jail. Would you come in with me for a few minutes? I'm afraid he might've showed up. He has no right to be here. He's not my husband, and he's no friend of mine."

This was not something Jerry had bargained for.

He'd been in the middle of way too many nasty encounters with his mother and her husbands. But Cleo looked scared enough that he nodded, got out, and followed her to the door. She unlocked it, stuck her head in, and said, "I'm home, Crystal. Everything okay?"

A sleepy looking black woman with orange dyed hair looked up from the television and an old Robert Mitchum movie. She got wearily to her feet, skinny as a scarecrow.

"Sorry I'm late. Damn battery died in the Steelhead lot. This is Jerry, a friend of mine. He gave me a ride."

Crystal glanced at him and nodded. "Nothing happened. Robert never showed. I wouldn't let him in, anyway."

Cleo relaxed a little. "Thanks, honey. I'll pay you in the morning, okay? Haven't even counted my tips yet."

"Need a ride?" Jerry asked.

Crystal smiled for the first time. "Thanks, but I just live up on the second floor."

She went out, and Cleo moved into the small kitchen. Jerry glanced around. The place was tidy but tight. A few Barbie dolls and stuffed animals lay scattered in a corner near a small bookcase and plastic dollhouse. The furniture looked handed down after years in other houses. Cleo obviously didn't have much, but she'd managed to make the place feel like a home.

"Would you stay a minute and have a beer?"

"I don't know…I better get going."

"Sit a minute, Jerry. I owe you a beer, at least."

"Okay, for a minute. No beer, though. Got a Coke?"

"How about some orange juice."

"That's fine." He was feeling nervous for some reason—about the old boyfriend showing up, maybe, or maybe about her. But at the same time the room had begun to feel as warm and comfortable as Cleo's smile. So he relaxed a little and watched her as she poured the juice. She was an ample woman, not fat but generously made. Comfortable seemed to be the word that fit her all around.

She set the glass of juice in front of him, but nodded toward a hallway off the kitchen. "I should check the girls. Want to see?"

He nodded and followed her down the short hall with

a bathroom at the end. She opened a door to the right and looked inside. A nightlight near the floor illuminated a double bed with two little girls sleeping back to back. Their floppy dark curls stood out against the white pillows.

"They sure look pretty," he whispered.

"Don't know where it came from," she whispered back. "Not from their mama. Must be their useless daddy."

"It's you," he said.

They returned to the kitchen and sat down. She drank a beer from the bottle, and he sipped his juice. He couldn't think of much to say. The only thing they really had in common was the Steelhead. But she had an easy way of just talking. He noticed she didn't do much complaining. She liked her job, she liked his dancing, she liked her kids, she seemed to like just being alive. She wove a cocoon of words around him, and he relaxed into it.

And then someone began rapping at the door. It was 2:30 in the morning, no time for visitors.

"Oh, Lord Jesus," she said fearfully. "Only one person'd be knocking at this time of night." She put her finger to her lips. "Don't say nothing. Let me go see." She took off her shoes and silently made her way to the door. She looked through the peephole, and her shoulders went limp. She returned to the table, leaned to Jerry's ear and whispered, "It's him. You go talk. Tell him I don't live here no more."

Jerry's heart started to pound. He wanted nothing to do with this, but he couldn't go walking out. He went to the door and stood close. "Who is it?" he asked sharply. He looked through the hole and saw Robert, a near-white-looking black guy with dreadlocks and a black coat with collar turned up. He wasn't as big as Jerry, but he looked rugged enough.

"I want Cleo. Tell her Robert's here."

Jerry opened the door to the length of the safety chain and peered through the crack. "No Cleo here," he snarled. "This is my apartment, and it's too damn late to be pounding on my door."

Robert swayed a little as if drunk and looked uneasy. "This is where Cleo lives. I been here before."

"She might've lived here once, but she doesn't live here now. Get the hell out. I gotta work tomorrow." He slammed the door and bolted it, went back to the table and sat down beside Cleo. They listened in silence for a few minutes, and then heard a car start up and go squealing away.

"He's gone," Jerry said.

"Maybe—but you don't know him. If he sees your truck is gone from my space, he'll be back in here for sure. You gotta do me one more favor, Jerry. I'm begging you. Stay here tonight. You can have the bed. I'll take the couch. He wants my money and a place to hole up. He's a bum, and I don't want him to have nothing to do with my girls. He's never paid a nickel for them. Won't even admit they're his."

His kindness was quickly turning into a bad dream. But it was hard to stop now. He stared at her and sighed heavily. "I'll text my mother that I'm bunking at a friend's. You take the bed, I'll take the couch."

Her life, he could clearly see, was every bit as messy as his mother's once was.

She got him two blankets and a pillow and then went into the bathroom to take a shower. He stripped down to his undershirt and boxers and folded his cowboy clothes into a neat pile that he stacked beside his boots.

In ten minutes or so, she came back into the room, dressed in a loose cotton nightgown. He was already on the couch with a blanket over him. "I didn't have energy to wash my hair," she said. "You're way too long for that couch, Jerry. Come and take my bed. I can fit on that."

"I'm fine," he said, "you need your sleep." So she went down the hall and into the room on the left.

The couch was hopeless. He finally slid to the carpet and stretched out beside a coffee table. He was pretty sure there was concrete underneath. He rolled around for fifteen minutes or so, groaning a little, until he heard her bare feet padding into the living room.

"Y'all come in with me," she said firmly. "There's room in that big bed for both of us. And don't worry, I'm too tired for playing around."

He got to his feet and followed her in his underwear, carrying his clothes. She pointed him into her bedroom. "I like the left side. Get in while I check on the girls."

He climbed into the big bed and turned facing the door.

Moonlight streamed in through an open blind, and he could see her come in and shut the door. She got in on the left and snuggled up against him. "You're a good man, Cowboy," she said. "I feel safe with you here. Thanks for helping me." Her breasts pressed like pillows against his back. She radiated warmth, and his heart began racing like a hamster in a wheel. For a few moments he could hardly breathe.

When at last he whispered, "I like helping you, Cleo," she was already fast asleep.

It was light when he woke up, well after 9. She wasn't there. He pulled on his jeans and cowboy shirt, made a stop in the bathroom where he found a toothbrush with a note on it that said "For Jerry," and then made his way to the kitchen. The twin girls, doe-skinned and pretty with mop heads of dark curls, were eating bowls of Cheerios with blueberries.

"My car broke last night, girls, and this good friend of mine brought me all the way home. It was too late, so I asked him to sleep here. His name is Jerry. And Jerry, this one with the little mole on her cheek is Nina. This one with no mole is Ella."

"Are you a cowboy?" Nina asked.

"Only a pretend one," he told her. "It's sort of a costume I dance in."

"Jerry is some fantastic dancer," Cleo said.

"Would you dance with us?" Ella asked.

"Hush now, you two. The man needs a cup of coffee. Then we gotta go out to the Steelhead and get my car started."

Ella jumped up, still in a long nightie, and turned on a cd player. The music was Ella Fitzgerald and what sounded to him like Count Basie. Ella began dancing and Nina quickly joined her. They improvised crazy, funny, jazzy steps with perfect rhythm.

Jerry laughed and clapped. "You girls can move!"

"Come on!" they said together. "Dance with us!"

"Some time I will," he said.

"Hush now," Cleo said. "He needs to get to know you better."

Jerry smiled, sipped his coffee, and ate an apple muffin. "I promise I will some time," he said.

By the next Friday, Cleo was back to being his favorite waitress and life was normal again. He'd gotten her a new battery at Discount Tire, and he'd installed it himself at no charge. At his suggestion, Cleo traded parking spots with Crystal, and Robert never reappeared. She let him know several times what a good friend he was.

Jerry's mother was still watching Hallmark Christmas movies, and his heart still yearned.

Three days from Halloween, the Steelhead was decorated to look like a haunted house with a big, fake spider web at the entrance. The cowboy costume would still be his trademark, but he acknowledged the holiday by wearing a black Lone Ranger mask. It seemed perfect, and made him feel even more mysterious.

By nine the place was packed—and with a fair number of people he'd never seen before. Some of the women wore costumes, here and there a sexy one like Cleopatra or one witch showing a lot of skin through filmy black cloth. The men mostly came as their disappointing selves.

The band was a pretty good rock group with a brassy female singer. But they cranked the music so loud, it was hard to talk. Halfway through the first set, he was still mostly dancing alone, the women doing their moves with friends. Out of nowhere, though, someone new appeared, a stranger, who pulled off her coat and took the floor with a girlfriend. Her hair was long and reddish blonde, pulled back loosely and tied. She wore no costume except a mask like his. She was tall and willowy, her jeans tight, her angora sweater fuzzy and low cut. And she could dance like no woman he'd ever seen at the Steelhead. He ignored her nondescript friend and spun in her direction; she smiled, and separated from her partner, picking up his moves. In only a moment, they were moving together, as if she'd learned from the same YouTube instructional video. The band was playing "Love in an Elevator," a song with very sexy lyrics even though you could only half hear them over the guitars. "Hi, there, masked man," she said, holding him with her eyes.

"Hello, masked lady," he said, his voice hoarse. "You sure can dance."

She just smiled and spun away. He followed her,

something he rarely did. Her lips were the color of burgundy wine, her cheeks faintly flushed, her body soft and fluid, her hair swinging to the rhythm of the song. She was the most graceful, perfect thing he'd ever seen. The song ended, but she didn't move away.

His heart was pounding hard. As always, when he wasn't dancing, his confidence went away somewhere.

"You're good," she said. "Let's keep going a little."

"Okay with me. I'm Jerry. In here they call me Cowboy."

"Okay, Cowboy. I'm Breanna."

The music started up again, sparing him the need for something wise and witty to say. They danced on, one song after another, even when her friends tried to partner up with her. As the set was nearing the end, he asked her for her phone number.

"We'll see, Cowboy," she said. Her smile had some mystery in it.

"Brown Sugar" was what the band chose to play before the break. Her body turned liquid as she began to sway. He followed her lead, caught in the spell of her flirtatious, reckless sexiness. She turned her back to him, moved against him, and began slowly grinding her hips. Grinding wasn't his kind of dancing, but as her heart-shaped rump moved against the front of him, all his inhibitions flew away. He danced her dance, bewitched, seduced; he had no awareness of other dancers stopping to watch the simulated passion. Their bodies fit like spoons, flowed together like molten metals, like silver and gold. For reasons beyond him, the lines of a poem from poetry class sounded again and again in his head: "The grave's a fine and private place, but none, I think, do there embrace..." and, peculiar as it was, he couldn't shut it off.

The song ended. Both of them were breathless and dazed. For an instant, he noticed Cleo across the room, looking at him. Breanna breathed a heavy sigh, touched his arm, and then quickly left the floor to join her friends who were already pulling on coats, planning to move on, even though there was one more set to go. As they shoved their way toward the door, he regained his senses and yelled, "Breanna—hey, your number."

She didn't hear him as they pushed through the packed

bodies. He went after her but the doorway was thick with costumed people. As he neared her, he heard her say, "Hey, come on, he's kind of hot in his own weird way."

"Jesus, Breanna, I've been here before. He always wears the same dumb cowboy outfit, and they humor him for laughs. It's a freak show."

Breanna looked at her friend and smiled, as if the comment didn't matter, and they disappeared into the cold darkness.

Jerry looked away from them and saw Cleo laboring with a huge tray of drinks. The sight made him inexpressibly sad. He went to his booth and fell into it. He had half a glass of Bud Lite still sitting there. He took off his hat and drank the beer in a swallow. When the music started, he didn't get up. Cleo came over, acting a little cool, and he ordered another Bud Lite.

"You never have more than one, Cowboy," she said.

"Well, tonight's different," he muttered.

She stared at him a minute and went off. Jerry's thoughts darkened as he sat. He tried to imagine himself in his 50s still playing the Cowboy, still dancing at the Steelhead. He snorted bitterly. It was pathetic. There were four billion women in the world, and nothing was ever going to happen with any of them.

Thanksgiving came and went. At this point, he usually decorated the front of their big old barn-shaped house with Christmas lights, but he kept putting it off. His mother was talking about skipping a Christmas tree this year, and he was okay with it, though he'd always been a nut for Christmas.

A week into December he was in a Discount Tire repair bay balancing a tire when Cleo showed up.

"The manager said I could come back here and see you," she told him, folding her arms. She had on some makeup, jeans and a heavy sweater with blue and yellow stripes, looking sharp. But she wasn't smiling as usual. "What the hell happened to you? I haven't seen you in over a month. Even Mel is asking."

"Nothing happened," he said, pounding wheel weights into the rim. "I got tired of dancing."

"I can't imagine it. Something else must've happened. "

He felt the back of his neck start to burn and knew his ears were turning red. "Nothing happened. Nothing ever does, Cleo. I'm just sick of the way things are."

She shook her head at that. "Who isn't, Jerry? Honest to God…"

"You having trouble with Robert or maybe with that new battery?"

"No, I'm not here looking for favors. I've been wanting to invite you over to dinner is all, but I never even see you any more."

He continued working on the tire. "I'm just not feeling very social these days."

"Is that a no?"

"For now I guess."

Her voice eased up, and he hoped she was back to her usual self. "Well, you promised my girls a dance. Don't forget that."

When he looked up from his work, she was already gone, and that made him feel surprisingly crummy.

Christmas Eve was on a Monday, so he worked a half-day and then went off to Target to find some sort of gift for his mother. She'd watched the last Hallmark Christmas movie of the season the day before, but he'd spent the time changing oil in his snow blower even though there wasn't much chance of a white Christmas. He was feeling bad that their house on the holiday was as bleak and cheerless as it was in mid-February. Maybe Target would have some kind of miniature fake tree he could put up. When he was a kid, his family had always put up a half price, ratty-looking tree on Christmas Eve, so there was precedent, but he liked getting a fresh cut tree early, the day after Thanksgiving if he could, and taking three days to decorate. He liked the sharp smell of a real pine tree in the house.

Target was loaded with last-minute shoppers, and he found his mother some silk scarves, which he knew she'd like. He bought an 18-inch artificial tree with lights already on it, a feeble gesture, but something at least to take the edge off the gloom. As he passed through the toy department, he saw something else, and he paused and thought about it.

It was three p.m. before he got to the York Apartments.

A rusty black Jeep stood in her parking spot, so he guessed it was Crystal's car. He parked across the drive in what looked like visitor spaces, and went to the door with three gift bags in one hand, his Cody James hat in the other.

Cleo opened the door, saw him, and looked puzzled.

"Merry Christmas, Cleo. Mind if I come in a minute?"

"Course not. I'm surprised to see you."

He entered and saw the girls playing with Barbie dolls on the couch. They gave him a look as if trying to remember. Beside the couch was a Christmas tree with way too many decorations but only a few presents underneath.

"Hi, there," he said to them, and then to Cleo, "You put up a real tree. I love the smell. I didn't do it this year, and it was a bad mistake."

"Yeah, we don't in go for fake trees."

He put his hat on so he could sort out the gift bags. "I brought a few presents. Nothing big, but I just got thinking about you ladies." He held out two of the bags toward the girls. They jumped off the couch and raced over to him. "This one is for Nina with the mole, this one for Ella with no mole. Go ahead and open them."

They both glanced at Cleo. She nodded, so they tore into the bags, and each came out with a white cowgirl hat. They held them and looked them over, a little mystified.

He handed the other bag to Cleo.

"I got nothing for you, Jerry," she said.

"You always got a smile for me."

"That ain't much." She opened the bag and took out something wrapped in tissue. She pulled it off and found a tree ornament—a cowboy kicking up one leg.

"You can hang that on your tree if there's room. Now if you girls put those cowgirl hats on, I'll dance with you like I promised."

Nina cried out, "He's that dancing cowboy, remember, Ella?"

"Now I do!"

"I got my cowboy hat on," he told them. "You put on yours if you want to dance with me."

So Ella pushed on her hat and switched on Ella Fitzgerald. Nina put on hers and began to spin like a dervish. Jerry started slow, with a faint, rhythmic bounce on one leg, then the other. One hand pointed to the ceiling, one hand reached for the floor. As he exploded into his YouTube routine, the girls whirled giddily around him, fascinated with his moves, shrieking with laughter, falling down with dizziness and bouncing up again. Cleo's laughter made its own sunny music. Before the song ended, Nina clamped onto one of his legs, and he kept on dancing. Ella grabbed onto the other leg, and he kept moving, hauling then both around the floor with what felt like elephant legs.

The Cowboy saw he'd be okay dancing with them. They were crazy for it, and it suited him.

DOWNRIVER

The three of them launched the large, flat-bottomed bass boat well below the last dam before the river reached Lake Michigan. It was a warm, windless early June day, the trees still glossy and looking new; spring floods were behind them, the water now as mild and clear as the Grand ever got this time of year. They took along an elaborate lunch with a large cooler of drinks, a thermos of coffee, and fishing poles just in case. Their spirits were unexpectedly high.

The boat excursion was the grandfather's idea, inspired by his decision, at 78, to start jotting down his memoirs in this, the final decade of the century. As he'd begun considering his earliest days, the old farm homestead beckoned as it never had. It seemed vitally important that he see the place again. The farm stood on a hill at a wide bend of the river, owned now by a family that raised acres of blueberries. The house had been remodeled, he'd been told, and a new barn built—a lucrative business with the latest equipment. The thought pleased him. From this point (some miles below Grand Rapids), they'd need to travel ten miles or more to reach the place by river. It was territory he'd explored as a boy, scouted in a canoe like an Indian brave. He'd shot his first deer with a bow in the woods near the shore of their property. It seemed fitting that this pilgrimage would take a water route.

It was still morning, and he had the whole day to motor slowly downriver with his son Mike and grandson Danny as company. The day felt like a gift, a blessing even though it should have happened many more times than just this once. There were so many puzzling barriers, so much mutual incomprehension.

But today would be otherwise. He stepped into the boat and took a padded swivel chair on the front deck. An electric trolling motor lay folded at the bow. It wasn't a cabin cruiser, but it was a comfortable boat for the river, stable enough to stand up in. His Chris Craft El Capitan Cruiser had navigated

Lake Michigan for years, all the way to Mackinac Island. Mike could have had it, but didn't want it, couldn't afford it, he said. His son hadn't wanted much of the life he'd built, especially a part in the banking business. He'd marched to a different drummer, one that moved to a jazz beat. He'd also marched in protest of the Vietnam War, of nuclear power, of racial injustice—chafing against his parents' conservative values.

The grandson Danny seemed to have that rebellious spirit, less coherent but multiplied by ten. Intelligent, amiable, but barely getting by in high school, he'd had a year of wrecked cars and drinking-related brushes with the law, driven by a frenetic energy he couldn't exhaust, like a dervish shooting out sparks in all directions. As a grandfather who enjoyed his company in spite of it all, who rarely had to deal with the consequences of the erratic behavior, he had become something of a friend. They weren't together often, yet when they were, he let the boy tell his side of things, and he simply listened. Let his parents take him to task. It wasn't his part, though he fully understood Mike's frustrations. Danny called his grandfather Papa Ben, and Ben liked the name. They both loved baseball, and Danny played it superbly, a hard-hitting catcher—though his behavior had put his senior season in jeopardy.

Danny was broad and muscular (as Ben once was), built for the position he played. He took a long, cat-like leap from the dock and slid onto the swivel chair at the stern. Mike, once he'd parked his truck and trailer, jumped aboard, settling into the cockpit in mid-boat to man the controls. Without being told, Danny squeezed a rubber ball on the gas line to prime the carburetor; in a moment they were off and running. The current in this spot was leisurely, and when Mike accelerated, Ben slowed him down.

"I want to enjoy this. For now just go at my pace. I need to see it all."

Mike nodded and slowed until they were mostly drifting, though he held them steady in the stream, circumventing all the large rocks and tree limbs near the surface. He knew the river well. He had once set traps upstream from the restaurant/bar he owned—traps for snapping turtles. His turtle soup was a specialty of the house. Now there was a law protecting the turtles, and Mike understood it and obeyed. He had a band there on the weekends, and customers danced in a space between the tables and the bar.

It was an odd way for a musician to make a living, but jazz musicians, Ben knew, needed something other than music to support a family. Mike's wife Sally, a peach of a girl, was hostess and bookkeeper. They'd somehow made a go of it, raised a family. Danny's two sisters were in college, and Mike had never come to his father for help.

"So this is where you hung out as a kid?" Danny asked his grandfather.

"Down from here a bit farther. I'll let you know when we get near. I was out on the river every free minute, like Huck Finn—exploring with my brothers in canoes. We knew all the islands, even slept on some of them—found arrowheads at times. We shot deer and caught fish. Always had plenty to eat, even during the Depression."

"Jeez, Papa. How'd you ever end up a banker?"

Mike laughed, and Ben smiled.

"Farm life just wasn't for me. Part of it was growing up in a Christian Reformed crowd of stiff Dutch people. As soon as I could, I ran—and my father never quite got over it."

"First I've heard that part," Mike said with surprise.

"He was pretty unbending about prodigal sons."

"I never knew him very well."

"That's because I stayed away. I regret it now."

Mike shook his head. "I don't think I've ever seen the farm except from a distance. Why have we waited so long?"

Ben shrugged. "Life gets busy, I guess."

Danny poured coffee for all of them and opened a bag of fresh doughnuts. He passed the bag and sang, "I picked up a doughnut/ and I wiped off the grease/ and I handed the lady a five cent piece."

It got a smile from Mike. He took a powdered doughnut from the bag. "Great song."

"Crummy singer."

"I know a lot of music, but I never heard that one."

"Burl Ives, I think." He bit a chunk from a chocolate doughnut and kept talking. "Lizzie and Grace both have great voices. So does Mom. Then there's you—the music man. I'm like a crow. I got none of those genes."

Mike tightened at Danny's longtime habit of underselling himself. "I'm a piano hack in a bar. Your gift is baseball… maybe Major League stuff. Who needs musical genes?"

Danny frowned. "Hell, Dad, you're no hack. You stayed home with us instead of going on the road and making a name. I know how great you are. You gave it up for us. That's amazing…or stupid. I'm not sure which." In one breath, he'd revealed more than he ever had on the subject and now was trying to backpedal into a joke.

A surge of emotion silenced Mike. Danny almost never expressed appreciation in any form, yet here it was, out of nowhere.

They drifted on, not talking, enjoying the doughnuts and coffee. Muskrats appeared here and there near the shore; herons waded in the shallows spearing minnows. Around one bend they came upon two raccoons digging in the mouth of a creek. They looked up, mildly startled, but a moment later resumed digging. Danny pointed to a barn owl in a beech tree. There were no homes or businesses at all through this stretch, just newly greening corn and hay fields, an occasional barn, thick stands of trees. The warm sun rose in a bright sky full of gauzy clouds. Danny had started out in a tee shirt. Ben stripped off his flannel shirt, and Mike did the same.

Mike thought about his father needing to escape the rigid confines of the Dutch CRC. It was hard to imagine him rebelling in any way. Mike had been the poster boy for that behavior. He'd been raised in his parent's moderate, urban Presbyterian Church—a stone edifice with soaring spire, spectacular pipe organ, huge stained glass windows, a sanctuary of rich, mellowing oak. It was a church of wealthy business leaders, lawyers, surgeons, heavyweights of the community. For years he'd faithfully attended Sunday school, including church camp, retreats, mission trips. He'd memorized Bible passages that sometimes astonished him— made him wonder if the adults of the church ever actually thought about them—lines aimed pointblank at their privileged world. Love thine enemies, bless those who curse you. Sell all your things and give to the poor. If anyone slaps you on the right cheek, turn to him the other also. Blessed are the peacemakers. You cannot serve God and money. Deny yourself and follow me. Whoever loses his life for my sake will save it.

What were they thinking of, filling their children with such subversive stuff? Was it that in time those children would (as they had) filter out the practical from the impractical, the conservative from the radical, the good-for-business from the bad-for-business? Was faithful church attendance mainly a way to beef up resumes? In college, Mike had left the church, though not the Christian faith. Once he married and had a family, he'd tried a liberal Unitarian Church, raised his kids there, but knew something vital was missing. He was the only one who still attended—mainly in the role of social justice advocate. Danny, he'd heard from Sally, was occasionally hanging with a friend's youth group at a large nondenominational church in the suburbs.

The boat's flat bottom lightly scraped over rocks as they skirted the outside of several fast-moving, shallow stretches. Mike navigated carefully, but the low water level made it tricky. Danny rigged up a pole and tossed out a spinner in hopes of a bass, but they were moving too fast to make it work.

"I remember an island a mile or so downriver with some deep holes," Ben said. "We could stop and fish there for a while."

"Great," Danny said and set his pole down.

A half hour passed and no island appeared. "A river changes a lot in 65 years," Mike said. "Maybe the island is gone."

"Maybe so." Ben wondered if his memory was the problem. Yet within another ten minutes, a wooded island appeared, the river splitting around it. It was smaller than he remembered, perhaps not the one he was thinking of, but he saw a shelf of sand, and Mike headed the boat up on it. Danny jumped out and pulled them ashore far enough that his father and grandfather could get out without soaking their feet. He ignored the water gushing from his own shoes.

Ben was right, there were some good holes, and bass were plentiful, though mostly undersized. They ended up keeping four of them. The solitude was so pleasant, they sat and ate their lunch there. Sally had made chicken, potato salad, and carrot cake. The cooler was full of beer and bottled water. Danny, the older men agreed, should have a beer with them on this occasion. They saw a small snapping turtle rooting around in the shallows. Danny told a story about his father hauling a big snapper in a gunny sack over his shoulder. The creature had clamped onto his back right through the sack. Danny, just a kid, battered the shell with a stick until the turtle let go.

"You can still see those beak marks," Mike said with a laugh.

Danny went on. "I could never eat turtle soup after watching him dress one out. It was gruesome." Danny finished his beer and popped another for each of them. The turtle story reminded him of other times—short visits he'd spent as a kid with his mother's parents. Grandma Krause hardly talked at all, but Gramp loved telling stories, a jolly German with a red nose and a taste for Pabst Blue Ribbon beer. They owned a small frame house in the country with a chicken coop and garden. When Danny was there, Grandma Krause usually caught a chicken, slipped its head between two nails in a flat stump, and lopped it off with an ax. The body ran in crazy circles for a few moments, spurting blood, wings flapping, and then went limp. Danny reluctantly accompanied her (Gramp didn't go) to mass at St. Anne's Catholic Church, where he watched her pray through her rosary, wondering what in the world she was doing. A sacred heart of Jesus painting—a deep red heart aflame and bleeding from a spear wound—hung above her bed. It made him uneasy, like the bleeding chickens. He noticed even back then how religion could get weird. His father's Unitarian Church had its own quirks. The pastor more often quoted Walt Whitman than the Bible. Jesus rarely came up, or blood. Still he held onto the odd shreds of belief that made some sense to him.

At close to one o'clock, Ben saw the farmhouse through the trees, prompting an unexpected rush of emotion. He had to clench his jaw to stay composed. "That's it," Ben said. "They have a dock—good. Pull up to it. They know we're coming."

The sight of the old house, now restored, with a large wing added to the back and a new barn atop the hill, both thrilled and dismayed him. It was impressive but also wasn't his any more. Acres of large, white-blooming blueberry bushes stood in rows on the high ground where corn had grown in his childhood.

"Amazing," Mike said as he cut the engine and Danny tied up to the dock. A pontoon boat was secured to the other side.

Danny gave his grandfather a hand up onto the dock. "Some place, Papa."

"It was a lot more basic when I lived here."

"At least it's not in ruins," Mike said.

"You mean like me." Ben laughed at himself and began to relax. As they walked an uphill path toward the house—built well above flood level—they saw a woman exit a side door, wave, and come toward them.

Nellie Ferwerda was blessed with a broad, welcoming Dutch face framed by blonde braids tied in a bun. She was young—Ben guessed in her mid-30s. He introduced his family to her, and she asked if they'd like to tour the house. Her husband had run into Grand Haven to pick up fertilizer but planned to be back to meet them.

"You go ahead with your business," Ben told her. "I think we'd like to wander around outside for a bit. We'll tour your house afterwards, if that's okay. Maybe your husband will be back by then."

She smiled, understanding, and gave them carte blanche to wander. "When you're ready, just knock at the side door," she said.

Ben led them in the direction of the new barn, the highest point of land. The six-foot highbush blueberries were full of white, bell-shaped blooms, and arranged in long, symmetrical rows of well-mulched, sandy soil. The farm was now a showplace. In July, people came to pick their own fruit.

"These folks know how to farm," Ben said. "Our old barn stood about fifty feet west of this one." The front doors of the barn were open, revealing a small fortune in harvesting equipment. He led them past the barn toward a stand of woods. Ben found a boulder marking the start of a path, which he took into the trees. They walked, and Ben watched carefully until he spotted an opening, a circle of sunlight. He knelt at the base of a large oak and brushed the surface of a round, massive, half-buried river stone. He could see, etched on it, the name BOB in faint, squared-off letters. "Well, here's proof of my existence."

Danny knelt beside him. "Who's Bob?"

"My dog. My dad and I buried him here when I was twelve. I etched his name with a hammer and cold chisel but couldn't figure out how to make the letters round. He was just a mutt but my best friend in those days. See this oak? It was small when we buried him. That was over sixty-five years ago. Jesus..."

"You don't look your age," Mike said. "People think you're my older brother."

"It's true, Papa."

They walked the woods down to the river shore. Danny skipped some flat stones, grabbed a crayfish hiding under a shallow stone and threatened his father with the flailing pincers.

"Cut it out," Mike said, momentarily irritated. "Jeez..."

Danny's look was quizzical. He tossed the crayfish back in the river.

They made their way along the shore until they reached the dock again.

"Anyone want another beer?" Danny asked.

"We probably should get up to the house," Ben told him. "She's waiting for us."

They returned to the side door. Nellie greeted them, and they set out on a guided tour. She was obviously proud of the decorating. Ben recognized the mud room, the kitchen (at least the shape of it), but not much else. The ancient gas stove, linoleum counters and floors, chipped porcelain sink with hand pump, had all been replaced by modern stone and stainless steel. The living room furniture was plush, much of it in dark leather, very comfortable and lived-in, not at all like the stark, simple furnishings he'd grown up with. The Ferwerdas had three children, but they were away somewhere—maybe because of this occasion. When they'd finished the tour, Nellie's husband still hadn't returned.

"He'll be disappointed. He wanted to show you around the working part of the farm."

Ben glanced at Mike. Danny seemed to be getting antsy.

"If your husband wouldn't mind driving me a few miles to my son's restaurant, I could stay and send these two back downriver. I'd like to meet him."

Mike and Danny continued in the boat without Ben. Mike felt the loss of an important buffer between them, but he was determined to hold onto the good feeling of the day. Their relationship lately had been precarious, full of long silences and stifled disapproval. Danny by himself had caused his parents more worry than a dozen daughters. Danny seemed to be aware of it, but it didn't change him. He could be charming but also sullen and chaotic, indifferent to school except for baseball. His friends were many, yet often the wrong ones. He lived recklessly. The girls had had their issues, but the issues were normal ones. Danny's were large and unpredictable, without clear motivation.

But Mike took a leap of faith. "Want to take it the rest of the way home?"

"Drive the boat? You mean it?"

"It's pretty clear sailing from here to the restaurant. Just go easy. I'll sit up front and watch for rocks."

"Cool," Danny said and held the wheel as Mike moved out of the cockpit. Mike had let him drive before on inland lakes, so it wasn't new. But the river took some patience, some careful navigating. He hoped Danny could manage.

The boy suddenly became more talkative. "I'm not sure how Papa felt about all the changes to the farm. It must have been hard for him." He guided them swiftly between two large rocks. Mike held his breath.

"At least he found his dog's grave," Mike replied, exhaling as they cleared the obstacles. "I hope he's okay. I never knew how unresolved his family stuff was. I hated leaving him alone back there. "

"Yeah. Me too. It was a good feeling with all three of us."

"Great idea to go downriver together. He and I have never been able to have much fun."

"What? You gotta be kidding."

"No. There's nothing much we've ever agreed on. He wanted me to live his sort of life, and I wanted my own. I think we're finally getting past our mutual disappointment."

"Wow, I thought I was the only one you had trouble with."

Mike laughed heartily. "Sorry."

The boat scraped over a rock, and Mike stiffened. "Damn," Danny said. "Didn't see it."

"My fault. I'm talking instead of watching."

Moving at Danny's pace, they arrived at the restaurant dock within half an hour. Danny finessed it into the pilings, and Mike tied up.

"How about taking it all the way to the big lake?" Danny asked. "We haven't done it since I was little."

"It's a good 40 minutes more. I need to clean these fish, and your grandfather will be back soon."

"What if I do the run myself?"

Mike hesitated, not happy with the idea. Danny was always pushing, but Mike didn't want to end a good day on a sour note. "Sure. Check the gas. I'll pick up the truck and trailer and meet you at the public ramp in Grand Haven. Remember—the bayous and channel are no-wake zones. The Coast Guard patrols there."

"Not a worry," Danny said.

Always a worry, Mike thought.

They unloaded the fish, the poles, the picnic basket, the cooler—everything but two beers hidden at Danny's feet. The gas was okay, Danny said, and in a blink he was off downriver, not once looking back.

He waited five minutes to pop a beer. This sudden freedom was brilliant, and he had to fight the impulse to open the boat up to full bore. He'd left all authority behind him. He felt a wildness in himself he couldn't contain, and it longed to express itself in speed. At the same time, he truly didn't want to wreck anything else. He'd already totaled his mother's car and banged up a friend's. His family didn't deserve it. He was a stumbling block to them, a stumbling block to himself. He was pretty sure he wasn't crazy, yet something was haywire, and he didn't know how to fix it. He prayed he'd grow out of it soon. He had a good and caring family. Today displayed it. Every person on earth struggled without exception, even his solid father. Even his banker grandfather. How utterly different the members of one family could be—yet always with some common thread binding them together. Danny had felt the pull of the thread at moments today. It was not something he'd expected.

He drank the second beer and hid the empty cans in a storage bay before he reached the bayou into Spring Lake and Grand Haven. He gunned it to see what a 50 horse Evinrude could do, passed a NO WAKE sign, glanced back at a canoeist struggling in the chop he'd left behind. He slowed suddenly to a crawl. In the channel, he passed a Coast Guard boat and waved. They returned it. The water between piers was rough from many boats passing in and out as well as turbulence on the big lake. When he reached the end of the piers, he leaned hard on the accelerator. Lake Michigan was a huge expanse, terrifying in its massiveness and power. His father's boat leapt up and pounded down against incoming waves, slamming them hard as if it might break in two. Danny breathed the chill air, breathed the speed and danger. He went straight out, wondering how long the gas would last. He didn't care.

As the boat plunged into the trough of a wave, his forehead caught the windshield's edge, and he came to himself.

The sun was in his eyes. He struggled to gain control of the boat, maneuvering a turnabout that narrowly avoided capsizing the whole rig and tossing him overboard. He was shaken as he re-entered the channel, proceeding again at no-wake speed.

He could see the public boat ramp. His grandfather was leaning against the truck. His father was there on the ramp waiting, just as he said he would be. Danny was back safely; in their faces he saw the relief.

THE GREAT 83 BASEBALL TOUR

(A travel memoir)

I can't remember whose idea it was initially, but I do know it was my son's energy that sustained the vision.

It began on a long walk downtown in early winter of 81. It was a sharp, sunny day, full of false promise. Matt was eleven years old, already a confirmed baseball fanatic—already yearning for spring training and his own Little League season to begin. The kid has somehow been blessed with the genes of a shortstop. I have no idea where he got them, but they've plainly been recessive for several generations. At seven he'd assimilated Rod Carew's batting stance and worked out his contract with the Tigers—in his head, at least. And now he was talking with great animation about how tremendous it would be for both of us to go to baseball games all around this country and Canada—26 stadiums, to be exact—and not as a life-long project but as the quest of one skylarking summer. I could drive. He could cook and put up the tent. We both could collect and file all the material for a book or movie that I'd write later. Maybe we'd collaborate. I remember thinking, what a sensible kid this is…I remember the sun beating on my head.

Well, 1982 was out. We'd already scheduled a big family summer trip. 83 seemed safe and distant. I had breathing room. By then he'd be an adolescent and likely would prefer anyone's company to mine. In the spring I smiled when he asked me to Xerox 26 copies of the following letter:

Dear Sir,

Would you please send me your 1983 baseball schedule and any other free pamphlets if you have any. Because my dad and I are going to every Major League Stadium (American and National).

Thank you.

Sincerely,

Matt Lockwood

Mail began arriving within two weeks. Each thick envelope contained bumper stickers, team literature, souvenir catalogs, and schedules—*1982* schedules. Not a single 83. The following November he had to repeat the process. He did it without complaint. Months came and went. I was hired to write a screenplay for HBO. It was the biography of a baseball player. At least half a dozen scenes were to be set in American League baseball stadiums, predominately Eastern ones. I now had stronger motive but could no longer afford an entire summer off. Three weeks at the outside.

He never faltered. An alternate plan was swiftly devised. "Now you *have* to go," he said. How could I presume to write about stadiums I'd never seen? We would hit Detroit, Toronto, Montreal, spend a couple of days recuperating with Uncle Doug in Maine, then on to Boston, New York, Philadelphia, Baltimore, Washington, D.C., to see where the Senators used to play, then back inland to Pittsburgh, Cleveland, Cincinnati if there was time, Chicago, and Milwaukee.

A massive logistical problem presented itself. Our schedule was tight. Would the teams be at home at the right times? He sat down and figured it out. We'd miss the White Sox and the Mets. The Sox we could see any weekend and the Mets this season were expendable.

I thought about contacting campgrounds and buying game tickets in advance. Too confining, I decided. We'd play this trip by ear. If by Montreal we hated baseball, we could opt for fishing in Maine. At the time I understood little of the energy of his dreams.

Suddenly, July 29th was upon us, and all I had ready was my camera with a dozen rolls of film to record this monumental, whirlwind, increasingly lunatic tour. My wife, who'd just returned from Scotland, managed to throw together most of the things essential to our survival and pack them in around us. My station wagon is the size of a small house, but by the time everything was in, we looked like dustbowl Okies starting for California.

An hour out of port we tacked into Lansing for the travel blessing of an old friend who wanted to go with us but couldn't find the time. Matt calls him Uncle Jim, though he's no blood relation. He's a baseball freak and a bachelor. My son idolizes him because he's a world-class baseball trivia expert. Everything that ever happened on a baseball field is stored in the junkyard of his brain. He has been known to spread the rumor that Matt is actually his kid. He buys him expensive baseball books, and when we complain that he's spoiling him, Jim says, "Leave me alone. It's the least I can do for my only son."

In recognition of our undertaking, Jim was wearing his Pony League uniform from 1955. Something was amiss in the fit. Cloth and man seemed to be doing battle. We took a bunch of pictures. He lent Matt a stack of baseball books so he could bone up on trivia, and after an hour we were off again for Detroit.

Of our twenty nights on the road, only three were spent in hotels. Detroit was the first—done for convenience. The other two were matters of personal hygiene and basic survival. As I checked in at the desk, the clerk handed me a message: "Emergency. Call Jim collect." I wondered what the joke was. We had a ball game to get to. I had to take pictures of the stadium before it was dark. I'd hoped for a shot or two of batting practice. Hell, it was late and we didn't even have tickets yet.

But in the room I lifted the phone and dialed. He answered on the first ring.

"You really didn't think I'd call collect, did you?"

"Hey!" he shouted, "how's it going?"

"What's the emergency?"

"How's the weather down there? Looks like rain here."

"What do you want?"

"Hey, you're a friend of mine, aren't you? I want you to do me a favor."

"Sure. If you can wait three weeks."

"You know that camera you've got? I'm crazy about it. I want one just like it. In fact, before the game starts, I want you to go out somewhere and buy me one."

"You're crazy. Buy your own camera. You think they don't have cameras in Lansing?"

"I'm not kidding. I want a Pentax just like yours. I've always wanted a camera like that. I want one of those little timer doohickeys on it that lets you jump into the picture before it clicks. You know…"

"You're nuts. What are you talking about?"

"You've *got* to buy me a camera."

"*Why?*"

"Because you left yours here, dimwit."

My heart sagged—I *heard* it. I muttered some obscenity and slapped my head. There was no time to go back. We had to be in Toronto at one the next day. We'd either miss the Tigers or the Blue Jays. We could catch the Jays a day later, but by then Montreal would be on the road.

"You've got no choice," he said. "Hurry up and buy it or you won't get seats."

"Hey, man…" I said.

"Forget it. I really want the camera. Break it in for me. Have a great trip. Take care of the kid."

There was a camera store beside our hotel, but it was closed. Okay, we'd get to bed early, buy the camera when it opened in the morning, and with luck we could make Toronto by game time. I was beset by doubts. Did he need a camera, or was this simply pure, shameless generosity? I think I knew the answer.

Tiger Stadium was jammed. We got seats—in the upper deck of left center field, beside a strange, disheveled young man who carried a brown shopping bag and looked like a hatchet murderer. He had a Boston newspaper, old clothing, and his dinner in the bag. During the first two innings he gnawed on a cold hamburger patty. I bought hotdogs and beer. He watched me out of the corner of his eye. Suddenly, lightning cracked. Rain began falling in buckets. Half of the 40,000 people made for the beer counters. The soggy lunatics in the bleachers sang, drank, and bounced beach balls off each other.

To use up time, I wrote down images in the program: "Rain against the lights gleams like a blizzard…Air trapped under the field tarp looks like whales undulating on the surface of the sea…" Matt glanced at my longhand scrawl and said, "Why are you messing up the program?" So much for sensitivity. An hour passed. Two. Three. I made friends with the hatchet murderer. He was actually a life-long Red Sox fan who had moved to Detroit and was trying to adjust.

"We'll sit here all night before they'll give out 40,000 rain checks," he said.

The crowd thinned by a third. Then half. No one would call the game. Then the rain began letting up. It was going on 11:30.

"We'll never catch a ball up here," Matt said. "Let's get better seats." He was wearing his glove. He had complete faith that the game would continue.

We moved down behind the Tiger's dugout. The hatchet murderer came with us. We wiped off the executive box seats with his Boston Globe. A cop was tossing out all the other squatters but never said a word to us. We sat down, the rain stopped, the grounds crew came out, the game restarted. There were men on first and third—Trammell had executed a perfect hit and run before the rain. Wockenfuss walked. Parrish came up and belted the first pitch into the upper deck of left-center field. It landed near our empty seats.

The crowd rose in awe. One drunk behind us performed an aria of riveting machine imitations. There was another hit. A walk. Lemon came up and rapped one into the lower deck in left. We all went crazy…bananas. George Brett kicked dirt and began carping at the third base ump about the long delay. The riveting machine imitator began razzing Brett about his hemorrhoids.

It was a joyous time, and Morris was never better. The delay hadn't fazed him. He made fools of everyone, including Brett. At 1:10, with an inning to go, the game was called because of curfew. The Tigers led 10 to 1.

We stood and applauded. My eyes were misty. I'd had a lot of beer. I remember thinking, this is going to be a great trip. When we crawled into bed it was close to 2 a.m. "Well, only 20 days to go," I said. Matt never heard me.

I'd planned ten minutes to buy the camera and it took an hour and a half. The salesman would not let me go until he'd demonstrated all 1232 features. So I found myself barreling 75 mph up the 401 to Toronto in a driving rain. Matt slept. By 1:30 I was still 45 miles from town. The sun broke through the clouds as I turned the radio on. Matt muttered something as the Canadian National Anthem came on. "I'm trying," I grumbled. I goosed it to 80 and was in the parking lot of Exhibition Stadium by the second inning. The sky had turned a hard, brilliant blue. And from our vantage point the game looked like a sell out.

A scalper approached—a big, smiling cutthroat. I bought two reserved tickets at face value—just above first base. They turned out decent tickets—they just weren't anywhere near each other. By the time I'd talked the box office manager into giving me two together, Cleveland was ahead 5 to 1.

But we were there. I focused the brand-new camera with automatic doohickey and realized suddenly that Jim now had a stake in the trip. It eased my conscience. I sat, watching these unfamiliar teams, trying to care about them. I bought a Canadian beer. The sun beat on my head. When my skull struck the knee of the guy behind me, I discovered I'd been sleeping. The game was in extra innings. By the 13th I felt I'd been sitting there half my life.

Someone won—Toronto, I think—and afterwards, in the midst of a traffic jam on the Gardiner Expressway, I blew a radiator hose. I made it to a service station just as the engine overheated but found no service. A bored, greasy kid in a Grateful Dead tee shirt was talking to his girlfriend on a phone. He took money and credit cards—didn't fix cars or pump gas…didn't have any hoses. I rummaged through the food box and found the vegetable knife, cut off the bad part of the hose and stuck the rest back on. It seemed to work.

Later, I sat in a McDonalds, staring out at the road.

"Where'll we stay tonight?" Matt asked. "I thought we were going to get halfway to Montreal."

"Shut up and eat," I said.

"Jeez, what's the matter with you?"

"Have you ever seen such a boring game? That stadium looked like a college football field. What do Canadians know about baseball? I hate Astroturf."

He glanced at me and shook his head.

We continued up the 401. I recall only a dim succession of images: a tent set up in the dark, a sky full of fuzzy-looking stars, a wild party down the road from the campground, two hours of sleep, leathery eggs on a Coleman stove, road signs suddenly in French rather than English.

The Montreal Olympic complex turned my mood only a little. The stadium looked like something designed to transport extraterrestrials. From car to ticket office to stadium, we never set foot out of doors. We found our seat near the top of one of the flying buttresses supporting the partial dome. The place was big league compared to Toronto, but there was still something wrong. This wasn't a *real* baseball field like Detroit. It was a multi-purpose facility covered with long strips of phony grass. Astroturf: the word itself shouts the unnatural, the *unearthly* qualities of the stuff. If God had meant baseball to be played on Astroturf, He would have said something to Abner Doubleday.

The place was *too big* for baseball. They looked like insects down there. The outfield fence was perfectly symmetrical—dull, dull. The crowd was well behaved—mannerly and disinterested observers. They cheered politely—God help us—in *French*. It bordered on sacrilege. The hotdogs were sad, skinny imitations of the real things. The beer softened my judgment—but only a touch. And I have to admit that Andre Dawson, the Expo's center fielder, was a miracle. But it wasn't baseball. I slept an inning or two while Matt spit in his glove, tensing at each foul ball.

"Don't let one hit me," I muttered. I calculated the chances of it at approximately one in 25 thousand.

"Don't worry," he said, pounding the glove.

But as time and miles swept behind us in the wind stream of the Ford, the blur of this new life slowly began to assume a shape. Without the shape, there would have been no sense to the brutal march of expressways and big city traffic jams. The life was thin and comfortless. By Montreal I had honestly reached the growling stage. But the kid was a paragon of patience. Inexplicably and by inches, the vision began to reveal itself to *me*.

Storms followed us toward Maine. As we wound down the narrow road through the middle of Lake Champlain, the sky exploded with strange, horizontal, soundless lightning. My eardrums throbbed from the pressure. Suddenly, the road was alive with creatures. We couldn't believe our eyes. For ten miles, with few intervals, we sloshed through hundreds... no, *thousands* of frogs. The tires played a melody of eerie little crunches. Then, as abruptly, they were gone.

When we slowed for a town called East Hero, Matt pointed out the window. A double bed sat in the front yard of a house. Two drenched, bedraggled people were lying in it under the sheets, watching the storm. Matt and I looked at each other. He flicked on a tape of Leon Redbone, and suddenly the world seemed as crazy and rich as our dreams of it. Later we stretched out in the car, read some of Twain's *Roughing It* aloud, and slept easily to the music of the rain. Sometime through the night I turned 42, and wasn't once troubled by the experience.

Maine: two days of fishing and an overdose of lobster left me—I could hardly believe it—antsy for a baseball game. When Matt approached me with a revised plan, I put up little fight. Detroit would be in Yankee Stadium for 3 days. We could go to New York first, back up to Boston, and then down to Philadelphia.

"That's 400 miles out of the way," I said.

"You're always bored by teams you don't care about."

"Yeah, but *400 miles*…"

"I know you have to drive, but I don't mind…"

So off we crashed into the fug and babble of the East Coast, pilgrims in search of America, or the meaning of baseball, or just whatever we could find. Yankee Stadium was a jewel amid the Astroturfed indecencies blighting the leagues. Center field is a great chasm (though less now than the 461 feet it was in the old days). You have to be an Arabian horse to play it. Everyone is close to the action. The grass is like a golf green, the seats new and blue, the center field wall imposing and impossible—like the wall of some Scottish castle. A New Jersey journalist sat beside me and drank prodigious quantities of beer. He offered to join us for the rest of the trip, then disappeared forever during the seventh inning stretch.

Sparky's managing was baffling that night. He pulled Rozema and brought in a secret weapon named Martin. When the dust had cleared, the Tigers had been skinned 12 to 3. They lay down even more generously the following night. It didn't matter as much as we'd expected. We were happy. We wandered Manhattan during the day—saw a man and his wife slug it out on the street, saw musicians, Mennonites, Hari Krishnas and Moonies, saw Iranian torture racks demonstrated, saw kids Matt's age selling sunglasses on every corner, saw a fat actress in a deli who left a bright red, wet ring on her straw.

And our New York campground—who'd ever believe there'd *be* one?—was a lesson in environmental determinism. Our tent site was 10 by maybe 15. New Yorkers were stacked about us, and the city had come with them. They'd lugged out kitchen chairs and tables, baby buggies, mattresses, televisions, tires, potted plants—and a thousand ghetto blasters that pounded me with disco rhythms through the night. The city had done this to them. Not one of them was secure without the noise and clutter of lots of his own kind about. What was hopeless chaos to me was music to them, as familiar as old shoes or faces in bathroom mirrors. Matt slept soundlessly through it all. I remembered that at home he went to sleep to WGRD bubblegum rock.

As we headed up toward Boston from the debacle in Yankee Stadium, we knew it was time for a motel. The sterile little room with shower and TV was a taste of pure heaven. The air conditioner sang to me as I languorously counted tiles above the tub. I flushed the toilet whenever I passed. It was ten times the price of a campground, and I'd never spent money any more intelligently.

Fenway Park was a turning point in my life. There I underwent conversion. My resistance to the trip dissolved entirely. There, for the first and only time, we sat in bleacher seats. The stadium was a marvelous anachronism, a genuine old time baseball park with stands that could just has well have been built for a county fair. The place will seat twenty-one thousand—miniscule by modern standards. Even in the cheap seats, Yastzremski looked close enough to slap on the back.

We were accompanied by a rabid Boston fan, a shirttail relative named Richard whom we'd spent the previous evening with in heated debate. The years of frustration as a Red Sox booster had obviously unstrung him. He'd asserted, wildly hammering knuckles on his kitchen table, that Boston always had the best bats in the league (if the worst pitching) and, furthermore, Rod Carew was a miserable wimp who hit only for average. I'd never cared enough to argue baseball with *anyone*, yet I found myself pitching into the fray like some street-corner evangelist. Carew, I'd always believed, was one of the game's few artists. I glanced at Matt, who joined my defense by providing the concrete statistics notably absent from my case. It ended in a jackassed, scoffing deadlock, but we one-upped him before all was said and done.

As we watched Boston struggle against the odds, a Texas Ranger named Larry Biittner came to the plate and cracked a low line drive at us. I ducked before it cleared the fence. When I looked up again, Matt was holding out his glove. The ball was buried in it.

"You lucky little wimp," Richard barked. "I've been here a million times and never came *close* to catching one! It won't happen again in a century."

As Matt flashed the ball to people around him, I offered to buy Richard a beer.

"The stuff in Fenway always gives me the runs," he grumbled. "The *Red Sox* give me the runs."

I laughed and realized how genuinely I liked the guy. Matt gave me a high five and handed me the prize. I ran my fingers around the tight red seams. "Official Ball – American League – Lee MacPhail, Pres." Above the "Rawlings" trademark was Biittner's bruise. It was like being plunked with a magic twanger. That home run had reached through some spectral barrier and touched us both. Neither of us could express it, but we both knew.

In his journal of the trip Matt wrote "I'd waited five games and didn't think I'd ever catch a ball. When I did it made me want to go to every stadium."

In my own I said: "The home run was an umbilical connecting us to this crazy game. Though I can't define what has changed, I know we are no longer merely spectators."

After that, the balls arrived at regular intervals; we were happy but not surprised. In Philadelphia a dishy usherette gave Matt a Phillies' Centennial ball because she loved what we were doing. Everywhere, we met with the same reaction. It was as though we were realizing some latent desire, touching something very American and very important. God keep me from exaggerating. Baseball is dull as sin most of the time, but it gets whoever watches it long enough.

It's a cutthroat business, granted, but there remains something mythic about it—as if it's, well…the individual and the team, independence and interdependence…an emblem of *democracy*. I'd heard it called an opiate of the masses, one beautifully orchestrated distraction from our troubles. I no longer bought *any* of that; the game had begun to smell of heroes and Horatio Alger to me.

Matt wrote: "In Pittsburgh I caught a ball that Dave Parker threw over some guy's head. I reached down and caught it. Then in Cleveland I got a ball in batting practice that rolled and stopped right in front of me. A guy held me by the pants while I grabbed it. Later on in the game I was sitting by the Blue Jay's bullpen, talking with Roy Lee Jackson (a great pitcher) who knows my Grandpa. A foul ball came to Dave Stieb. Jackson pointed to me and Stieb threw it to me." We had balls coming out of our ears.

We walked the streets of all these jammed and frantic cities. We drank them in—museums, monuments, graveyards, people. But baseball never left center stage. We arrived a little bit earlier for each game. At Three Rivers in Pittsburgh we were the first ones in. We'd waited an hour for the gates to open. It got to be a habit. Matt would run down to the fence while I bought a beer. By the time I found my seat, he usually had a ball. Batting practice came to be a very sweet time for us.

The trip had become an absorbing endurance test. It was like climbing Annapurna—with the motives just as obscure. I know it was a beautiful time to go—catching Matt in transition, riding through the last days of his childhood with him. He still played his made up baseball games and dragged me out to toss a ball around at every rest stop and filling station. If he's never a major league shortstop, if I'm never a great writer, we *have* realized this dream together—pursued it and seen it through to the end.

Our final stats were impressive: 4000 miles, 14 states, 2 provinces, and the District of Columbia; 33 border crossings; all of the American League East; two-thirds of the National League East; 15 games; a bag full of baseballs; pennants, programs, and pencils from every team; 250 photographs indistinguishable from each other; 3 motels, 8 campgrounds, 1 house, and a night in the car.

Baseball is a grand game. The trip convinced me, and I returned a devotee. But the real heart of the matter was something else, something simpler: it was the two of us, meeting the challenge and seeing it through. If I faltered at moments, Matt never did. I toughened as I went.

And I'm left with these images, this rich gallery of green, real moments. Life, I think, *is* these moments, trapped in the amber of memories. I see this skinny kid down at the right field wall, waiting for a pop foul. I feel him pressed against me through a sleeping bag and breathing gently. I hear him waking in the night, lost in the black void of the tent, calling for me, relieved at my hand on his face. I feel the silence in the car during long stretches of road—the comfort of it. I hear our laughter at some absurd thing we saw: the hag in the housecoat who watched TV all day at the picnic table beside her tent; the wildlife museum in the Pittsburgh campground with mounted heads of squirrels; the man in the ticket line at Three Rivers who told everyone the hospital was giving free enemas; the old wag in the New Hampshire rest stop who said it was good I'd gone 18 miles in the wrong direction since I wouldn't have met him otherwise.

Matt bothered to make a list of things he loved…"smelling French toast in the morning…walking into the stadium and looking out onto the field for the first time…seeing the Green Monster in Fenway…watching people get into fights at Yankee Stadium…catching my first ball…buying steak, potatoes, and sweet corn with my Dad and cooking it all in the fire at our campground."

And a few things he didn't: "Living in a campground and having no kids to do something with…getting carsick and knowing I still had four hours to go…going home and watching baseball games on TV." But his conclusion confirmed my own: "It was my best trip. I wish Uncle Jim had come along…" and ended with a quantum leap beyond me: "…and maybe he *will* next year when we go West to see the rest of them."

We spent the final night in Milwaukee—a twinight double header at County Stadium. At 5 p.m. we arrived at what we expected to be a near-empty parking lot and found it full—full of Milwaukee fans having tailgate parties, grilling bratwurst, steak, ribs, drinking gallons of beer. In the stadium was an even bigger party. The crowd was huge and unabashedly partisan. I got a strange feeling that nearly everyone in the stadium *knew* each other. I bought a brat on a bun and grilled hotdog called a plumper, and immediately knew I'd found the food Mecca of organized baseball—worlds beyond the others. In New York Matt had looked at his hotdog and pronounced it dead.

We left in the seventh inning of the second game because of the suffocating heat. Outside, the stadium was a blazing, roaring spectacle against the night. While we watched in awe, some Brewer hit a grand slam and an explosion shook the sky.

Later, on the road that in the morning would take us to Wrigley Field and at last home, Matt was silent—asleep, I guessed, or depressed. But after a while I heard his earnest, disconcertingly deep voice rise from the back of the car. The message was a simple "Thanks, Dad." My heart bumped. I watched the road for a moment, and then glanced back, managing a smile. It was simple, eloquent—everything I needed to know.

And farther down the road, hearing only the dark humming of the wheels, I thought, my dear son...I want the world to be good to you, but I can't guarantee a thing. You believe in me, but I'm not as tough as you think. Listen to me: remember, always, this crazy, beautiful thing we've done. Whatever else may happen, it's ours. It belongs to us. *Remember*.

9 781957 169156